THE MYSTERIOUS GOVERNESS

by

BEVERLEY OAKLEY

Publisher's Note: This is a work of fiction. Names, characters, places, and incidents are a product of the author's imagination. Locales and public names are sometimes used for atmospheric purposes. Any resemblance to actual people, living or dead, or to businesses, companies, events, institutions, or locales is completely coincidental.

Ordering Information:
Quantity sales. Special discounts are available on quantity purchases by corporations, associations, and others. For details, contact the "Special Sales Department" at the address above.

The Mysterious Governess/Beverley Oakley -- 1st ed.
ISBN 9781520665436

For Sophie and Dagny

Chapter One

Lissa watched Cosmo from the shadows of the schoolroom, reluctant to reveal herself, for the young master only visited the third floor when he wanted something. She'd come to fetch a pile of mending, one of the many "extras" Mrs. Lamont had added to Lissa's governessing duties.

Finally, curiosity got the better of her. Even from three yards away, Lissa could see that the cast of the nose Cosmo was attempting to sketch—or rather copy—of the angel framed upon the wall was all wrong.

He must have become aware of her, for turning suddenly, his expression suggesting first embarrassment, then pride, he beckoned her over.

"What do you think?"

Cosmo was always quick to crow his dubious triumphs. As quick as he was to anger. Lissa had learned to temper her responses.

"Beautifully rendered," tripped off the tongue, followed by a hesitation, her frown indicating the considered, critical response of a fellow artist to a great work that might be made greater with just a charcoal stroke here or a blending there.

The gentle snoring of Clara, the nursery maid, sleeping in the next room beside the cot containing the youngest Lamont child, was reassuring. It reduced the need for Lissa, who was becoming increasingly uncomfortable in Cosmo's uncertain company these days, to manufacture a reason to scuttle away. However, courting Cosmo's professional regard had its benefits, she'd realized, and was one way to ensure the security of her job.

Overseeing the education of the two middle Lamont children had its trials but it was better than the fate that had been forced upon Lissa's sister. Poor high-spirited Kitty had been required to remain in the tiny village where they'd grown up and were branded the local "bastards", caring for their mother in the final term of her latest pregnancy.

Another full-blood sibling. Another Hazlett bastard. Or Partington by-blow.

Cosmo looked smug. "I thought the same," he said, studying his work with, if possible, even greater appreciation.

Lissa, a bad liar, was reminded of the fact when Cosmo glanced at her, his self-satisfaction wiped away by suspicion before Lissa affected sudden astonishment.

"Why, it looks just like Miss Danvers!" she exclaimed. "Miss Danvers in the guise of an angel." It had been fortuitous that she'd gleaned from conversation that this young lady was the object of Cosmo's current interest and therefore quite possibly the subject of his artistic endeavors, for in truth, Cosmo had not a jot of painterly talent in his little finger.

"You think so?" Placated, he apparently strove to sound insouciant. Since attaining his majority, Cosmo had worked hard to cultivate an attitude of sophistication edged with patent boredom. Lissa's brother, Ned, had been the same, though he had fortunately grown out of it. He'd had to, since unlike Cosmo, he had no pretensions to respectability. "Well, it so happens, Miss Hazlett, that is indeed who it is, and it is my plan to present the painting to Miss Danvers when I see her on Friday."

"Oh, but she *will* be flattered by your attention and impressed by your talent, sir." Lissa gathered up the mending and had taken several steps toward the door when Cosmo called her back. Inwardly she groaned, for she knew what was coming; and she had so hoped to have an early night.

"A moment, Miss Hazlett." The supercilious flare of Cosmo's nostrils and the disdainful cast of his mouth could not hide his inner desire that Lissa help him. Twice in the past two weeks she had, with a few artful brush strokes, transformed Cosmo's work-in-progress from hopelessly inept to a strikingly faithful rendition of his subject. She was not vain; she simply knew it was so.

Cosmo tapped his fingers on the wall beside the painting as he apparently gave thought to his next words. Lissa knew this was all part of the act. Wearily, she waited for what was to come.

Predictable as ever, Cosmo frowned as he turned toward her, biting his lip as if in the grip of great deliberation. "I am extremely busy over the next couple of days, Miss Hazlett, and I barely know where I shall find the time to finish my painting, though as you can see it is all but complete." He stared at her, no doubt waiting for her bright offer of assistance.

Lissa hesitated at the door, a polite smile upon her lips. She remained silent.

Cosmo shifted his weight. Clearly he'd expected she'd blithely offer to assist, as she had the last time. And the time before that. Now she merely raised enquiring eyebrows.

The silence lengthened. Upon a gusty exhalation, Cosmo muttered, "There are but two days before I see Miss Danvers and I cannot find even five minutes from the pressures of my busy life. However, you, Miss Hazlett, enjoy a leisured lifestyle in the employ of my family. I wonder if I could prevail upon you to sacrifice just several minutes to order this painting with the minor details I have not the time to manage so that I might present it to Miss Danvers."

Lissa pretended to give the matter thought, then shook her head and said upon a sigh, "I'm terribly sorry, Master Cosmo, but I'm on call with the young girls all day for the next week and, in the evenings, your mother has been assiduous in ensuring I have not a second to call my own, much less to help others."

She could see the thunderclouds gathering. His gaze darkened and his brow appeared to protrude over his angry eyes. When in fine temper he was a good-looking man. More often he resembled a sullen gargoyle. Master Cosmo did not like being crossed.

Well, Lissa might be a lowly paid governess but she was not going to be taken advantage of more than she already was.

Fortunately the storm didn't break. Perhaps he remembered the sleeping baby, or was sufficiently cognizant of the likelihood she'd not help in future, for he kept a lid on his temper. "An inducement, then, Miss Hazlett?" Cosmo's smile looked more tortured than pleasant. "You are busy, as am I, but perhaps I might be in a position to offer something that might make it worth your while."

Lissa had never thought along those lines. An inducement? Goodness, a couple of shillings would go a long way toward the new gown she'd been saving for. Not the kind of gown a governess would wear, either.

She was about to accept when she glimpsed her opportunity. Money was not the only currency to get her where she wanted to go in life.

With her eye on the prize, she pretended to deliberate even

more. She was not calculating by nature, but since becoming a governess in this middle-class household, with its pretentions and aspirations, she'd learned how much more people wanted something when it seemed they could not get it. "An inducement, sir? When I am so very content with my lot? What could possibly serve as an inducement?"

When she saw him open his mouth she added quickly, adopting a dreamy look, "Though now I reconsider the matter, and the fact that you're so kindly offering to facilitate my desires in order to further yours, then yes, there is one thing." She wondered if she dared voice it. Cosmo had no imagination. He'd dismiss the idea out of hand as simply preposterous if she didn't follow it up with how he might achieve it.

Her heart beat quickly, despite her pretense at whimsy, as she whispered, "Oh, Master Cosmo, the only thing I've ever truly wanted is to go to a ball. Yes, you have every right to look shocked that I harbor ideas so above my station, yet all I lack is a ball gown. A ball gown that does not mark me out as what I am: a poor governess." Lissa raised her eyes heavenward and swayed slightly as, in truth, her dreams threatened to overcome her.

She knew her half-sisters went to balls regularly. Araminta, the elder, was in her second season—her first having finished under a cloud, Lissa recalled, after a young man had put a pistol to his head and pulled the trigger. The younger, sweeter one, Hetty, was now a regular on the dance floor, hoping no doubt to secure a husband before the season ended in a few weeks.

How wonderful if Lissa could secretly observe how these half-sisters, who did not even know of her existence, deported themselves in society. How wonderful to have just one night of seeing how her own life might have played out had her father, Viscount Partington, honored his promise to her mother, a lowly solicitor's daughter, and made her his wife.

Instead, he'd left Lissa's mother at the altar and married the earl's daughter his parents had chosen for him, a decision he appeared to have immediately regretted, since he was quickly back in his true love's arms, foisting upon Lissa's mother four bastards during the next twenty years.

Though he could not be faulted in his attention to their mother, he showed more inclination to discipline rather than show affection toward his illegitimate children. All were expected to go out and make their livings. Lissa as a governess, when she longed more than anything to be a renowned artist; Ned, who'd been apprenticed to a goldsmith, as that conventionally led to a financial career; and Kitty, who frequently scandalized her parents with her declarations that the only living she was prepared to countenance was a career upon the stage.

Hiding her anger, Lissa fluttered her eyelashes in a gesture she hoped Master Cosmo would regard as more helpless than flirtatious and turned her face appealingly toward his. "How I would love one night to dance beneath beeswax candles and partake of champagne and thinly sliced ham, pretending I am not the lowly creature I know myself."

Predictably, Cosmo was already shaking his head, his look making no secret of the fact he thought she'd taken leave of her senses. "Even my father, who as you know is a good deal plumper in the pocket than I am, balks at the cost of my sister's ball gowns. I really do not think, Miss Hazlett, that you can be serious."

Cosmo had no imagination. It was clear why he'd never be an artist.

But Lissa had both imagination and cunning and she was determined that somehow these would aid her.

Still wistful, she went on as if she'd not heard him. "I once heard a young man declare he had the cunning to achieve the impossible: get the kitchen maid into Lady Rutherford's ballroom decked out and behaving like a lady so she'd be asked to dance by Lady Rutherford's son." Lissa was conscious she had his attention as she went on with her story. He stiffened as he appeared to study the angel painting.

Clutching the mending more tightly to her breast, she went on, ingenuously," You see, the young man's sister was the same height as the kitchen maid, so he decided he'd borrow one of his sister's ball gowns and accompany the kitchen maid to the ball. All he had to then do was effect an introduction…and after the dance was requested, he would win his bet."

"How much was the bet?"

"A hundred pounds. He'd boasted to his friends at White's that he could do it, and it was in their betting book. Oh, but there was such anticipation over whether he could be so clever…"

She *really* had his attention now. No doubt the possibility of making some money was very appealing. His eyes bored into her as he waited for her to conclude her story, finally asking a trifle acidly, no doubt because he had to, "Well, did he?"

"Sadly he was *not* so clever. In fact, he couldn't even get so far as borrowing one of his sister's gowns, because she caught him and quizzed him and point-blank refused to let him take what wasn't his." Lissa sighed and leveled her gaze at Cosmo. "Young ladies in high dudgeon can be formidable. And as I mentioned, he'd thought he was so much cleverer than he was but I'm afraid one has to be exceedingly clever to successfully put one over one's sister. And *your* sister would be impossible to bamboozle."

Lissa inclined her head. "Good night, Master Cosmo. I hope Miss Danvers likes her painting."

Chapter Two

While the orchestra played, Lissa tweaked the lustrous folds of her silver-flecked evening gown—well, Miss Maria's ball gown—and tested her smile, reflected in the enormous silver epergne, from which protruded at least three dozen lilies on the center of the refreshments table.

"One dance, and that's all. Then the evening's over," Cosmo muttered as he plucked a glass of champagne from the tray of a passing waiter and handed it to her. "I get few enough invitations to such events and I won't suffer you to ruin my chances of more."

Cosmo had gone to great pains with his appearance. His hair, short at the sides, had been brushed upwards to gain him even greater height, while plunging south into a pair of razor-thin sideburns. Lissa glanced at the nipped-in waist of his royal blue swallow-tail coat and wondered if he'd resorted to his sister's corsetry. Well, perhaps not Miss Maria's stays, but lately he'd been adopting, more and more, the accouterments of style favored by the tulips or pinks of whom her brother Ned—a true nonpareil himself these days—spoke so scathingly.

Fingering the ridiculously high points of his collar, which looked like it was choking him, he muttered, "Drink up, Miss Hazlett, and then we shall dance a set before I take you home. It was pure chance I was invited here tonight and I don't want to be exposed." Cosmo glanced nervously over his shoulder as Lissa responded with a forced smile, "Others might have considered me an asset, Master Cosmo."

She wished she'd been cleverer at negotiating terms. Certainly, it would be a scandal if it were discovered the governess had slipped unnoticed into such hallowed precincts, but Master Cosmo was an accomplished liar and Lissa knew how to conduct herself in such a setting. However, if her duplicity were revealed, Cosmo would no doubt find a way to turn to it his advantage while Lissa might well lose her position.

"Excuse me…"

Both turned at the interruption, Lissa experiencing a sudden and curious reaction that certainly wasn't admiration as a lean, dark-haired man gazed at her through a pair of speculative dark eyes.

"My apologies. I had thought you someone else." Despite his error, the gentleman still asked Lissa to partner him in the quadrille once he'd introduced himself and ascertained she was free for that set. Within minutes, Lissa was close enough to smell the whiskey and tar soap that impregnated his inky locks and dark wool coat, and to wonder why she felt so uncomfortable in his company.

"Miss Hazlett?" As they waited for the head couple to perform their figures, he stared at her intently. "Is it possible you are related to Miss Araminta Partington?"

Shock rendered her speechless. How could he possibly have guessed at a family connection? But of course, he had not, she reassured herself. He was merely commenting upon a resemblance that had been remarked upon before, as resemblances were remarked upon in many families. However, with Lissa and Araminta on opposite sides of the social divide, Lissa had never—until now—considered it could be a complication.

She hoped he didn't notice her fiery blush as she replied, faintly, "I'm a visitor to these parts. I have not heard of the young lady."

He nodded, his thin lips tightening, turning to bow to the lady on his left, as the dance required, before turning back to Lissa, the music and figures of the quadrille sedate enough to continue their conversation. "Interesting. When I glimpsed you across the dance floor, I thought you were she. Not that I am disappointed, of course."

He smiled suddenly, as if it were a prop intended to make him appear disarming, as he led her in a short promenade. He exuded confidence and entitlement—and danger—and Lissa, who was not one to suffer nerves, was frightened her carefully cultivated façade may suddenly dissolve.

"This is my first season, Lord Debenham," she murmured, returning to her place beside him after the ladies' chain. "How interesting that I have a double."

"Yes, and there she is." His Lordship raised a thin eyebrow as he clasped her in a waltz hold, ready to gallop her across to the other side of the set. "Dancing with the very undesirable Sir Aubrey, in fact. You've surely been in town long enough to know he is someone of whom to beware."

Lissa followed the direction of his gaze and her heart lurched. Not on account of the sudden requirement for energy or fear at not knowing the steps. Though the quadrille in its modern form had been introduced relatively recently to the upper classes, Lissa and her siblings had been taught to dance. Their mother, not the most maternal nor ambitious of women, had nevertheless insisted her offspring receive a classical education, which included dancing and watercolors, even if there would be no occasion to flaunt these refinements. Having the accouterments without opportunity until now to practice them in public was one of the many reasons Lissa was enjoying every moment rubbing shoulders with the rich and titled.

Well, she *had* been enjoying every moment, until she saw her half-sister. There she was dressed in virginal white silk with a pale green sash to match the green feather in her simple headdress. Miss Araminta Partington, living the life Lissa would have lived had her father followed his heart, not his parents' dictates.

The young woman's supercilious glance about the ballroom did nothing to ameliorate the raw hatred that surged through Lissa, though fortunately when Araminta looked pointedly at Lord Debenham, her gaze didn't encompass the unknown Lissa.

Araminta's interest in Lord Debenham immediately made him more interesting. Certainly his dark, cruel looks were not to Lissa's taste. She could tell that, in his own way, he was as self-absorbed as Cosmo; but the fact Araminta was clearly sizing him up as a prospect was unexpected. Lissa immediately wanted to know more. And of Sir Aubrey, with that striking streak of blond hair in his otherwise dark locks, whom Lord Partington clearly held in aversion. A rival, perhaps?

"Why should I be wary of Sir Aubrey?"

A glance down his hawk-like nose would have made lesser girls quail. As if her question singled her out as utterly ignorant.

"You really are from the country if you've heard nothing of the scandal attached to our lowly baronet. The blackguard is barely received. But I shall leave it at that for what would you know of politics? You only have to read the gossip sheets to understand it would be wise to steer clear of the villain."

Lissa bristled at his dismissive tone. In fact, she followed politics with great interest and regularly purloined her employer's newspaper when he'd finished with it.

"I am interested in politics, Lord Debenham," she said. "I'd like to hear the details."

Lord Debenham stroked his snowy cravat, then shrugged. "Sir Aubrey drove his late wife to take her own life—though others suggest he played a more personal role in her death—when he learned she was preparing to reveal his involvement in a group of Spenceans suspected of plotting the assassination of Lord Castlereagh."

Lissa gasped. "He's a *Spencean*? A murderer? And he's received?"

Lord Debenham shrugged again before taking her hands to execute the next figure of the set. "Only because there is as yet insufficient evidence to convict him, but mark my words, Miss Hazlett, it will not be long before Sir Aubrey is brought to justice."

"And Miss Partington is dancing with him?" Lissa was truly shocked. She knew her sister enjoyed taking risks, but surely she'd think associating in any way with a suspected traitor and murderer would be unacceptably damaging to her reputation?

Lord Debenham sent a narrow look in the couple's direction. "Sir Aubrey likes to look the Pinkest of the Pinks but the truth is, he's shockingly loose in the haft, if you'll pardon me coining a phrase your brother might use. Sir Aubrey thinks he can get away with anything if he puts up enough front. He's certainly cunning and desperate enough to be a danger to anyone who falls foul of him."

"Are you going to warn Miss Partington?"

Lord Debenham raised an eyebrow. "I suspect Miss Partington's actions are designed to invite just such a warning from me. Thank you for the dance, Miss Hazlett. Here is your cousin. I shall bid you adieu and do exactly as you suggest."

Lissa's high spirits came crashing down as His Lordship deposited her with Cosmo before he immediately set off in Araminta's direction.

"You've had your dance and now we must go." Cosmo was

waiting anxiously by the edge of the dance floor, ready to whisk her through the crowd and into a waiting hackney cab while Lissa had had but a mere taste of what she had been hoping would be the substance of her young life before too long. She knew she looked beautiful. That in fact, in looks, she rivaled her half-sister.

What a cruel twist of fate that it was Araminta who was living the life that should have been Lissa's; Araminta who was anticipating a glittering marriage and a life of ease. For Lissa, the only life-changing event she could anticipate would be to graduate from her role of governess to Cosmo's two little sisters to that of unpaid companion to her mother in her old age.

With a grim look, Cosmo caged her hand on his arm, as if the touch with someone so lowly were utterly repugnant.

The double doors that opened into the lobby grew closer, and now the bewigged footman was ushering her outside, into the cold. It was *not* where she belonged. Always on the other side of these doors. Her throat thickened and tears formed behind her eyes.

"Stop looking so Friday-faced. I have fulfilled your wish, Miss Hazlett." Cosmo turned to her as they descended the stairs. "Now you must fulfill your part of the bargain. I need to give Miss Danvers' miniature to her in the morning."

Lissa, who'd not put it past him to steal it, had hidden it beneath her pillow as further protection against him reneging on his promise. She suspected he'd already rummaged through her room trying to find it.

Now, she weighed up whether to push the advantage as Cosmo helped her into the waiting hackney he'd flagged down as they'd rounded the corner from Lady Stanely's Bruton Street residence, for he couldn't be observed, in public, putting a lone woman into such an equipage. She decided against it. Cosmo could turn nasty if he felt he was being taken advantage of.

"Never fear, the miniature will be waiting for you in your bedchamber when you return, Master Cosmo. And now you must return to the ball. You won't want to squander the invitation. As you yourself remarked, they do not happen regularly, do they?" She did not hear him respond to her jibe, for the jarvey shut the door at that moment before jumping onto the box.

With a "Gee-o", he whipped the horses into movement and as Lissa lurched forward, she was filled with the determination that she would not always be a governess. She'd witnessed enough of her half-sister's behavior over the years to know that Araminta, vain and proud, did not appreciate her life of ease and plenty.

Well, Lissa was as well versed in the requirements of being a lady, and certainly behaved in a more ladylike manner than Araminta, an observation backed up by her sister, Kitty, who took an even greater interest in their half-sister than Lissa did.

Surely, with her unusual palette of talents, Lissa could carve out a niche for herself that was more rewarding than the usual destiny allotted to the illegitimate and unacknowledged daughter of a peer of the realm?

***

Cocooned alone in the musty, uncomfortable interior of the hackney, now that Cosmo had, with clear relief, washed his hands of her, Lissa had gone only a couple of blocks when she was jerked out of her unhappy musings by a terrified cry, a head-rattling lurch, and the grinding of wheels accompanied by a deafening whinny.

Disoriented, she flailed in the dark for something she could grip as she felt the hackney round a bend on only two wheels. The side window smashed inward as it veered too close to a building and Lissa screamed as she was thrown against the door. For a moment the vehicle slowed, then, suddenly gathering speed, it sped on. Now she could hear the shouts of others in the street as they either leapt clear of the runaway horse or perhaps tried to arrest its progress.

Hunching her shoulders, she covered her face and braced for the inevitable impact, a prisoner in this capsule and under no illusions it would end well.

Despite her flights of fancy, Lissa was pragmatic by nature. Either she would be snuffed out when the hackney came to a final, messy stop or went into the river, or she would be looking for a way to explain her multiple injuries and damage to Miss Maria's ball gown while hoping she still had a job.

If the outcome were too bad she may have to return home to her mother. She felt ambivalent about this. While she'd never been more lonely than in the six months she'd spent as governess in the Lamont household—not good enough to be spoken to civilly by her employers and too good for the other servants to offer friendship—she did enjoy the bustle of London.

The inevitable impact came, truncated by a terrible sound of splitting wood and grinding metal, and Lissa was thrown against the side of the carriage, hitting her head on the window frame before slumping to the floor.

For a few moments she lay curled up in a ball, breathing heavily and waiting in case there was a dramatic codicil to her terrifying adventure.

Tentatively she flexed her hands and feet and opened her eyes, screaming when she found her right eye without vision as she drew away her fingers, sticky with what she knew must be blood.

Seconds later the carriage door was forced open and she found herself staring at three goggling men, two with blackened faces half covered by filthy, ragged mufflers, the third startling clean by contrast, with chiseled elegant features, a thatch of flyaway brown hair beneath his topper, and an expression of concern that blazed her into renewed life.

"Are you all right, Miss? Here, let me assist you. Are you alone?" The clean, handsome gentleman elbowed his way forward and extended his hand into the gloomy interior, and as she gripped it, she felt an almost overwhelming sense of safety and relief.

Lissa was a quick thinker, and had her excuse ready in answer to his surprise. "The horse bolted before my chaperone had a chance to enter the carriage."

Now she was outside, being assisted to stand, shivering in the darkness. The young man divested himself of his coat, which he wrapped around her, and as the other two characters melted into the darkness to assist the cab driver, Lissa's gentleman protector lowered his face to study hers.

"You have a cut just above your eye," he said, whipping a snowy-white handkerchief from the pocket of the coat he'd just relinquished. "Ah, not deep, fortunately. Now, what shall we do with you? You're probably in shock, in which case a little brandy would be just the thing, but of course I must return you to your chaperone immediately. She'll be in a panic. Here, lean against me. You're shaking."

Lissa's knees felt they might give way any moment. A short distance away the jarvey was urging his horse onto all four legs while the two men in mufflers had recruited help with righting the smashed equipage.

"Where have you come from and where did you leave your chaperone?" asked the young man, adding before she had time to answer, "But where are my manners? Introductions are in order."

His grin by the light of a nearby lamp post was enough to do what any amount of brandy might not have achieved. It warmed the cockles of Lissa's heart. Shyly, she introduced herself.

"A pleasure to meet you, Miss Hazlett," he said, caging her hand on his arm as he led her to the pavement. "And I am Mr. Ralph Tunley, parliamentary secretary and confidante to all manner of rakes and rogues but, sadly, in my own right, a poor, struggling hopeful with not a feather to fly with. Which is why I am unable to offer you a carriage ride home, since it is quite beyond my means. Shall I accost the driver of this passing hackney and send you back to your chaperone, or dispatch a note to your family immediately to let them know what has happened?"

Lissa shook her head as she glanced at her ball gown, nearly doubling up with dismay when she saw the damage inflicted upon it.

"I'm sure you have plenty more just as lovely," he reassured her. "Not that a great beauty like you needs silk and diamonds to enhance what nature has so abundantly bestowed upon you. There, wasn't that a pretty speech? I can practice such courtly sentiments without fear of censure since you will shortly be whisked out of my orbit and I will never see you again, though perhaps I shall hear news of your marriage to some great scion I could never hope to rival. Goodness, though, but I think that you *are* a beauty beneath the grime and blood."

She saw he was grinning as he moved her a little closer to the illuminated glow cast by the nearby gas lamp. "You're welcome to slap my face if you wish."

Finally, Lissa was able to utter something coherent. "I shall forgive your impertinence, for you rescued me," she sniffed. "And this gown is not mine. It belongs to the daughter of my employer." She thought she might burst into tears as she contemplated the repercussions of the damage it had suffered. Several bows had been torn off the trimming at the hem when she'd been pulled from the wreckage, though in the dim light she could discern only a few dirt smudges. "She doesn't even know it's gone," she admitted. "I'm just a governess, and the family I work for thinks I'm in bed, asleep." She balled her fists, trying not to cry. "If they find out what I've done, I'll lose my job."

Mr. Tunley looked properly concerned for the first time, no doubt perceiving the enormity of losing one's position when one had no financial backing. Then his mouth stretched wide into a warm smile.

"Just the governess? Why, isn't this my lucky evening? I get to rescue the beautiful maiden and perhaps not lose her within a fortnight to some unworthy wastrel with more money and address than I have. Where do you live?" Then, when she told him, he added, "Allow me to escort you home, since we're so close. I must satisfy myself that both you and the secret of your truancy remain safe, and I also will pledge that your gown gets the very best attention. The good woman I lodge with is a seamstress. She'll know what to do."

Lissa slanted a dubious look at him as they began walking, and he laughed. "You *are* the suspicious type, aren't you? But of course, to be alone with any gentleman must be highly distressing. Don't worry, no one will recognize you with such a dirty face."

Lissa liked his easy-natured humor but she was wary, too. "Without wishing to be rude, Mr. Tunley, I haven't met many people who don't expect to be more than handsomely rewarded for doing one the slightest good turn. Might I just warn you that while I'm very grateful you've rescued me, I will also be saying a very firm goodbye when you deposit me at the garden gate."

"You do speak your mind—and I like that in a young lady!" He raised his hands and took a quick sidestep, wearing an expression of mock alarm. "I assure you, Miss Hazlett, my first impulse is to help you. Though would it be such a terrible thing to further our acquaintance? Once you're inside and have changed, you can toss down your poor ruined dress. I promise I shall return it to you by tomorrow evening in pristine condition. If anyone can work miracles with clothing, my landlady can."

'No!" Lissa gave an emphatic shake of her head. "I am permitted no followers, Mr. Tunley. Besides, I've only just met you and that gown is worth a pretty penny. I'm quite capable of managing to do what must be done in order to rescue it from total ruin."

To her astonishment, she choked on the final word, stumbling against the low railing of the neighbor's house as a great sob wracked her body. Good Lord, what was wrong with her? She was not one to succumb to displays of emotion, and she wasn't even afraid.

Well, not really.

"I hope it wasn't something I said." Mr. Tunley looked alarmed. "I was just trying to offer a helpful solution."

Lissa tried to draw in a breath but there seemed to be some blockage. "I know you were, and it's not you," she managed, realizing that the sobs that were suddenly choking her must be due to the kind of shock that afflicts one after a terrible event has befallen them. The same thing had happened unexpectedly when she'd fallen off a horse once. She'd thought she was fine at the time, only to succumb to the vapors half an hour later.

When she glanced up, she saw the happy smile had been wiped from the poor young man's face. He was standing, uncertainly, as if he didn't know whether to take off, fearing she might be mad.

Lissa pulled herself together and managed to stammer, "Little wonder you look like you'd rather be running a mile in the opposite direction. First, you're so good to me, helping me out of the carriage, seeing me safely home, and then offering to salvage my poor ruined dress so I don't lose my job. And what do I do? Behave like a cry-baby."

He gripped her hands and helped her to stand straight. "You mistake me. You're suffering from shock but I don't want to appear to take liberties. You have every reason to shed tears, Miss Hazlett. I'm surprised you didn't before. You've been lucky to escape a horrible accident with just a scratch. You're probably half frozen to death, and if I weren't a gentleman who's already given you my coat, I'd offer you the warmth you need right now."

He looked suddenly abashed, as if he wished the pavement would swallow him. "Pardon me, that came out terribly wrong. I meant I wish I had a decent abode close by with a blazing fire where you could warm yourself but of course, even if I had, I couldn't, for I really am a gentleman, and I'd never dream of sullying your reputation by getting closer than is seemly—well, except to rescue you from a crushed carriage, that is."

Lissa continued to tremble, though she smiled at his little speech. "You have been very kind, and yes I am very cold, though I will have to give up your coat in a minute."

"No, no, I insist, you must keep it."

Lissa shook her head. "I shall throw it down from the window, then. With my dress. I've decided I do trust you, after all. And since we've gone this far, and I am so beyond the pale, I will allow you to very quickly put your arms around me so that I may warm *you*, for you are trembling from the cold and, shocking as it may be, I am not in my ordered mind, but it's all I can offer as my thanks for taking me this far so safely."

His irrepressible grin lit up his face as he wasted no time in stepping forward and, in a gentle yet quite firm embrace, he held her to him for a second.

A charge of such warmth seemed to fill Lissa's veins that she gasped. He was not tall and broad-shouldered, yet he felt dependable, and he smelled of almonds and coffee overlaid with tar, perhaps some concoction he used on his thatch of brown hair.

It was the briefest of hugs, already he'd dropped his arms and stepped back, but his expression perhaps mirrored hers for he looked as if he too had been overcome by something quite unexpected.

Lissa blinked rapidly several times and then glanced up at the Lamonts' townhouse. Feeling completely tongue-tied, she said the first words that came to mind. "I hope Master Cosmo ensured the kitchen door remained unbolted." She cast a dubious look at the stairs that led from the pavement to the basement. Then in enquiry to the young man's look, explained that her employer's son had taken her to a ball in return for a painting he'd asked her to do for him.

"What an enterprising young lady you are. And an artist, to boot," remarked Mr. Tunley, before insisting he do the "gentlemanly thing" which was to descend the stairs to try the door.

A moment later he returned to her side. "I must say, your Master Cosmo is very neglectful since he's clearly given no thought to how you might get in once the servants had gone to bed. You can hardly knock, can you?"

Lissa was feeling distinctly forlorn by now, and Mr. Tunley gave her a bolstering pat on the shoulder. "If I could look forward to imminent elevation in my job, I would suggest that we eloped this very minute. Not only are you beautiful but you're clearly wondrously talented, and sound as if you'd be a great asset to a young man trying to make his mark in the world." He sent her a self-deprecating grin, then shrugged. "The fact is, *I* cannot offer you anything, and *you* face the prospect of being thrown out onto the street without a character if you don't gain access."

Lissa put her hand to her mouth. The truth was terrifying.

"I'm not sure whether to be flattered or not, Mr. Tunley. Though of course, it's easy to make extravagant declarations when you follow them up with the caveat that they're entirely impossible." She liked this young man, whose humor and lightness of being was so different from what she was used to.

He raked his fingers through the thatch of hair that flopped over his forehead. "One day I shall be a man of influence and plump enough in the pocket to make spontaneous offers of marriage to beautiful women I rescue from carriage accidents. Sadly, though, for now, I'll just have to be ingenious enough to find a way to breach the stone fortress that stands before us."

Mr. Tunley might not have been flush with funds but he was incredibly daring, climbing the drainpipe and entering the house through an open window. Lissa had never been so frightened, watching his precarious ascent and then perilous acrobatics as he'd struggled to push up the sash while balancing on the narrow window ledge. It took all her willpower not to hug him again when he triumphantly opened the kitchen door and greeted her with out-flung arms and a grin of self-congratulation.

***

Lissa had not expected thanks but she was surprised by the force of her feelings when, the following day, Cosmo flaunted the portrait he claimed to have painted while his mama and sister gushed their admiration. Lissa, who was passing the breakfast room to take her two charges out of the house for a walk, hesitated in the passage and looked through the half open door. The eldest Lamont daughter, eighteen-year-old Maria, thought her brother's talent prodigious, while Mrs. Lamont declared her son's brilliance sufficient to ensure him all manner of lucrative commissions amongst the haut ton.

"You tell your Miss Danvers that she's to show it to the company when her mother entertains that new MP, Lord Debenham and his friends," cried Mrs. Lamont as she held the painting up to the light. She patted her ringlets as she sighed pleasurably over the family's future prospects. "I read all about His Lordship in the gossip sheets and he'd be just the man to help advance you, Cosmo. He's not married but he has the look of someone in need of a wife, eh Maria? Or perhaps he has a nearly-betrothed in need of painting."

Lissa tried not to cough and thus alert Cosmo to her outrage at the smooth manner in which he accepted his family's praise, with not one word to indicate he was not the lone architect of his masterpiece. Instead, she had to satisfy herself with a very brief but focused glare as she passed by while she digested the rather disconcerting news that Mrs. Lamont was familiar with the very man her governess had been dancing with the previous night. It was some small consolation that the Lamonts only *aspired* to the social ranks that would enable them to invite a man like Lord Debenham to the house.

Lissa's revenge upon Cosmo for his arrogance came in a most unexpected manner about an hour after his return. She was on her hands and knees in the drawing room, turning down the hem of one of Miss Maria's older morning gowns and wondering if she'd have the chance of conversing with Mr. Tunley if he returned her damaged ball gown that afternoon, as he'd promised.

Thanks to Miss Maria's father's success as a broker in the city, the young lady had a fair selection of evening gowns for her debut, but she'd put on an unexpected spurt of growth and the family was not wealthy enough for luxuries like new morning gowns, which were only for lounging around in at home, besides. The lady of fashion was an expensive creature, with so many changes of clothing required, but Mrs. Lamont was, in addition to being frighteningly ambitious, extremely enterprising. And ruthless.

Miss Maria, prettier than her mother had ever been, Lissa suspected, was not nearly as clever and did not do much in the way of lounging. When she wasn't being drilled in deportment, she was to be found flitting around, checking her appearance in her hand mirror and scanning the street from the drawing room window for a sign of the various men who might have caught her interest at the few social events to which she was invited, or taking visits with her family to the theatre or the National Museum.

Lissa was terrified her eldest charge would discover the absence of her silver-flecked ball gown and every minute that ticked by was spent in an agony that the charming young man she'd met the night before would let her down. It wasn't too much to say that her entire future rested in his hands, for if he reneged on his promise to return Miss Maria's dress properly mended before its disappearance was discovered, Lissa would be out of a job. Without a character, she had no hope of securing another position.

When the parlor maid put her head around the door a

moment later and announced with a frown that a gentleman wished an audience with Miss Hazlett, all three heads jerked up. Not Lissa's for she could only stare at Maria's daintily shod feet while heat burned her cheeks.

"Gentlemen callers are not allowed," Mrs. Lamont responded in warning tones, rising and taking a few threatening steps toward Lissa. "Miss Hazlett, can you explain what this is about?"

"Excuse me, ma'am, but the gentleman—a Mr. Tunley—says he's here on behalf of his employer, Lord Debenham." The girl looked confused, as if she had no idea whether this might be a man of importance or not.

Mrs. Lamont's reaction left her in no doubt.

"What would Lord Debenham want with you, Miss Hazlett?" It was an accusation, not a question, and Lissa made to rise without an answer, though in truth her terror threatened to overwhelm her.

Mr. Tunley worked for Lord *Debenham*?

It was Cosmo who strode forward, smoothly taking charge and saying, "Tell this gentleman we shall see him in the conservatory."

Lissa shook her head, shrugging off his hand upon her shoulder. "But he wants to see *me*." Whatever the gentleman had to say must be said in private. Dear Lord, had Lord Debenham learned she was the mere governess and Mr. Tunley was here to warn her? If it were about the dress only, he'd have been more circumspect about it, surely?

"I was speaking of Lord Debenham to an acquaintance and of His Lordship's potential interest in a portrait just an hour ago," Cosmo hissed to Lissa under his breath when he'd nevertheless propelled her toward the doorway that opened into the passage. "You've got a message to him, haven't you? Telling him that *you* painted the portrait of Miss Danvers when it was really me!"

Lissa stepped back at the vitriol in his eyes as she defended herself in a whisper, "Truly, Cosmo, I have no idea what this is about. I've said nothing to anyone about... You know." She trailed off at the warning look in his eye. "It's just that I met Mr. Tunley last night when my hackney was in an accident. He must be here to see if I'm all right."

Cosmo looked first mollified, then assessing. "So you met Lord Debenham's equerry, or whatever this servant calls himself, last night, did you? Well, Miss Hazlett, you'd better be careful what you tell this gentleman."

Lissa squared her shoulders. "I value my position, Master Cosmo, besides which, I have nowhere else to go. Ah, Mr. Tunley, what a pleasant surprise."

She was relieved he was dressed like a gentleman of fashion and not a lackey, and unprepared for the lurch she felt in the region of her heart as he was invited at that moment by the maid to step into the drawing room Lissa had hoped to vacate. She certainly did not wish the family to witness her meeting—or her suddenly disordered wits, for such feelings were new to her, as was this young man's response.

His easy open grin and the way he tossed his unruly thatch of hair back from his face were signs of an open heart, she thought, liking him even more in the daylight. The only man apart from her brother that she'd had dealings with were Cosmo. Most other gentlemen didn't deign to look at lowly governesses.

Mr. Tunley inclined his head then, with a glance at the assembled company, said with all the aplomb of the consummate diplomat, "Is there somewhere Miss Hazlett and I might speak in private? I have something to communicate on behalf of my employer…in confidence."

After the rather bemused Lamont family had watched Lissa lead Mr. Tunley to the conservatory, Ralph thrust the parcel he carried under his arm at her and said triumphantly, "I pledged to return your gown—or your mistress's gown—none the worse for wear."

"And managed to set tongues wagging in the process."

"Adding to your consequence. You should be grateful to me. The Lamonts will never look at you in the same way, wondering what business you have with the esteemed MP, Lord Debenham."

"I just pray I never see him again," Lissa murmured, stroking the fronds of a large potted palm before smiling up at him, "for he was the only man I danced with at Lady Stanley's ball, and no one must ever know I left the house and did such a thing."

Mr. Tunley cocked his head and looked at her with renewed interest. "You danced with my employer? One of London's most…*dangerous* bachelors?" The gleam in his eye faded and he sighed. "I hope you didn't prefer him over me. That would not be wise, and I'm not saying that only because I'd *prefer* you favored me. The fact is, I would caution any young lady against falling in love with my employer, even at the risk of my job."

Lissa stared at him against the backdrop of exotic greenery and London's gray London skies through the window in the background. She'd sensed something she hadn't liked when dancing in Lord Debenham's arms, chaste though the contact had been.

"Dangerous? Pray, why is he dangerous?"

"So you know nothing of Lord Debenham? Of his vendetta against his late cousin's husband, Sir Aubrey, whom he accuses of being the ringleader in the plot to assassinate Lord Castlereagh?"

"Good heavens!" Lissa cried, shaking her head. "But surely it's Sir Aubrey who is the man to beware? At least, that's what Lord Debenham told *me*." She narrowed her eyes. "And why work for a man you clearly do not admire?"

Mr. Tunley looked abashed for the first time as he played absently with the frond of an overhanging fern for Lissa had not invited him to be seated. She was too nervous for that. "Needs must, my dear Miss Hazlett. I could ask you the same. Why work for a family you clearly have no respect for? I'll answer it for you. Because where else could you go? As for myself, I'd need a very compelling reason for leaving my present employ without my reputation being tarnished. I'm afraid Lord Debenham would not be kind in letting me go. So, I make myself absolutely indispensable to him. He'd be lost without me, and that's a fact."

He grinned suddenly. Lissa liked the way his smiles lit up his face, as if he possessed a great radiance within. "Deuced coincidence that you danced with him. Not that—as you say—you want the Lamonts to find out about that." He looked thoughtful. "Or, to in fact, see Lord Debenham in case he says something."

"That's not likely, for I rarely leave the house except to take the little girls to the park. However, Master Cosmo hopes to render His Lordship's likeness, which means he plans to make some awful sketch and then have me fix it up. His mother thinks it a splendid idea." Lissa smiled, tilting her head and feigning entreaty. "I don't suppose you could find out for me whether Master Cosmo's request was conveyed to Lord Debenham? It would help to know so I had something to convey when I returned to the drawing room where the family is no doubt agog to hear what you've had to say."

Ralph stroked his chin, thoughtfully. "I've been on business about town all morning so I'm afraid I have nothing to report. Nor will I have anything to report in the future as I see how unwise it would be to communicate further with you. The Lamont family will not tolerate their governess entertaining," he shrugged, "a follower—dreadful word, that is—and I do not wish to make things difficult for you."

Disappointment flooded her though she knew this was ridiculous when she'd only just met the young man.

"You see," he went on, "I'm in great danger of liking you altogether too much, but as I have nothing to offer, our love is doomed."

She tilted her chin, glad he'd been able to inject humor into the situation. "Mr. Tunley, we have met but once. There has never been talk of…"

"Love?" He looked abashed. "No, it's true. Ah well, until last night I'd never met a young lady I believed I could hold in such high esteem. You were brave as well as beautiful, even with blood all over your face. I couldn't sleep for thinking about you, only now I'm in danger of appearing ridiculous. You seem far too sensible to believe in instant attraction."

Lissa dropped her eyes. "No," she whispered.

"No, what?"

"No, I'm not too sensible to believe in that."

"Oh…"

Clearly her whispered admission had taken him by surprise. For a moment he was lost for words. Then he grinned. "Well, it's quite unfair to make you fall in love with me when, at the risk of repeating myself, I've already said I have absolutely nothing to offer you."

He took her hand and bowed over it, the touch of his lips causing a tremor to travel all the way up her spine.

"And so I bid you *adieu*, my fair Miss Hazlett, with the greatest of regrets, but wishing you all the happiness in your life that a maiden as bold and beautiful, yet modest, deserves."

Rising, he tapped the parcel she now held. "Tell them this is for your father, a country solicitor or some such, with whom Lord Debenham does business. How's that for cunning? It'll satisfy their need to know what our meeting was all about while adding to your consequence."

Lissa watched him bow his way out of the door and disappear from, she presumed, the rest of her life.

A great sense of tragedy weighed heavily on her—until it was replaced by pleasurable astonishment when she unwrapped the parcel in Maria's room a short while later, intending to return the beautifully cleaned gown to its rightful place. For as the wrapping fell away, a beautiful silver comb encrusted with tiny, sparkling gems of colored glass tumbled to the floor.

Attached to it was a card on which was written: *Always remember the man who would have rescued you from more than just a hackney accident, had it been possible –Ralph Tunley.*

Her delight was sudden and brief but the crushing disappointment that followed was more long-lasting. She tossed the card and comb on the bed in order to concentrate on ensuring the gown was perfect. Only when she'd reassured herself on that score did she return her attention to the lackluster message—and find that more words had been written on the inside of the fold.

If you ever need a knight in shining armor—albeit a poor one—you can find me through Mrs. Nipkins, mantua maker to the nobility, Coopers Alley, Soho.

***

Cosmo adopted a different approach the next time he saw Lissa. She was walking with the younger girls in the little park in front of the Lamonts' townhouse. The evening shadows were long and Lissa was glad of the girls' company as she became aware of him creeping up behind her. When she felt his hot breath on her cheek and his soft words in her ear, she knew he was trying to unnerve her. He would not succeed.

"What do you really know of Lord Debenham?" There was both envy and concern in his tone. "He wishes for a charcoal sketch, you know. A likeness." Master Cosmo matched his steps with hers.

Lissa gripped his younger sister Nellie's hand as she answered blithely, the lies tripping off her tongue, "Lord Debenham is a friend of my father's. I have never met him, personally, until we danced at Lady Stanley's, however, I barely looked at him, I was so overcome with fear he might recognize my name, though of course he did not. But I'm sorry, Master Cosmo, I am quite unable to render his likeness, if that's what you want."

She had determined already that she would not submit to any amount of bullying just to bolster Cosmo's reputation as a painter. The young master had no concern for Lissa's welfare. If Ralph hadn't helped her gain admittance to the house last night, she might well be on her way back to her dear mama's without a job right now.

Cosmo was silent for some moments, apparently not expecting such intransigence, so Lissa was surprised when he said pleasantly, "I've been invited to attend Mrs. Gargery's garden party tomorrow and I would like you to accompany me."

Nellie and Harriet had run on ahead so he added, "Not that anyone will be made aware of your lowly position. I can't afford to have it known you are what you are, however, I thought you may enjoy the diversion."

"And because Lord Debenham will be there?" But he'd found her weak spot. A garden party. It would be a chance to mix with her social superiors.

Immediately she corrected herself. Her social superiors? Her father was one of these people. So were her half-sisters, Araminta and Hetty.

She'd always held out the smallest hope that somehow she'd find her niche. That she wouldn't be a lowly governess forever.

Then she thought of lovely Mr. Tunley and her stomach turned over. If only he wasn't as poor as a church mouse, though his fulsome compliments had been quite safe to declare as he'd so clearly put himself out of contention for being a suitor. Even though she'd tried not to think of him all morning, the image of his handsome, smiling face with its unruly thatch of brown hair kept intruding.

But a garden party, where eligible young men might be similarly taken with her, was too irresistible to refuse. She was not being vain but at twenty, she needed to direct her future where she could. She had no intention of being a governess or living as a spinster with her mother for the rest of her life.

"I want you to enjoy what is not generally within your reach, Miss Hazlett." His smile was false and cloying as he stopped to wave at his sisters before turning back to her. "And I want you to sketch Lord Debenham, though that will have to be achieved from a distance."

Oh, but how she wanted to go. If Lord Debenham were going to be there, it was possible Mr. Tunley might also.

"What can I wear?"

He shrugged. "You're enterprising enough to solve that problem yourself, surely? Mind, though, you can't wear that." He cast a disparaging look at her serviceable blue serge skirts.

"Miss Maria?" She knew it was hopeless, even as desperation prompted her to ask the question.

He shook his head. "I dare not try that again. No, Miss Hazlett, you must find a way to clothe yourself. If you're as anxious to go as you appear, you'll be enterprising enough to find a way."

"I see you know nothing of how the world works. Of its impediments such as decent clothing, the want of which precludes those respectably born, but without funds, from mixing with their class. Perhaps you don't really want me to accompany you after all." Lissa glared. "You know I shan't be able to sketch Lord Debenham unless I have a gown that is suitable."

Cosmo cast her a look of frustrated despair. "Miss Hazlett, I am completely unable to provide you with a new dress. You know that. I have very little in the way of ready income, not that I'd spend it equipping you with new clothes when I think my offer of attending a garden party with a better class of people than you're used to is generous enough. Now please, use that pretty head of yours to secure yourself something suitable for just two hours."

Chapter Three

Araminta stared at the two bonnets lying on the bed. Deciding which one to wear might be the most difficult decision she'd have to make in a day. The bonnet of vermillion-colored satin, embossed with straw and surmounted by a bouquet of full-blown damask roses? Or the simple, leghorn bonnet, which would highlight her innocence when teamed with her demure sprigged muslin?

Her sister, sitting morosely on the bed behind her, had been no use in helping her decide. Hetty had appeared plainly bored by the question and apparently more concerned with how to conceal a pimple on her jawline. Araminta had offered her advice but Hetty's mood seemed only to have grown darker at Araminta's bolstering suggestion that patience and acceptance were far more becoming than petulance in one who did not have the striking looks to turn the heads of the gentlemen, and that such virtues may even be rewarded.

Despite Hetty's lack of response, Araminta considered herself a caring sister and made a final attempt to ease her plain sister's concerns. Deciding upon the more striking vermillion bonnet, she turned, tying the scarlet ribbons beneath her chin, and said with a reassuring smile. "Just wait another year, Hetty dearest, and your skin may well improve, not to mention your figure. You're only in your first season out, and remember that Mama said she was more comely after a year of marriage than when she was making her debut. Now, what do you think of this now that it's on? It favors my complexion, don't you think? Certainly not a color you can wear, though."

"All I know is that it's a color favored by Jezebels wanting to get their claws into certain gentlemen. *Dangerous* ones," Hetty hissed.

Araminta was truly shocked. This was not like Hetty at all. Hetty was generally sweet and pliable, as she needed to be when she lacked the benefit of Araminta's good looks. "What do you know of such things, Hetty? Two evenings on the ballroom floor and it appears your innocent mind has been corrupted when that's the only attribute you really have." She shook her finger at her sister and tried to soften her rebuke with a fond smile. "Just don't you let Mr. Woking hear you speak like that or he'll run a mile."

Hetty, who was now tying her garter, looked up with a glare. "I wish he would," she muttered. "Better still, I wish *you'd* marry him. There! That would be poetic justice when you've set your cap at his wicked, dashing uncle."

"What? Lord Debenham?" Araminta laughed, despite the discomfort that rippled through her. She'd caught Lord Debenham's eye the first night she'd danced at Lady Knox's ball, and the knowledge that he found her attractive had put steel into her spine and fired her with the conviction that here was a likely catch. Then she'd been favored by his attention at Lady Stanley's ball a few nights previously. Lord Debenham was dashing, in a lean, spare and dangerous way, titled with expectations, and he was handsome. What more could an aspiring debutante want?

When she'd made mention of his lordship's interest during a few minutes in the mending room in the hopes of soothing the mood of a certain woebegone Miss Hoskings—who, with the face of a roly-poly pudding and a body to match, would be lucky to catch a bald eagle—the response had been far from expected.

Apparently Lord Debenham "did things", according to the wide-eyed Miss Hoskings. The young lady's patent horror at the mention of Lord Debenham's name had been followed by the whispered admonition that her very own aunt had been ruined by the gentleman, who did not deserve the moniker, and now it was a crime in the household to even speak her aunt's name.

At first, Araminta had been skeptical, since surely any relative of Miss Hoskings could not rival a sprouting potato in looks. Then Miss Hoskings had risen from the chaise longue and declared in rather dramatic tones, "Five years ago, my aunt was tipped to marry the Marquis of Donley, she was so beautiful. But Mr. Carruthers, as he was then, before he became Lord Debenham, ruined her."

"Obviously, your aunt was very silly and careless with her reputation," Araminta had replied, earning a predictable glare and then the rather uncomfortable response. "I'm not supposed to know this, but they were going to elope and she'd gone to the inn where they'd agreed to meet and set off," Miss Hoskings had paused, looking first uncertain, then shifty, before whispering in a rush, "the next day! While she was waiting, Lord Debenham remembered something important and went off to fetch it, only he suffered a delay of some hours and in the meantime, her father caught up with her... *tied* to the bedposts!"

Araminta could not hide her horror. She'd heard that Miss Hoskings was prone to the vapors and that she spent a great deal of time in the ladies' mending room during these entertainments. Araminta wondered if spouting tall tales about gentlemen who'd spurned her or family members was an antidote to the inevitability of sitting out most dances as a wilting wallflower. Araminta sniffed and adopted her most haughty tone. "It might have been wise for your aunt to have thought more carefully about the potential damage to her good name if she was so easily compromised."

Still, it was a salutary tale, though Araminta wondered—if it were true—why Miss Hoskings was the one banished to the country, never to be heard of again, and Lord Debenham had gone on to make his fortune and to cut quite a dash in the fashionable world.

Nevertheless, Lord Debenham's lack of regard was enough to make Araminta think twice about courting His Lordship's interest. A girl had to be strategic. Perhaps the very handsome and rather enigmatic Sir Aubrey was_a better bet, despite the rumors flying around of some kind of scandal attached to him. But as he was still received, that was really all that mattered.

Hetty, having tied her garter then straightened her dress and bonnet, hesitated in the doorway. "You think you can charm the birds from the trees, Araminta, and maybe you can, but mark my words, you're going to land in a bramble bush," she said softly. "I predict that by the end of the season you'll be marrying either Mr. Woking, and spending your days pleasing a fool for your pin money, or you'll get your just desserts and have no choice but to wed evil Lord Debenham and be miserable."

But Araminta had just decided at that very moment what she was going to be doing by the end of the season.

She flashed Hetty a smile. "No, I'm not, Hetty, because I've decided to marry Sir Aubrey. Thank you so much for laying out my options with such exquisite acuity. Indeed, I *shall* marry Sir Aubrey! You just see if I don't."

Her sister's outrage was marvelous to behold—and it also

made Araminta think that if Hetty had indeed lost her foolish, susceptible heart to Sir Aubrey, she needed to be taught a lesson so she was less careless of it in future.

***

The afternoon was to become even more entertaining, however, with the arrival of a strange and rather shocking note delivered by Araminta's maid, Jane.

At first Araminta was so scandalized she could only imagine it a hoax. But on the heels of her indignation came curiosity. Of course, the writer—a young woman, claiming to bear an uncanny resemblance to Araminta that had been remarked upon by a certain member of high society—could only be a thief or a confidence trickster. How could she possibly imagine Araminta would just hand over a dress on the spurious claim the two had been mistaken for sisters, and that this young lady had an important mission to undertake which might benefit Araminta?

Araminta was always ready to take advantage of something that might benefit her, but this was going too far.

However, a few minutes later, Araminta couldn't help herself. She hadn't responded to the note, but yet she was at the bottom of the garden at the stipulated time, and when the young woman, a governess out for a walk with her two young charges, stopped by, Araminta was struck by both fascination and revulsion as she realized the truth of the young woman's claim. She did indeed bear a striking resemblance to her. More than that, she was disturbingly familiar, and while Araminta had pledged to remain ignorant of the strange undercurrents of her father's household in the country, the temptation to learn more was too tempting.

Especially when she learned it was Lord Debenham who had remarked upon the resemblance between them.

Upon further consideration, Araminta decided that if this young person was required to sketch His Lordship and needed a decent dress to do so, Araminta was ready to facilitate something that would gain her a greater insight into His Lordship's conduct when Araminta was not around.

Sir Aubrey would also be at Mrs. Gargery's garden party. Araminta was to be accompanying her mother to see the wild animals at the tower of London, but having Miss Hazlett keep an eye on the competition might serve Araminta rather well.

Miss Hazlett. Araminta asked if she were related to the

Hazletts in her village, as her father had bought a pony from a Mrs. Hazlett who had lived in the cottage by the bridge.

Miss Hazlett had been vague, only saying that a great many tears had been shed over that horse.

***

Lissa, for her part, had regarded the proceedings with more dispassion. After all, she'd long known of Araminta's existence. And no, she refused to refer to her in less than familiar terms, at least to herself. Araminta was no better than Lissa, just more fortunate.

It was their father whose sins had condemned three of his five surviving children to live lives shadowed by shame. Lissa's brother, Ned, was more accepting than either Lissa or the fiercely spirited and dramatic Kitty, who said she would rather die or become an actress than be condemned to living out her life and branded a bastard in the village where she'd been born.

For the moment, however, it was in Lissa's interests to keep up the charade that she had no idea of the real identity of Miss Araminta Partington; that she simply was trading on a chance likeness.

Araminta had cast her supercilious gaze over Lissa and clearly found her wanting before she summed up, "So, you're asking for the loan of a gown, in return for information on a certain gentleman in whom I believe you have an interest. That's a bold statement. Who do you suppose I'm interested in?"

"Lord Debenham. I was at Lady Knox's ball and I observed you dancing with him immediately after he'd claimed a dance from me. You were interested but you were unsure, too. Now you'd like me to help you ascertain what kind of gentleman he really is, otherwise, you'd have chosen to ignore my note."

"Oh, you are good." A gurgle of genuine mirth bubbled up from within the other girl. "I shan't pay you a penny, if you're hoping for money, but I shall lend you a gown—and if you don't give it back you will regret it, I promise you that. But here."

She handed a parcel over the fence and Lissa took it with a plethora of feelings warring within her. Anger at the world for putting her in the position of supplicant, anger at Araminta Partington for having the life Lissa should have had, and simple curiosity as to what might transpire tomorrow.

"Well, aren't you going to thank me from the bottom of your

heart?"

Lissa only just managed to refrain from rolling her eyes. "I haven't seen the dress yet. It's possible you've set out to humiliate me and the gown is too short or else in screamingly bad style."

Araminta shrugged. "Take it and see for yourself. Though not before you pledge to give me a full report within two days' time."

***

Lissa met Cosmo on the corner of the street, where he was waiting in a hackney. She'd left the house wearing a drab brown pelisse, but the afternoon gown Araminta had lent her had been a perfect fit and was in the first stare though, to her surprise, it was not a gown a debutante would wear. A bold cerise color, adorned with ruffles of a lighter hue, it clung to her curves in a way that, while perfectly decorous for a garden party, nevertheless highlighted Lissa's finer attributes.

And even though she had no full-length looking glass, she could tell by the way it molded her body and, later, the flare of interest in the glances of gentlemen of all ages, that she cut a fine figure. So while she smiled and nodded in response to the greetings she received, often coupled with the hopes that "Cosmo's fair cousin enjoy her sadly too brief stay in London", she was painfully aware that the pleasure of the moment was a cruel contrast to her reality.

A perfect summer's day had created an idyllic backdrop to Mrs. Gargery's summer entertainment. Trestle tables beneath the trees overlaid by white tablecloths carried an abundance of delicious food. Sweet and savory pies, strawberries and cream and syllabub were just some of the mouthwatering fare on offer. The gardens of the elegant house were exquisite, with terraces and rosebushes and sweeping grassy hills. The hostess herself seemed to take a shine to Lissa and was quizzing her with great interest over her "background", as she tried to recall a certain young lady she'd met recently whom Larissa strongly resembled.

"I'll have to introduce you to my nephew when we meet in the ballroom," she declared. "Indeed, there he is. My darling Roderick. Mr. Roderick Woking. That's Lord Debenham's nephew on the other side of the family. The poor boy has lost his heart to a dark-haired enchantress but a blind fool could see Roderick is out of his league and will get nowhere."

Lissa liked Mrs. Gargery's unaffected friendliness and was

sorry when Cosmo reclaimed her to point out his quarry. "There, you see, is the gentleman your father does business with and who danced with you though he doesn't remember it for I beheld him look at you a moment ago, quite blankly."

Lord Debenham was conversing with a much younger gentleman, whose brisk and enthusiastic manner and bright and eager expression instantly brought a pang to Lissa's vulnerable heart. For indeed, as she had hoped, Mr. Ralph Tunley was in attendance.

"Lead me to them. You can introduce yourself to Mr. Tunley and remind him of his visit to the house," Lissa urged, to Cosmo's surprised horror. Adding, when her employer's son demurred, "I can't possibly get Lord Debenham's eyes right unless I look into them. Please, Master Cosmo, I've not disgraced you up to this minute and I shan't start now."

The patent shock in Mr. Tunley's eyes when Lissa was introduced by Cosmo as his "cousin from Little Paisley enjoying a couple of weeks in London" was adequate reward for Lissa executing Cosmo's commission. In her reticule, she had a pencil and small sketchpad, of which she would avail herself shortly. In the meantime, she made sure to take in every detail of haughty Lord Debenham.

But it was Ralph who really interested her; whose bright blue eyes remained wide with delighted amazement and whose kind, generous mouth did things to her insides that she'd never experienced before.

Lord Debenham was particularly assiduous in making her feel that London was indeed a richer place through her presence, at which point Lissa decided she trusted him as much as a stoat in a henhouse. His response was in direct proportion to the level of humility she had shown, and she was sure that if she'd had more experience, she'd have understood a greater subtext in his smooth words. He found her worthy of more than a cursory greeting, that much she knew, but there was something about him that made her recoil. Certainly he was handsome in a commanding way, but there was a cruel twist to his mouth and a look of entitlement in his eye that she did not like at all.

Ralph, on the other hand, was clearly longing to say things that current circumstances prevented, and she was ridiculously delighted when a little later, she found herself part of a much larger group, and that Ralph had somehow managed to inveigle himself between two dowagers so that he could murmur without being overheard, "You are clearly the mistress of subterfuge, Miss Hazlett, but I fear your Master Cosmo must be your chosen consort."

Above, the enormous branches of an elm tree shaded them while clusters of guests picked at the sumptuously laden food table or sat in comfortable wicker chairs or strolled amidst the lovely gardens.

Lissa recognized the longing tinged with jealousy in his voice. It made her feel powerful in a way she'd never experienced. "Master Cosmo sees me as no more than the lowly governess, whose talent he wishes to exploit in order to add to his consequence."

She hoped she didn't betray her shocked delight when she felt the quick, surreptitious squeeze of her new admirer's hand before he added, softly, "Perhaps such enterprising minds as ours could change our hopeless situations."

When another guest arrived, they both turned away to the food table where they pretended great interest in the selection.

"You're the man with all the experience, Mr. Tunley, and tomorrow I must return this which was the only decent dress I was able to procure by less than honest means," Lissa whispered. "You tell me how we might alter our—as you put it—hopeless situations, though what you would like to alter it to, and what your motivation is I can only wonder at."

"My hopeless social and financial situation never felt so hopeless until I discovered myself hopelessly in love with a lowly governess in an even more hopeless situation, Miss Hazlett. What are we to do?"

He slanted a suitably agonized expression up at her as he speared a piece of ham and Lissa laughed. "Oh, my, but you have perfected the star-crossed lover look to the finest degree. I think your calling is the stage if you want to really be noticed, though I doubt that will bring the necessary financial rewards." Nevertheless, his words reverberated through her and filled her with warmth and, yes, hope.

Mr. Tunley pretended to look slightly offended before the light returned to his eyes and his mouth quirked. "I am rather good at charades, I'll admit, however in this instance, my sentiments are a true reflection of what I feel here." He tapped his heart and suddenly there was nothing but raw feeling in his gaze.

Adding a plover's egg to his plate, he said a little wistfully, "It's true that I can get beyond myself in the excitement of the moment, Miss Hazlett. Forgive me. You are beautiful and clearly clever and enterprising. You can—and I suspect, will—rise above the shortcomings of your birth. Forgive me for putting it so bluntly. I hope you will make a fine match and one that will make you happy. Sadly, I have five older brothers. I am required to prove myself before I can inveigle myself into some rewarding sinecure. Perhaps in ten years I'll be in a position whereby I could make you a respectable offer, but you'll be long married by then."

She was about to respond with all the intensity such a declaration demanded; indeed, she was about to put her hand on his sleeve and tell him that her feelings echoed his and not to despair, for there must be some way, when Cosmo suddenly appeared.

"Miss Ha— I mean, Cousin Larissa, it's time we departed. Are you ready?"

Would he really speak to a cousin with such cavalier disregard for whether she might share his desire to leave, and when she was in conversation with another? Yet she was his servant when all was said and done. With a quick nod at Ralph, and a look which she hoped conveyed that her heart was in accord with his, she responded to Cosmo's summons.

"Please, Master Cosmo, I need but two minutes to sketch Lord Debenham without his realizing it," she whispered when they were out of hearing.

He cut her off. "Lud's sake, you've had all afternoon to look at him." He was clearly agitated and eager to go, making his reasons clear when he said, "Can't you do it from memory? You've created far too much interest already. I don't know how I'm going to explain it if you come up in conversation at some later date. One gentleman thought he recalled seeing you at Lady Stanley's ball whereupon Lord Debenham announced you were a fine dancer. Fortunately, the subject was changed at that point."

"Please, just two minutes more." Lissa scrabbled in her reticule and brandished her sketchpad then took refuge in the shade of a tree a few feet from the rose garden, but so she had a clear view of Lord Debenham, who was once again in a group that included Ralph.

True to her word, it took only two minutes to sketch a rough draft she could work from later, with another thirty seconds to sketch a quick one of Ralph. She was just closing her book when Mrs. Gargery's voice intruded.

"My dear, so you're an artist, please let me see what you've drawn."

Lissa was aware of Cosmo's horror when she slanted a glance to her left, and was pleased to compound it as she flipped open a page, asking, "Do you think it a fair likeness?"

Mrs. Gargery gasped. "Why, you are a master. It's superb."

"Pardon me, but we really must be leaving. Mrs. Gargery can't possibly be interested in your idle doodling. Larissa, please come now!"

The sharpness in his tone made the kindly Mrs. Gargery widen her eyes in surprise but Lissa obediently returned her sketchpad to her reticule and followed Cosmo out of the garden, saying placatingly, "I showed her a drawing of a rose, Master Cosmo, which I had ready for such a situation."

When he merely glowered, she produced her sketchpad, turned to the appropriate page to show him in case he didn't believe her and wanted to cause trouble later.

Cosmo visibly relaxed, though his tone did not lose its edge as he climbed after her into the waiting carriage. "Just make sure you do a good job of your rendition of Lord Debenham, and don't make me appear a fool, Miss Hazlett. You know what will happen if you do."

Lissa was surprised as she tilted her head to look at him in the dim interior of the carriage. He'd dented her enjoyment of the afternoon, when she'd thought he'd be pleased.

She hesitated to suggest that gratitude might be in order, but was taken aback when Cosmo muttered, "I rely on you, Miss Hazlett, and I don't like it. However, if you let me down, I'll see your reputation shredded."

Chapter Four

"Really, Araminta, it's not like you to be so agitated. Who are you waiting for? A lover to signal you from the apple tree?"

Araminta swung back from the window to glare at Hetty, who was relaxing in a chair and looking over the top of the book she had in her lap.

Hetty's charge was too close to the truth and it irritated Araminta beyond measure that her little sister could so easily read her. And others, according to their mother, who claimed Hetty's sweet and empathetic nature made her a good gauge of people's feelings. She'd added that this was something Araminta could learn to her benefit, which had done nothing to endear the apparently remarkable Hetty to her, if that's what dear Mama had hoped.

Hetty, Araminta had quickly pointed out, was only able to observe things and people unnoticed because she was such a timid little dormouse in both looks and temperament that no one ever noticed her.

The reflection, though, gave Araminta pause. In fact, it was something that was beginning to trouble her more than a little lately, when she stopped to consider it. Hetty seemed less and less the plump pudding she'd been when she'd set her cap at cabbage-headed Edgar, their late, lamented cousin, who'd drowned after rushing off into the night with that designing piece, Lady Julia.

No, it wasn't so much that Araminta had observed an improvement in her sister's looks, but that she had observed Hetty seemed to create far more interest from the male contingent than she ought.

Araminta stepped back into the center of the room and stretched languidly. "A lover, Hetty?" She affected a lazy smile though her heart was beating just a little faster than usual.

"'Wouldn't you like to know? But," she cocked her head as if in great thought, adding, "didn't Cousin Stephen say he and Mama would love your company for their afternoon walk?"

"Is it that time already?" Hetty leapt up, obviously forgetting any suggestion Araminta might be engaging in a possible assignation so that, when Araminta glimpsed in the distance from the window, the dark-haired governess in her drab clothing approaching the property, she was in good time to make her way to the fence to greet her.

The girl looked surprised to see her, for the agreement was that Larissa was going to simply leave the parcel in the crook of the apple tree for Araminta to fetch.

But Araminta was eaten up with curiosity to learn what had transpired the previous afternoon. Immediately she began to question the girl. Had Sir Aubrey been there? To whom had Lord Debenham spoken? Had he mentioned Araminta directly to Miss Hazlett? What were Miss Hazlett's impressions of him?

At this question, the young woman's eyes narrowed. "He's a dangerous man. Even my employer says he's eaten up with vice, and he's one to talk!"

Araminta smiled. Since she'd decided she was going to marry Sir Aubrey, Lord Debenham's character didn't matter, unless he posed a danger to Sir Aubrey's prospects or reputation. Rumors swirled around Sir Aubrey, she knew, but they'd never been substantiated. No, she was more concerned that His Lordship had remarked upon similarities in looks between Miss Hazlett and herself. For Araminta had to concede that they shared the same glossy dark hair and similar bone structure. Not that Miss Hazlett possessed Araminta's flawless beauty, to be sure. But now, even more, Araminta wondered how such a resemblance could be utilized to her benefit.

"You were successful in aping your betters, then? What do you know of how those in high society conduct themselves? You're just a governess." At first Araminta was annoyed by the young woman's self-composed response, before realizing that if she did indeed succeed in utilizing Miss Hazlett, such self-confidence was just what was needed.

"Wearing your dress enabled me to imagine I was you." Miss Hazlett paused, her green eyes—certainly not the striking color of Araminta's—going cloudy. "Though I don't know why you were so amenable to the idea when you should despise me. I was certain you'd send me away with a flea in my ear."

Araminta frowned, not wanting to understand her. "Why should I despise you?"

The girl looked surprised. "Surely you're not going to deny that you know. Why, we share the same father, of course. I'd thought you'd hate me for it. I do *you*, after all."

Araminta's mouth dropped open. She'd not wanted to hear the girl put it into words. She gasped and stepped back as if Miss Hazlett had physically assaulted her. "How dare you?" she managed. Her tongue felt swollen and her heart beat erratically as she stared at…this baseborn imposter.

"Surely you knew?" The girl looked momentarily abashed before she raised her chin proudly. "Don't pretend to have a fit of the vapors. You cannot have misunderstood my reasons for contacting you."

With difficulty, Araminta regulated her breathing. How clearly she remembered the young woman's visit to The Grange all those months ago, on the pretext of requesting funds for the village school. Her father, she recalled, had acted most strangely as he'd sent Miss Hazlett into the room where the servants were generally required to wait.

So this, indeed, *was* her father's bastard standing right before her. Larissa Hazlett was the daughter of Mrs. Hazlett in the village, whose horse Araminta had insisted her father buy for her, despite knowing how much it would upset her mother, for even then, deep down, Araminta had known the truth. Lissa was the girl who'd sat in church with her fellow base-born siblings—her father's bastards— in a pew behind the first family of the district, Lord Partington's wife, Lady Sybil, and his daughters, Hetty and Araminta. Even yesterday, when Araminta had spoken to the girl, she'd pretended ignorance. But she had known. Yes, she had known.

Indignation and anger were followed by a great sense of superiority. This poor, stained creature before her could never compete with Araminta, no matter how beautiful she was. They might share a father but Miss Hazlett was a bastard, and a bastard could never rise in the world.

Fortunately, Araminta was as adept as the young woman before her at keeping her wits in check. It would be best not to gloat if she wanted the girl to be useful to her, which she certainly did. "So, telling me you hated me and that I should lend you my gowns whenever you want something in the first stare was your reason for wanting to meet me? I must say, this is all rather a shock."

Her half-sister—she choked on the term—was gazing anxiously at her as she obviously decided to alter her approach. Oh, Araminta could sense her insincerity a mile away as she said demurely, "I am sorry I said that. However I'm truly grateful that you saw fit to allow me to wear your dress for an afternoon. Besides, I've always wondered…about you."

"Have you indeed? But let's return to this important gentleman you were required to sketch. Have you told me everything? You look like the sort who would keep secrets." Araminta decided she could dismiss the threat she'd originally feared that Miss Hazlett might pose. With no social status, Miss Hazlett could never be a likely prospect for any gentleman upon whom Araminta set her sights. Certainly not anyone in Sir Aubrey or Lord Debenham's league.

In the meantime, there was this unexpected foray into subterfuge to enjoy. Life could sometimes be so deadly dull, even when she was feted by admirers at every turn. And decidedly, this Miss Hazlett was going to be useful in passing on information regarding the more interesting of these admirers. Like Sir Aubrey.

"So, this sketch you clearly executed with passable results…" Araminta considered the information, thoughtfully. "You will no doubt be doing more of this sort of thing in future." She tapped her fingers upon the top of the garden fence that separated them. It was not hard to see how desperate the girl was to sample more of what she'd tasted the previous day. Perhaps she'd already set her cap at some out-of-reach nonpareil. Well, that would be interesting to observe, though could only result in disappointment for Miss Hazlett.

Araminta took the parcel from her and leaned her head closer. "I cannot but be repulsed by who you are, but the fact remains that we can, I believe, be useful to one another." She gave a decisive nod. "Yes! You can be my little spy in return for the means I provide that will enable you to gain entry to similar entertainments."

The girl cut her off. "I see little chance of that happening. I'm a governess and I have two little girls to take charge of."

Irritated as she always was when anything interfered with her plans, Araminta glowered. Then her brow cleared. "So this Master Cosmo fancies himself as a portraitist, does he? Oh, don't look at me like that! Of course, I guessed the truth." Araminta laughed. "And that he wishes to be one of us. His family aspires to be like us. Like me, I mean. Oh, do say he has a sister about to make her debut? Good Lord! That's too marvelous. In order to achieve my aims, I shall work my magic so that you're given the time off to do as I require. Never at the same entertainment as me, you understand. But there will be occasions when you will be useful.

"Meanwhile, you can help Master Cosmo see his way to becoming London's finest portraitist. You can sketch his portraits for him and I can have you supply me with the information I'm interested in. And I thought this was going to be the dreariest second season ever!"

***

Despite concerns over the potential pitfalls of Araminta's plans, Lissa returned home in high spirits that were quickly quashed.

One minute she'd been imagining herself the belle of the ball, dressed in her half-sister's glorious diaphanous creations, the next minute her arm had been snatched by Cosmo, who hauled her into the gloomy cavity beneath the stairs.

His eyes were black with anger in his pasty white face as he raked his fingers through his fashionable 'Titus' coiffure. "Lord Debenham is highly pleased by his sketch, which I presented this morning." He pursed his thin lips. "I told him I'd executed it from a brief study of him yesterday and now it seems half of the ton wants something similar! What am I to do?"

Lissa drew back at his agitation. She'd seen him in such moods when he completely lost control and now that she was alone with him, she was frightened. First, he paced between the stairs and the end of the corridor, then he loomed over her, clearly using his height and bulk to intimidate her. "A pretty state of affairs this is, isn't it?"

"I thought that was what you wanted."

This didn't seem to be the right approach. Lissa thought quickly. Cosmo was volatile and she'd seen him smash the nearest item at hand during his temper tantrums. But now she had an answer that she was reasonably sure would placate him.

Careful that she gave no sign of being intimidated, she managed calmly, "I carried off yesterday's charade with no one being the wiser, and, only today, I've ensured a regular supply of suitable gowns for any occasion, Master Cosmo. Moreover, I have befriended a viscount's daughter, who has promised to introduce Miss Maria to any potential suitor whose interest she cares to engage. There! I hope you are as delighted as your sister will be. Just tell me who you wish me to sketch and I'll find the means to do it."

She swallowed, for this was the difficult bit. "I'll just need some pin money for my pains."

Instead of greeting this with relief, his face turned red. "Pay you?" He looked horrified. "But you're a governess. You live under our roof, enjoying our food and shelter and protection. Why should I pay you?" His shoulders slumped. "How can I when I have no money?"

A surge of anger stiffened Lissa's spine. "Didn't you and Lord Debenham come to some agreement over 'your' sketch of him? Are you to paint or sketch half of London for no return?" She turned to go. "I'm sorry for your predicament, Master Cosmo. Perhaps someone else can help you."

"No!" Once again his unwelcome touch was upon her as he snatched her wrist, pulling her back to him. "I'll give you a shilling for each painting."

"I want half of the agreed amount, and if I am clever enough to rub shoulders with those you paint, then I will find out what the going rate is."

"One-third."

"Agreed." Lissa stepped back, out of his hateful aura. She'd won this round, and soon she'd enjoy a taste of all the wonders that had been denied her. She'd also have a little money for the first time in her life. Money that might in some way pave the way for the life she'd always wanted: a husband she cared for and a family. And definitely a carriage.

She didn't need the trappings of high society but in her present dowerless state, bearing the indelible stain of illegitimacy, she hadn't, until just now, seen how she could possibly ever have a husband, much less a carriage.

Chapter Five

On this gray, drizzly and miserable afternoon, it wasn't the poor state of the weather that accounted for Ralph's dismal mood but the task set for him by his employer.

For over a year, he'd done Lord Debenham's bidding. Well, his master had been Mr. Carruthers back then, newly returned from the West Indies with pockets lined with gold. A cousin's death had elevated him to the peerage, and Ralph's mother had been in transports when Ralph had secured the position of secretary to the soon-to-be-elevated Lord Debenham.

Her distress had been almost comical when Ralph had declared some months ago he simply couldn't continue; that the demands were so overreaching and the man's contempt of his supposed inferiors so strong, it made Ralph's daily job a nightmare.

In the end, his mother had prevailed, telling him quite rightly that to leave would invite Lord Debenham's revenge, surely, and where else could Ralph go?

It was the truth. Ralph was a prisoner of circumstance and he had no other means of respectable work if he ever hoped to marry and have a family—which indeed he did. The tragedy was that the perfect contender had just waltzed into his orbit, tantalizing him with everything about her, from her lovely dark hair and sparkling green eyes to her gentle wit. Her unavailability.

Of course, Miss Hazlett hadn't meant to taunt him. She was not that kind of young woman. But her innocent determination to make something of her own miserable circumstances had sparked something to life within him.

He'd always accepted that his older brother bore the greatest burden. Teddy was the nicest natured of all the brothers, and he'd never quite recovered after the inexplicable desertion of the woman he'd hoped to make his wife. But he would marry, for even without money he was highly eligible. And handsome to boot.

John, the next in line, was following a career in the church. He had a modest living and was already happily ensconced in a well-appointed vicarage with a pretty, if demanding, wife.

The next two brothers after John had had army commissions bought for them while Harry, the black sheep of the family, had run off to sea.

Ralph was the youngest and the one over whom his mother despaired. Now she was pinning her hopes on the fact he'd be rewarded for serving well an important member of the House of Lords. It was a job Ralph had come to despise with greater feeling every day.

But he was in no position to give it up. And if there were any chance that he would somehow be granted a handsome sinecure that would put him in a position to make Miss Hazlett an honest offer, he would stay.

The fact she'd succeeded in infiltrating the garden party so successfully proved her determination and ability to rise beyond the usual obstacles. She would make a fine wife.

Some day. The sad fact was it might be years before he could take a wife without the risk of driving them both into poverty, should they have a large family. Or any family at all.

At this present moment he was occupied with writing the eviction notices that would send a number of his employer's cottagers into worse despair than Ralph could ever imagine, and there was not a thing he could do about it. Lord Debenham had taken a firm hand in the matter of those who didn't—or couldn't— pay their rent on time, and had determined that henceforth there would be no second chances.

Ralph was to see that the letters were dispatched, and was then to follow up himself to ensure that no families hung on to what was no longer theirs. He felt sick as he dipped his nib once more into the ink and signed the final eviction notice on behalf of Lord Debenham.

After such a painful afternoon's work, Ralph decided a brisk walk was needed to clear his heavy mood once a chance presented itself. Hyde Park was only a short walk away and looking at the lovely ladies promenading there was always a pleasant diversion. His mother liked to be informed on what fashions were being worn by whom, and Ralph, apart from being a dutiful son and enjoying the sport in any case, had a good eye for an ensemble in the first stare.

The sun was dropping lower in the sky, the birds were singing in the trees and he was dreaming, impossibly, of a future with Miss Hazlett, when he was shocked to see a familiar profile come around a bend, chattering with great animation to Sir Aubrey.

It was only when she was within a few yards of him that he realized it *wasn't* Miss Hazlett. Certainly not the Miss Larissa Hazlett with whom he was acquainted, though surely the two must be related.

The pang that squeezed his heart also made him realize how much it would have pained him to have seen *his* Miss Hazlett so clearly entranced by a gentleman other than himself and again he was fired with the determination to find a way to enable them to be together.

Immediately this was followed by the painful reality that his hands were tied. Short of an unexpected inheritance—and none of his infirm relatives were remotely well-heeled, though all were respectable enough—or committing highway robbery, Ralph was completely dependent upon Lord Debenham for a paltry salary.

Leaning against a tree trunk, he gazed at the young lady talking to Sir Aubrey and his misery increased. She was clearly making a determined play for him and Ralph wondered how Sir Aubrey could still be so successful at winning female interest when he was dogged by Lord Debenham's allegations.

His employer had an almost pathological hatred for this gentleman, and it was intriguing that Miss Larissa Hazlett's relative—for they surely *must* be related—should show such singular interest in someone whom rumor painted as a murderer and plotter of treason. Thanks to Lord Debenham, it was widely whispered Sir Aubrey had been involved in the plot on Lord Castlereagh's life. Unsubstantiated rumors, certainly.

When the young lady turned so that her face was no longer concealed by her bonnet, he realized with a start that he'd seen her before at several high-society entertainments. He struggled to recall her name. Surely it was Miss Partington? Yes, the debutante who'd ended her last season under something of a cloud but who appeared to have bounced back, the way she was talking with such joyful animation to Sir Aubrey.

Returning to his office, it was harder to concentrate, but after he'd finished his unpalatable duties, Ralph took a circuitous route past the large home where Miss Hazlett worked. He suspected she'd be in the habit of taking her young charges for a walk in the afternoons in the little park opposite, and so he dragged his heels in the hopes she'd appear.

He was in luck, for indeed there she was, and not only that, her face lit up with unadulterated delight when she saw him loitering beneath a plane tree.

"Meet me on the opposite side of the park, where we are not in view of the windows," she whispered as she passed by him, not pausing.

Ralph's heart beat a rapid tattoo in his chest as he discreetly followed her with a surreptitious glance over his shoulder to ensure he wasn't being watched. He hadn't liked what he'd seen of her employer, young Mr. Cosmo. He was jealous of the young man's proximity, too, and couldn't imagine he'd not have an interest in the young governess that went beyond wishing her to sketch his paintings.

Waiting impatiently in a shaded corner of the park, he wondered if the chance for intimacy beyond a smile might present itself, should Miss Hazlett manage to send the little girls off to find fairies in the nearby bushes.

However, the moment she appeared before him, she clasped her hands in entreaty, whispering, "Mr. Tunley, I am really at my wit's end as to what to do, and I hope you can advise me."

His pleasure that she should consider him in a position to assist her was quickly displaced by his sense of failure. How *could* such a poorly situated young man as himself help the goddess of his heart's desire?

Before he could respond, she began without preamble, "My half-sister, a young woman who looks extremely like myself, lent me the gown I wore to Mrs. Gargery's garden party because she wanted me to learn what I could about Lord Debenham, amongst other certain gentlemen in whom she's interested. Now she has again visited me, with the request that tomorrow I accompany her to an assignation with," she gave a furtive look about them before whispering, "your employer's *valet*."

"Good God!" The words were out before he could stop them, so great was his shock. "Lord Debenham's valet? Jem? And you have a half-sister?"

"Yes, one who looks exceedingly like myself. Even Lord

Debenham remarked upon it, though he'd not look twice at me, dressed as I am now." She seemed to be concentrating on her own clearly tumultuous thoughts rather than registering his shock. Tentatively, she added, glancing up at him, "You see, Mr. Tunley, I did not mention it before, as it seemed of no consequence at the time." She dropped her gaze, as if overcome suddenly by shame and Ralph wished he could put out his hand and offer what bolstering courage he could. But it was possible they were being watched. He was always conscious of being watched, with an employer like Debenham.

She took an audible breath, then raised her eyes, appealingly. "I am ashamed to tell you this, but I want you to know the truth. It won't make you think any better of me because, after all, a bastard is a bastard, whoever her father happens to be. But my half-sister is Miss Araminta Partington."

"Miss Partington is your *sister*?"

"My half-sister, for Lord Partington is my father, and he has two natural-born daughters. He abandoned my mother on the eve of their nuptials to marry the bride his parents had chosen for him. Nevertheless, during the intervening years, he's spent most of his time with my mother, as if in fact they *were* married. I also have a brother and sister, with another one on the way."

She sighed, adding softly, "Another one to share my shame, and to have to make its way in the world with no status. But as I was saying..." She returned briskly to the subject at hand. "It was my half-sister, Miss Araminta Partington, who lent me the dress I wore to the garden party, and, as I said, she contacted me, unexpectedly, and asked me to accompany her on this visit."

"To visit my employer's valet? Good Lord, why? She's a...*lady*!"

"Precisely." Miss Hazlett smiled. "This is the extraordinary thing. Apparently Miss Partington believes this young man...the valet, Jem...is in possession of a letter written by Sir Aubrey's late wife, which implicates one of the men—Sir Aubrey *or* Lord Debenham—in the attempted assassination of Lord Castlereagh."

Ralph could not have been more astonished. He gripped the wrought iron fence though his concern was entirely for the lovely young woman opposite him. If it hadn't been, he'd have gripped *her*, but it was quite possible Cosmo Lamont might choose that moment to take his daily constitutional and appear around the corner.

A week ago, this same lovely creature was like a beautiful butterfly beating her wings against the nebulous periphery of his life, a mere governess and he a simple clerk. There was nothing to bring them together. Then suddenly she was rubbing shoulders with the ton. Now she was growing ever closer to his decidedly wicked employer.

"My belief is," she went on, "that my half-sister wants to discover the contents of this letter so she can focus her attention on the gentleman whose reputation is not smeared by it. If I were to hazard a guess, I'd say that if this letter exists, Lord Debenham may have a very good reason for not wanting it in the public domain."

"You are a sharp young lady." Ralph could well countenance the possibility of Lord Debenham being involved in shady dealings, perhaps even Lord Castlereagh's attempted assignation, though the thought had never occurred to him before, for it was Sir Aubrey's reputation that had been so damaged. But then it was also true that Sir Aubrey's late wife was Lord Debenham's cousin. And lover, it was suggested. There may well be more to it than Debenham had relayed to the world but such a sordid affair should under no circumstances involve his precious Miss Hazlett.

He was afraid for her.

"You cannot accompany Miss Partington on such a mission," he added firmly. "It may be a trap. You can have no idea what kind of man Lord Debenham is. Ruthless and cruel. He'll not differentiate between a villain whose interests run counter to his own or a defenseless female such as yourself." Impulsively he gripped her hand and was jolted by the connection that ran between them as strongly as if the bond were the warmth of their bodies joined as one.

This was too much. How could he breach the divide that yawned between them without harming Miss Hazlett or her reputation? If he was unable to offer marriage, he was unable to offer *anything*.

He felt her yield a moment before she pulled back, practicality once again the order of the day. "I *will* go, though I do not feel comfortable going alone without telling anyone, which is why I'm telling you. I merely wanted your advice on what I should do if the letter indeed exists."

"But you can't go!" The idea was preposterous.

"Why?"

"I've told you. It's not safe. Lord Debenham is a...debaucher."

"My half-sister is meeting his valet, not His Lordship."

"Then she no doubt will induce him to give her the letter. My advice is that you at least glean the contents of the letter before it changes hands. Then tell me and we can decide from there."

"I knew I could count on your support." She reached out quickly and, with both hands, gave his a squeeze.

"I still wish you would not go. It could be dangerous."

"I feel obligated. Also, Araminta is the kind of spoiled young lady who is quite likely to flounce off in high dudgeon if I refused. She'd never lend me another gown again." She smiled. "But the truth is, if there were something important in that letter pertaining to Lord Debenham, it could assist you, Mr. Tunley."

He shook his head, thinking how sweet she looked when she nibbled her lower lip as was clearly her wont when she was worried. "I cannot imagine how your sister knows of such a letter? One that, I gather, must be supposedly incriminating? *I've* certainly heard nothing, and I work for the blackguard."

"The misses Partingtons' lady's maid, Jane, is sweetheart to Lord Debenham's valet. Jem told Jane that Lord Debenham_took the letter out of Sir Aubrey's dead wife's hands to use in case he needed it. Jane, I believe, then told her mistresses."

"But this must have happened years ago. And Jem has only just now decided to reveal the existence of the letter, only he's not sure if it incriminates Debenham or Sir Aubrey?"

Lissa shrugged. "I have no interest in either gentleman, but I do have an interest in being useful to you. And to Miss Araminta, though from a less altruistic point of view. She's a cunning piece, but I don't believe she's as clever as I."

Ralph chuckled. "Not many young ladies are, I'd wager. Well, I suppose there can be no harm in seeing Jem," he conceded. "He should not have taken a letter that didn't belong to him—if indeed it exists—but I can see why Jem wanted to shore up his position. Lord Debenham is a cruel employer. Fortunately, he doesn't beat *me.*"

Miss Hazlett's pretty mouth opened, then she frowned. "It all sounds rather grubby. Imagine, the two men fighting over the same poor lady who took her own life. But who am I to judge what is sordid, being what I am?"

"Never say such things! You are perfect!" Ralph declared, gripping her hands once more with a quick look over his shoulder. "I shall always think it, and never for a moment must you consider yourself stained with the sin of your parents!"

Conscious of the risks they ran, he dropped her hands, which, he was pleased to note, had returned the fond pressure. "I wonder what Jem will have to say for himself," he mused. "I've seen him only briefly once or twice when I've gone to Lord Debenham's house to deliver messages or to have documents signed. He is a handsome, confident young man, who I imagine would be quick to seize an opportunity. So he wants money for it, then?"

Miss Hazlett shrugged. "I gather Jem can't read. Anyway, he's keen to profit from the letter and I daresay hopes to blacken your employer's name."

The little girls were returning from their foray to look for pixies at the far end of the park. Ralph saw the worried glance Miss Hazlett flicked first at them and then in the direction of the house. Although Ralph was confident they could not be observed from its windows the danger remained that one of the Lamonts might walk around the corner.

"You feel spied upon?" he asked.

"Always," she replied. "You must leave now, I think. If Cosmo or Mrs. Lamont saw you, I could be dismissed upon the spot if it pleased them. Though Cosmo needs me too much."

"Have you done more work for him?"

"I managed another sketch, which was received with apparent enthusiasm yesterday. Not that Cosmo would tell me that, though he's quite happy to tell me of the flurry of commissions he's received, which he expects me to execute."

She looked suddenly excited. "Perhaps I'll become rich. I negotiated with him to receive a third." Daringly, she touched Ralph's sleeve for the briefest moment. "Yes, perhaps I'll become rich, Mr. Tunley, and then…" She blushed before dropping her eyes but her sentiment was clear—and it flooded him with desire and determination.

"Somehow, Miss Hazlett, we shall find a way to proceed beyond mere words we know carry no weight when there is no possibility of deepening our acquaintance." He didn't like to dwell on the thought of Miss Hazlett providing for them and changed the subject back to the matter at hand. "Before you go, tell me the details of this assignation between you and your sister, and where you are to meet Jem. I shall keep a watchful eye over you, if it is at all within my power, for to be truthful, the notion of what you're about to risk fills me with dread."

Chapter Six

Araminta felt very pleased with herself as she made her way down a narrow cobbled road to her assignation.

Lately, she'd been feeling more than just concerned that Hetty seemed to be increasingly well received amongst the circles that had hitherto been *her* domain. In the past, no one had seemed to notice her silly little peahen of a sister. Now, when Araminta observed the way some of these handsome, rich and titled gentlemen looked at Hetty, she no longer saw pity in their faces.

No, she saw interest.

Of course, yesterday's carriage ride with Sir Aubrey had cemented her precedence over her sister. Sir Aubrey had positively glowered at Hetty, just as he had when the entire Partington family had met him during that terrible walk her father had proposed the day before, during which he'd told them of his dire financial straits.

Perhaps Sir Aubrey suspected Hetty was sweet on him and was using bad temper to convey to her that he could have no interest in one so beneath his notice.

That's what Araminta had to believe.

But then she'd learned about the letter, which apparently Hetty was planning to secure from Lord Debenham's valet. Good Lord, what was the girl about? How on earth had Hetty learned such a thing but, more concerningly, *why* should she want to do anything about it?

Araminta's first impulse was to tell their Papa but when she gave the matter greater consideration she realized there were far greater potential advantages if she matched Hetty's cunning.

In the first instance, if such a letter existed, why did Debenham not pay his manservant what it was worth? Then Araminta got to wondering if in fact the letter was this manservant's insurance. If that were the case, then the letter must not paint a very complimentary picture of Lord Debenham. But if that were so, it must somehow exonerate Sir Aubrey, and why would Hetty want a letter that would do that? Oh yes, Araminta had seen the occasional longing look or remark that suggested her sister had an interest in Sir Aubrey but surely she'd never truly imagined her interest could be returned? Especially, after yesterday's carriage ride? Besides, Hetty *knew* Araminta had set her sights on him?

What was more concerning was the realization that if Hetty did, in fact, discover the means to exonerate Sir Aubrey—for apparently all this nonsense about the Castlereagh affair was quite important—her little sister would have very good reason for attracting Sir Aubrey's attention. And even though it would be due entirely to gratitude on his part for her helping him out of a sticky situation of his own making, Hetty would be the one getting all the glory.

Sir Aubrey had been foolish to have married a woman who had taken her own life. Furthermore, all this talk of his being part of a Spencean club sounded very havey-cavey, and Araminta didn't quite understand it, but if the letter was something he did or didn't want in the public domain, then it must be Araminta who did the clever work required to hand it back to him.

Fortunately, Jane, the lady's maid Araminta shared with Hetty, had been very forthcoming as she'd brushed Araminta's hair this morning. Especially after Araminta had told her that Hetty had confessed to Araminta all the details concerning the letter and had asked Araminta to see Jem on her account, as she was frightened.

So now, instead of Jane accompanying Hetty to an assignation with the lowly valet, Jem, to fetch the letter, Araminta had located that creature to whom she was related and resembled mildly: Miss Hazlett. For who else could she get to accompany her for the necessary chaperonage on such a forbidden mission?

Delicious tingles of excitement curled their way through Araminta as she thought of the happy conclusion to this adventure. Sir Aubrey was more than likely to ask Araminta to do him the honor of becoming his wife on the spot. He'd already made clear his interest during a tender encounter in the corridor of Lady Knox's townhouse, after Araminta had been returning from the mending room during the ball.

Of course, Sir Aubrey was a mere baronet at the moment, but only a sickly cousin stood in the way of Sir Aubrey becoming a viscount, and there was even a doddering earl in the wings who'd neglected to secure the family line to whom he was related. Araminta was nothing if not a betting girl.

"No need to look so downcast, Miss Hazlett, no one will take the slightest bit of interest in you, the way you're dressed," Araminta reassured her as they waited in a dim booth in a tavern, a place no respectable lady would be seen. It was very exciting. Araminta had dressed herself for the part in a veiled bonnet. She'd chosen a flattering gown, for she wanted people to admire her without being able to recognize her. And she was not disappointed. Men of all stations positively leered at her.

Miss Hazlett, veiled too, did not seem to be reveling in the attention nearly as much but then, she was probably uncomfortable at being shown up by Araminta's superior manner of dress and carriage.

When Araminta demanded that she tell her why she was looking like a frightened rabbit, the girl replied, "If I'm recognized I'll lose my position, and then what will become of me?"

"Your father will take you in." Araminta wasn't in the mood to pander to such lily-livered whining. It rankled that her papa chose to spend so much time with his forbidden family. For now, she realized, that was why he was absent so often from home.

Miss Hazlett fiddled with the button at the wrist of her gloves. "He won't support me forever. I'm expected to work for my living. It's unlikely I'll make a match that will secure me the clothes and comforts you take for granted."

Before Araminta could respond, Jem, the lowly valet, slid into the booth, and my goodness he was handsome. Araminta didn't think she'd ever seen such a handsome man. His hair was the color of corn and his eyes—a hazy, dangerous gray—sparked with a speculative glint when he ran them over Araminta.

The most extraordinary spasm in the region of her lower belly kicked her into an awareness both disconcerting and incredibly exciting.

Briefly, she raised her veil to smile at him, just so he could see how truly beautiful she was. But as no one must know she was here, she lowered it again and began proceedings in a formal and businesslike manner, which Jem didn't seem to appreciate.

With a grunt, he thrust the letter in front of her and the contents could not have pleased her more.

In black and white, Sir Aubrey's late wife branded Lord Debenham the villain, and her Sir Aubrey the falsely accused, unfairly maligned husband.

This document was exactly what was needed to prove Sir Aubrey's innocence, and once Araminta could get it into Sir Aubrey's hands, her future happiness with him was assured.

Unfortunately, the greedy Jem wanted more than the half a crown she had to offer him for it and didn't seem to trust her when she said she'd send him the rest but that she needed to take the letter with her now.

Rudely, he rose before she did, indicating their discussion was at an end.

Araminta was for the first time in her life speechless. No gentleman had ever spoken so roughly to her on any occasion she could ever remember. Her thundering heart was also not something she was used to, but she ignored that. Her needs centered on the letter—and she'd get it, one way or another.

Glad of the protection of her veil so that Miss Hazlett couldn't see how much Araminta was affected by this rude but handsome young man, Araminta said haughtily, "This is not our last meeting, Jem, I can assure you. I always get what I want."

She thought she saw a flare of admiration in the other girl's eyes as she rose, but now her anger was getting the better of her, and she didn't care she was in a public place. She informed Jem over her shoulder that she reckoned a fine lady would be believed over a mere footman, and that he should consider himself lucky that he wasn't going to swing over this, since she was now in possession of important evidence the government would wish to know.

There! she thought with a mixture of anger and pride in her abilities to reduce him to a quivering jelly, for she was sure he was quaking while she was striding out into the street with all the power.

She was not prepared for the sudden assault as her wrist was gripped and she was whisked back into the inn and into a small antechamber, just before she reached the exit.

In the dim light, she found herself face to face with Jem, his angry eyes staring right into hers, only inches away. And she was consumed by a feeling of such fearful excitement she really could imagine she was about to swoon—properly—for the first time in her life.

"You want that letter real badly, miss, don't you?" His eyes darted over her and his breathing was shallow and rapid. "Now you know what's in it, how do I know you ain't going to blab to the world that it's me what has it? Me neck's at risk here."

The power she felt to see that he was frightened of what she could do was like an aphrodisiac, and the most enormous thrill of superiority, coupled with something deep, dark and wicked rose up from the depths of her being.

Before she even knew what she was doing, she'd closed the distance between them and cupped his face, murmuring against his suddenly trembling lips, "Here is my reassurance."

She'd never kissed a man of such low birth before, but nor had she kissed one who was as extraordinarily handsome and whose proximity unleashed such madness in her. The brief kernel of rational thought that floated within her consciousness for a second was extinguished by the mad desire to show Jem who was master. The sudden raging desires of her body made her head swim when his arms went round her and he roughly kissed her back.

The scrape of his stubbled cheek upon her tender skin, coupled with his strong male smell of sweat, dirt and horses aroused even fiercer passions within her, and even though a faint caution sounded in the recesses of her brain, she was buoyed by the knowledge that the justification for her actions was pure.

"No one's neck—or anything else—is in danger," she whispered, "as long as I get that letter." It was so good to feel in control and to know he was her slave.

Soon her tongue was tangling with his, her own breathing was deafening her, and the sensations he was evoking with his wandering hands were for some reason making her want to feel the heat of his naked flesh against her own.

She could barely get the words out. "You'd better give me what I want, Jem."

He chuckled. "Indeed, I will, miss."

It was he who finally broke them apart. His mouth curved into a sly smile and Araminta frowned as she smoothed her hair and clothing, for it was too self-satisfied for her liking. She'd like to...well, kiss that smile right off his face. Her heart was still racing and that strange, unfulfilled feeling in her lower belly was making her want to do all kinds of unheard-of and unladylike things.

Muffled shouts of laughter and the serving of drinks could be heard nearby, and when a shrill cry from a drunk patron made Araminta startle, the mood was broken. She knew it was time to leave before Larissa conducted a thorough search for her.

After a regal exit, having laid out the terms of their "arrangement", which would have him meeting her shortly with the letter, Araminta went in search of her next quarry: Lord Debenham.

**

Where on earth had Araminta gone?

In a panic after she was unable to locate her in or around the tavern's environs, Lissa finally went to Lord Partington's London townhouse. Though she was in danger of losing her place if her truancy was discovered, she loitered under the plane tree across the road until, finally, she caught the attention of the younger girl, Hetty, who had her nose pressed to the window.

Succumbing, obviously, to curiosity, Hetty came into the garden and for the first time Lissa properly made the acquaintance of her other half-sister. Immediately, she liked her. Hetty was sweet and unassuming, where Araminta was venal and calculating. It was hard to imagine they could even be related, so different were they.

Lissa was indignant on Hetty's behalf when she learned the full story of Araminta's deviousness in going behind Hetty's back to get Jem to hand over the letter. She was glad to tell Hetty that Araminta hadn't had the money on hand to secure it.

The girl's smile at this piece of information had transformed her into a beauty. "So Jem still has the letter? Why, all is not lost then!"

But all seemed lost for Lissa, and any possibility of a future with Ralph Tunley, she reflected dolefully after she'd traipsed home.

Mrs. Lamont was shouting for her and the nursery maid, whom she had begged to cover for her, was in tears.

"Oh miss, where have you bin? I've told ever so many lies about you being took sick of a sudden and going to visit your aunt for some remedy." Clara had the youngest child on her lap while the elder was demanding that her governess do drawing with her. Meanwhile, Mrs. Lamont's heavy footsteps were pounding up the stairs, and soon both she and Master Cosmo were in the room, their fearsome expressions suggesting what it must feel like to be confronted by an enemy battalion.

Oh, but she hated life here.

An image of domestic felicity with Ralph floated up before

her but was dissolved by Mrs. Lamont's fierce, "Perhaps I shall dismiss you on the spot, Miss Hazlett." Her multiple chins wobbled and her ringlets bobbed as her son glared malevolently at Lissa from behind his mother's shoulder. "Leaving the house with not a word! Why, Nellie was beside herself when you were not there for her usual drawing lesson. What possessed you to show such blatant disregard for the kindness this family has shown you?"

The knowledge that for the past six months very little regard had been shown to her by this family welled up in Lissa's breast, and for once banished all common sense.

"Very well, I shall go then!" she declared angrily, brushing past the gathered group and intending to go to her tiny attic bedchamber. At least her mother could use her help during her advantaged stages of pregnancy. She'd not cost much to keep.

"Pray, have a thought for the girls who need you." Cosmo's fingers were digging into Lissa's shoulder, and when he turned her to face him, his expression was both angry and frightened. Mama…"

He turned to his mother, who was trembling with an excess of emotion and who seemed unable to articulate the tumultuous state of her thoughts.

"Miss Hazlett has taken grave advantage, it is true. However, her imminent departure will cause far more disruption than is warranted, and although she is an ungrateful creature, she should be offered one final chance." He lowered his voice and there was a clear subtext in his expression as he added, "So that she might see there are…*benefits* to realizing the error of her ways." He put his lips close to Lissa's ear. "We will discuss this further when we are alone."

The idea of being alone with Cosmo was repugnant so Lissa ensured she was with Nellie and Harriet for the rest of the day.

Inevitably, though, he came, indicating for her to leave the girls to their drawing so he could speak to her in private as he led her to the window alcove.

"I have spoken to Mama, and you don't have to go, Miss Hazlett. I have two commissions and you're to have them all completed by Friday," he said without preamble.

Lissa waited for some kind of conciliatory addendum, or at least an indication that he was grateful and recognized his rising reputation was purely due to her.

Finally, she asked boldly, "How much will that earn me?"

Fury clouded his brow. "I ensured you kept your job. How dare you ask me now for money? If you wish to remain under this roof and enjoy my family's hospitality, you will need to show a little respect."

His cold, angry eyes were suddenly right in front of her nose. "Don't think I don't know what you're up to, Miss Hazlett. You have a young man, don't you? Well..." He looked gloating. "I have a good deal more influence than the specimen you clearly favor, so if you want him to continue to enjoy his fruitful employment, I suggest there be no more talk of something so unsavory as payment for doing only what you owe this family."

Lissa raised her chin with a fury to match his and was about to hiss a suitable response when suddenly she turned, nursing her right hand as if it gave her great pain.

"Ah, but I knew it would come to this, Master Cosmo," she whimpered, massaging the limb and pretending great sorrow. "As an honest and virtuous servant of this household, I feel I must go and confess all to your mother. I have deceived her, and both my conscience and the hand I use for sketching, are smiting me."

He looked confused. "Miss Hazlett, really, I don't think..."

"No, you really *don't* think, Master Cosmo, do you? Otherwise you'd not bite the hand that feeds you," Lissa flung back at him. "Are you so pudding-headed that you can't imagine I would happily tell the world of our little arrangement before going elsewhere? You think the lack of a good character from your mama might hamper my employment chances? I'm confident I have the proof to back up my testimony that I am the artist, not you. The only reason I remain is because I need you to secure the commissions. So why not reconsider the merits of honoring your pledge to pay me as agreed? Then we can put this unfortunate episode behind us."

She'd never spoken so forcefully but she'd been emboldened after watching Araminta conduct business.

And Lissa knew that she was cleverer than Araminta and more talented than Cosmo.

Chapter Seven

Highway robbery or a clever legal plan. These were the two choices which faced Ralph. Although he felt the former a more exciting option, and an antidote to his misery in Lord Debenham's employ, his steady common sense ultimately favored the clever legal plan.

Pacing his small office, he tried to establish what he had to work with. Clearly he must verify for himself what was in the letter Miss Hazlett had told him her half-sister had failed to secure. And in the interim, he must ignore the fact that his beloved was the illegitimate daughter of a viscount. His mother would be horrified at Ralph's choice when there were so many respectable ladies of middling rank with reasonable dowries, unstained by their accidental birth as poor Miss Larissa Hazlett had been, through no fault of her own.

But this letter. If it contained what Miss Hazlett said it did, then Ralph held Lord Debenham in the palm of his hand—and that was no bad thing, though he'd have to be careful. Ralph knew how ruthless his employer could be in his public life. It certainly did not end there. There was talk of a penchant for perverted activities involving a veritable bevy of lower-class women in the basement of his townhouse. Debenham was also a regular at Maggie Montgomery's Nunnery, a high-class brothel where, it was rumored, she sifted through the freshest, most innocent of London's new arrivals, and indentured them as virtual slaves for the pleasure of her high-paying clientele. Yet this, somehow, was not illegal.

At last Ralph found a pretext of speaking to Jem, his master's valet when he went to deliver some papers at His Lordship's townhouse and found the master not at home.

His arrival was fortuitously timed for Jem was on his way out to take one of his master's coats to the tailor for repair when he met him on the pavement near the servants' entrance.

During their hasty discussion around the corner, Jem was

initially cagey about his recent meeting with Miss Partington but when he realized Ralph shared the same distrust of their shared master, he became infinitely more forthcoming.

With a great sense of relief and not inconsiderable self-congratulation, Ralph returned to his office. Jem was clearly in terror of his master, much as Ralph was. The agreement they'd arrived at regarding the letter would, for the moment, preserve the status quo and leave everyone none the wiser. That is, until the other parts of Ralph's plan slotted into place. The letter was now Ralph's insurance, as much as Jem's.

In the meantime, there was nothing for it but to return to normal duties and wait to see how, and when, his newfound knowledge could be used.

***

Lissa knew life was an unfair business. Having met Hetty in order to pass on her concerns regarding Araminta's strange disappearance from the tavern, it was clear that the younger of her half-sisters was far sweeter and more deserving than the elder, and yet it was the devious Araminta who looked likely to win the man of her dreams, though Lissa wasn't sure that either Debenham or Sir Aubrey would make the ideal husband. Debenham she found terrifying, while Sir Aubrey appeared arrogant and distant. Hetty, however, was clearly smitten, though she'd not said anything directly to that effect.

As for Lissa, she was too poor to be more than of passing interest to her half-sisters. Perhaps they felt anger or revulsion. Nevertheless, she was only useful for the small services she could render, particularly to Araminta. She'd been relieved to learn that Araminta had finally returned home after she'd mysteriously disappeared following their meeting with Jem.

What was of graver concern, however, was learning of Jem's disappearance within hours of that meeting. In fact, so concerned was Lissa that immediately upon learning the news, she wrote a note to Ralph.

She was just drifting off to sleep when the sound of a small stone hitting her window caused her to leap out of her bed and run to the window, her heart pounding with the fear of retribution, then with delight that it was in fact Ralph she could discern in a pool of moonlight.

Snatching a shawl from the hook on the back of the door, she hastened down the servants' steps, pulled the bolt, melted into the night and, for the first time, into Ralph's strong embrace, as if it were the most natural thing in the world.

"Oh!" she cried as his lips touched her hair briefly before he set her apart from him.

"I was afraid you'd slap my face for taking such liberties."

The warmth in his voice was like a drug. He put his finger beneath her chin and tilted up her head. In the light of the yellow, waxy moon, his eyes glowed like liquid amber and desire pooled in her belly. She wanted him to continue to hold her but he stepped back with a smile, adding, "I'm glad you didn't. Just as I'm glad you told me about Jem. Have you heard anything further?"

"No, and I won't until I visit Araminta in the morning and ask the question for myself, but I gravely fear for his safety, having heard some of the things your esteemed employer is apparently capable of."

Her heart swelled when he stroked her cheek. It was a strange, disembodied sensation, and she wanted nothing more than for him to simply hold her and keep her safe. She rarely felt safe under the Lamonts' roof, and although she was fond of the little girls, it had been drummed into them to regard her as a servant and not, under any circumstances, a confidante. They were closer to their nursemaid, Clara.

Ralph's transparent admiration was balm to her barren soul but now he was deadly serious.

"This is a grave state of affairs," he told her, chafing her hand between his, perhaps to soothe himself as much as her. "Naturally I know you'll keep this entirely to yourself, but I saw Jem just before he apparently disappeared, and I saw the letter myself. I won't tell you the arrangement I made with Jem, and that's not because I don't trust you, but because if you are in some way implicated through having accompanied your…Miss Partingon, it will be safer for you to be ignorant of its contents."

Deep furrows crinkled his brow. Lissa wanted to smooth them away, and run her fingers through the springy brown hair that he was continually raking back from his eyes.

Instead, she told him her greatest fear: that Ralph would somehow find himself in similar danger to Jem. "I don't know how Cosmo knows about us, but earlier this afternoon, he threatened that if I didn't paint for him, harm would come to my," she blushed, "young man."

To her surprise, Ralph looked remarkably chuffed. "I say, 'young man', is it? Well, if that's what I am, then, I haven't yet enjoyed all the perks. May I kiss you, Miss Hazlett?"

Lissa gasped as delight and trepidation speared her.

He must have noticed the furtive way her eyes darted to the windows above, for immediately he looked contrite, retreating slightly and dropping his eyes. His voice was heavy, as if he greatly feared he'd overstepped the line. "Please forgive me, I had no right to make such an ungentlemanly request."

But barely had he finished the sentence than, in the greatest act of bravado in Lissa's life, she raised herself on tiptoe and touched her lips carefully to his.

They were soft and warm and immediately she was consumed by the greatest desire to lose herself in his embrace and the intimacy of his kiss. A desire kindled by the feeling of his arms tightening around her as his lips yielded to hers in a bonding that quickly grew in intensity.

A kiss that transported her beyond the realm of her narrow existence and filled her heart almost to bursting.

Her hands, which had been resting against his breast, now twined behind his neck and she pressed herself against him, just as she felt him retreating.

When she opened her eyes in disappointment, it was to see the sentiment echoed in his. "Oh, Miss Hazlett, this is far too dangerous." He was breathing heavily and he shook his head in agitation.

Embarrassment swamped Lissa. "You think I was...too forward? Please don't assume the accident of my birth makes me that kind of woman."

The misery of her dreadful origins threatened to swamp her. Her shoulders heaved and she didn't resist when he wrapped his arms about her once more and gently kissed the top of her head.

"You are the most virtuous, delectable armful I've ever had the good fortune to meet. The accident of your birth means nothing." His voice was a soft, cathartic murmur. "You are my angel, Miss Hazlett. I recognized it from the moment I laid eyes on you, but it's only now that I realize the danger you place me in."

A note of amusement crept into his voice at her predictable gasp, and he went on, "A danger that has nothing to do with my unsavory employer and everything to do with the fact that such close proximity to you makes *me* a danger—for I want you, Miss Hazlett." Sparks of light radiated from the depths of his gaze. "I want you with every particle of my being—oh yes, for my own selfish reasons, but also to keep you safe and protected."

Reluctantly he dropped his hands. "And I cannot do that when I cannot trust myself not to kiss you with a passion that would be dangerous for both of us. There's only one thing for it." His tone became brisk and businesslike. "I must go away to think, Miss Partington."

"Think?"

"Of how to expedite this bold and cunning plan I've only just now put into motion. I'm not rich enough to offer you marriage at this moment and anything else is quite out of the question. This morning I'd thought to rob a coach—not a thought I entertained for long," he quickly reassured her, "for that would be as counter to achieving the respectable, happy and long-lasting union I desire as succumbing to what I really feel here." He touched his hand to his heart and Lissa blushed at the allusion.

"You see, when I saw Jem, I came up with a plan to safeguard certain individuals from harm. In fact, it was more the *beginning* of a plan, depending on how other events transpired." He sighed. "Now I realize I must exercise my mental faculties more than I ever have and perhaps *tinker* with events. For so long I've been a lowly secretary, so there's not been much of a requirement to use this." He tapped his head. "But my unbiased mama tells me I'm the cleverest man she knows, and I'd like you to think it someday, too."

Placing his hands on her shoulders, he leaned close and kissed her chastely on the lips, stepping back and shaking his head when Lissa moved forward.

"Not yet, Miss Partington, but I promise you, our time will come."

***

Araminta felt her time had come.

The evening she had planned at Vauxhall Gardens was going to cement what she had worked toward for so long: the perfect marriage.

She'd told herself she could have any man she wanted and, during her first season, that had probably been true.

Then there'd been the disastrous incident with that stupid young man blowing his brains out. She'd only agreed to marry him after too many champagnes had led to a quick fumble in a carriage; but she'd not been found out, as she'd feared at the time, and there'd been no witnesses—and no consequences—so she wasn't going to marry any gentleman she didn't want to, unless she really had to.

Of course, she'd been very sorry that her disappointed suitor had been so addle-pated as to have used a loaded pistol. She fully agreed with everyone who wanted to talk about it with her that it was a tragedy and so thoughtless of him to have made such a mess for his poor mama to find, but that wasn't Araminta's fault. The trouble was, more and more she was gaining the impression that *others* in society felt it was. At least to the extent that the more glittering prizes tended to shy away from her when it came to forging a more long-lasting union.

Then she'd met Lord Debenham, who was clearly mad for her; and she did find him intriguing, with that edge of danger that did something to her insides. Yes, the letter Jem had shown her was troubling. Lord Debenham had been painted a villain by his very own cousin, Sir Aubrey's wife, while Sir Aubrey was, apparently, the wrongly maligned society gentleman.

However, Lord Debenham was only in danger if that letter were discovered. Araminta's meeting with His Lordship immediately after she'd left the tavern had made it clear how far he was willing to go to ensure that the letter was never made public. Araminta might even have agreed to be his wife that very moment if he'd asked her.

But then, when Hetty had dragged her into the drawing room just after she'd returned from her secret meeting with Lord Debenham in the hackney, there was Sir Aubrey pacing up and down. And after he'd kissed her knuckles and said such sweet things to her after telling her how important it was to give *him* the letter, Araminta's heart had fluttered all over the place.

So, really, Araminta had her choice of two suitors—Lord Debenham *and* Sir Aubrey.

Now Araminta had chosen. Sir Aubrey might be a mere baronet but only a sickly, childless cousin stood in the way of an earldom and, equally important, Sir Aubrey would make a far more manageable husband than Lord Debenham.

Although Hetty would be disappointed, and might even blame Araminta for acting improperly, she must know that a union between herself and Sir Aubrey was impossible.

Sir Aubrey's smeared reputation had apparently made him *persona non grata* in the higher echelons of government and society, so he needed a wife like Araminta whose beauty, charm and grace would assist in him being embraced by society.

All she had to do was give him the letter.

Tonight, dressed just like Hetty—as a Spanish dancing girl for the masquerade at Vauxhall—Araminta intended that by the end of the night, the elder Miss Partington was going to be all but Sir Aubrey's wife.

If he didn't make Araminta a formal offer, she had a plan that would give him no choice.

Chapter Eight

Lissa's relief was short-lived. News had come to her that Jem had been discovered alive but that he'd been knocked about badly, and now lay at death's door.

When she had a moment to spare, she scribbled a note, which she entrusted to the boot boy, waited a few moments before she snatched her cloak, then hurried the two blocks to where her half-sisters lived. Araminta was not smiling when she greeted her beneath the apple tree.

"What do you suppose might have happened if someone had intercepted that note?" she demanded.

"Is Jem going to live?"

"You risked my reputation to ask me that? Besides, why should you care?"

"Because I met him and liked him, and because of you—*us*—his life was put in danger. Of course I should care! I see you're going to a masquerade."

She stared at Araminta's Spanish dancing girl costume, trying unsuccessfully to withstand the spasm of envy that, she feared, was plain for the other girl to see.

Araminta looked smug. "Tonight is very special. I intend a certain gentleman to make me an offer."

"Lord Debenham?"

"Good Lord, no. Not after what I saw in that letter! No, Sir Aubrey. Although his reputation is somewhat tarnished, Sir Aubrey will have me to thank for restoring glory to him."

Lissa gasped. "I thought you didn't have the money to obtain the letter?"

Araminta looked uncomfortable. "Hetty has gone behind my back and somehow acquired the letter…but she won't have it for long. I intend to retrieve it tonight. Lord knows what she was about, thinking he might look at her twice if she was the one to triumphantly brandish it in front of him. Now I really must go, while you no doubt have your governessing duties to attend to."

She turned, saying over her shoulder, "Your concern is really most touching, but I'm sure Jem will be quite all right. He's not dead, at any rate."

***

Lissa dashed back to the Lamont household and had reached the first landing when a hand darted from seemingly nowhere and landed on her shoulder. She squealed and Cosmo stepped into the light, laughing. She hated his habit of accosting her from the shadows.

"Methinks only someone with something to hide could be so all-aquiver. What? Been to see your lover, have you? Well, that's of no account to me, as long as you abide by our agreement."

She shrugged off his hand and started to climb the stairs again, ignoring him, but he called her back.

"Clara is putting the girls to bed. I've told everyone you've been given the evening off to seek a remedy from your aunt." At her open-mouthed shock, he went on, "That's because you're coming with me."

She drew back, frightened, as he made to reach for her, and instantly the sneer on his face told her she was unwise to make her distaste so clear.

Before she could ask his meaning, he repeated, "You're coming with me to Vauxhall Gardens. It's a masquerade, the perfect opportunity for you to do those lightning sketches you're so good at, since you'll be in disguise like everyone else."

Excitement mixed with trepidation, for although Lissa had been envious of Araminta minutes before, the idea of being anywhere in close proximity to Cosmo was terrifying.

"My reputation—" she began, but he scoffed.

"Really, Miss Hazlett, you're a governess, that's all. Mama has an ancient domino rig-out she wore to a masquerade ball last century. The old-fashioned gown and cloak will fit you with room to spare. No one will ever know it's you, and I'll see you're served ham so thin you can see through it and partake of all the Bristol Milk you desire. Don't you want to know how the other half *really* lives?"

Lissa thought she heard resentment in his tone, for he was

only a few steps farther up the social ladder than she was, looked down upon by those whose portraits he painted. His money was not inherited.

Her final, faint objections were made to his retreating back. However, when a little later she returned to her bedchamber and saw, lying upon the bed, a voluminous domino and a sculpted mask adorned with black feathers, she could not deny her excitement. Despite its antiquity it did offer Lissa the anonymity she needed. She whisked it up and saw that it came with voluminous pockets she could tie about her waist, enabling her to easily access her sketchbook. If she'd been wearing the narrow fashions of the day she'd have had to carry a reticule.

Of course, she should feel angry that Cosmo had given her no choice but to dance to his tune, but a night of rubbing shoulders with the haut ton, doing sketches for which she'd be paid, eating and drinking things that were not governess fare, did not come her way every day.

Clara appeared in the doorway rubbing her eyes, and Lissa quickly tossed the Domino upon the bed and stood in front of it.

"Master Cosmo said as you'd gone to visit your aunt."

"I'm leaving shortly," Lissa said quickly. What a rare opportunity to be granted a reprieve from her work. One arranged by the difficult-to-please young master who'd had it sanctioned by the rest of the family.

Nodding, Clara turned and left her in peace while Lissa dreamed of the excitement ahead of her tonight.

She would make the most of her freedom and she would do what Cosmo required of her, but she would not be at Cosmo's beck and call all evening. Not when he'd neglected to pay her for all her sketches, as promised.

There were difficulties. Lissa had no hope of changing, indoors, without any of the family or servants observing her in costume, and Cosmo was virtually breathing down her neck the moment she tiptoed out of the schoolroom with the ensemble hidden in a hessian sack.

He took her to a tavern and directed her to small room, where she hurriedly donned the costume. The domino was a princess shape, made of black brocade, with a Watteau plait with cape, voluminous hood and wide sleeves. It was large and long enough to slip over her own dress and hide it completely.

With pretended nonchalance she returned to Cosmo's side and, in silence, they travelled in a hackney to the Gardens.

"I have two commissions I must complete tonight," he told her as they walked side by side through the throngs of revelers wearing all manner of outlandish and fantastical garb. "Make sure you stay near, but in the background, and make your drawings as quickly as possible."

Lissa was not going to be ordered about in such a cavalier fashion. The delicious aroma of roasting pig reminded her of how hungry she was, and there was also Cosmo's promise of refreshment and fun to compensate for the work she would do for him—in addition to the payment of a third of what he received. "I would like something to eat and drink, first," she said in a manner that brooked, she hoped, no refusal. "You took me away before supper, and I've had nothing since luncheon. I can't sketch without food."

He stopped to stare at her, as if she'd uttered an outrageous impertinence, but Lissa did not flinch before his jutting brow. Cosmo was a bully but not so stupid he didn't understand when it was unwise to court a falling-out. Without a word, he resumed walking, shouldering his way through the crowds to the refreshments tent after finding her a seat at a table where she could wait in view of him.

The food was delicious. She'd never enjoyed such rich and exotic flavors, and the atmosphere was intoxicating. The night was young and it was not fully dark, but the drink was flowing. Lissa saw women throw back their heads, eyes shining with promise, and young men transformed into gallant swains in their quest to strut their manliness before their lady loves. It was like being part of the theatre itself.

On the other side of the rotunda she saw Araminta and Hetty, *both* dressed as Spanish dancing girls, flanking their cousin Stephen. In their wake trailed a couple of country-looking misses dressed as shepherdesses and a young man in a cassock whom Lissa took to be their brother.

The country cousins looked as Lissa felt: as if they'd never encountered such a place. By contrast, Araminta appeared used to this kind of lark as she sauntered with confidence along the busy thoroughfare. Her confidence was in contrast to Hetty's obvious discomfort at being dressed in the same garb as her flamboyant sister. Lissa was in no doubt that Araminta had chosen the Spanish dancing girl's costume. She wondered if Hetty knew of her sister's plan to obtain the all-important letter before she could present it to Sir Aubrey, and she hoped an opportunity would arise whereby she could warn her.

Whatever revelations might be the outcome, both girls apparently had a decided preference for Sir Aubrey, and little wonder. Lord Debenham was terrifying.

By the time she and Cosmo had finished their meal, darkness was closing in and the shadows were lengthening but a large waxing moon shone a golden glow upon everything. Lissa leaned back on her bench and stared into the gloom. Araminta, she saw, had returned to listen to the orchestra, but of Hetty, there was no sign. Which one of them, she wondered, had the hitherto secret letter?

Her preference was that Hetty should be the unlikely victor and find love in Sir Aubrey's arms, if that was what she truly wanted. Araminta had shown the greater boldness but Hetty was, Lissa was certain, the more deserving.

If Lissa were required to melt into the shadows and slyly do Cosmo's bidding with pencil and paper, perhaps she could find a way to help Hetty.

"Who are we to sketch?" Lissa asked as Cosmo pushed aside his plate. Araminta had just disappeared, swallowed up by the crowds of revelers on the Serpentine Walk. Lissa frowned. She was sure she'd not seen her in company with her Cousin Stephen. Or any of her cousins, for that matter.

"I have a commission from Lord Smythe's wife to render her husband's likeness for a small charcoal etching, with which she wishes to present him as a surprise. She asked me to observe him without his knowledge, which is of course ideal."

The idea, which had pleased him a moment before, now appeared to have a caveat, Lissa feared, judging from the sudden downturn of his mouth. It was only after a little prodding that he finally confessed.

"Lady Smythe is holding a ball on Thursday night, to which I'd hoped to be invited so I could present her with the sketch. But no offer was forthcoming. I shall therefore deliver it to her tomorrow. She may be only too pleased to show it off during her entertainment later this week and thus I can garner more commissions."

Lissa nodded. A quick sketch of Lord Smythe should not prove difficult. "And the other?"

Cosmo looked evasive. Then Lissa realized it was embarrassment. A gentle breeze ruffled his light brown curls and he looked for a moment terribly young and not the cruel employer and manipulator she knew him to be. "Mr. Crossing believes his wife is…er, being unfaithful, and has planned an assignation with her lover in a supper room here tonight. He wants me to sketch her with whomever she is with."

Lissa clutched the folds of the domino at her throat. "That's spying. We can't possibly! No Cosmo, I won't do it."

"It's a commission worth three times the usual money, and yes you will." No longer did he look young and vulnerable. "My ability to render an uncanny likeness with just a few pencil strokes has been highly acclaimed."

"You mean *my* ability."

He ignored her. "This could become a lucrative business if you are canny enough to carry it off. Or will your nerve or talent fail you tonight? Mr. Crossing is justified in wanting to know if his wife is true. You'd not condone deceit, would you, Miss Hazlett?"

Cosmo knew how much Lissa wanted the money and gave her no opportunity to object further as he pulled her to her feet. "Goodness, I believe that is Lord Smythe heading past the orchestra in the company of two other gentlemen."

He relaxed in disappointment. "I'm sure it was, though he is gone now. No matter. We will be vigilant. And tonight will mark the beginning of a long and fruitful partnership, Miss Hazlett."

"With the financial rewards to be meted out before the end of the week, or it will be the last time we are in partnership, Mr. Lamont."

"I think we need each other too much for me not to accede to your money-grubbing sentiments, Miss Hazlett." He gave a disappointed sigh. "A lady's preoccupation with filthy lucre is so unbecoming."

***

Araminta leaned against the trunk of an elm tree, hidden in the darkness, and stared across at Sir Aubrey's supper box. She'd gained possession easily enough of the letter, snatching it from Hetty's reticule earlier that evening during a fortuitous moment when it had fallen to the ground after her sister had been jostled in the crowd.

The sense of victory had been supreme as Araminta had tucked the valuable missive inside her stays. What Sir Aubrey wouldn't give to have that letter? It would finally reveal to the world the truth of Lord Debenham's treachery, and thus her future husband's innocence. Yes, Sir Aubrey was, without a doubt, the man of her dreams. With the incendiary, incriminating letter detailing Lord Debeham's depravity pricking into her skin she wondered how she could for one moment have entertained ideas of allying herself with wicked Viscount Debenham.

She adjusted the veil that ensured her anonymity, ran her clammy hands down her red and gold flounced skirts and shivered with the thrill of simply being alone and unchaperoned. Any guilt or doubt about what she was about to embark upon could not be entertained. Of course, her Mama would be horrified if she knew what Araminta was about to do, and in fact Araminta did feel a trifle uncomfortable about sending Hetty off in the direction of Lord Debenham's supper box.

When Hetty had discovered the letter missing a few minutes ago, Araminta had told her she'd given it to Lord Debenham, whereupon the silly girl had immediately run off to beg him for its return. It was almost as if Hetty had imagined that by presenting the letter to Sir Aubrey, he'd convey his gratitude through a marriage offer.

Yes, Araminta acknowledged it had been wrong to send Hetty off, alone, to confront such a dangerous man as Lord Debenham, but what choice had she had? She'd rather share dreadful Cousin Edgar's fate and drown in a duck pond than finish a second season without an offer.

And it was unthinkable that Hetty might receive an offer first.

Araminta took a final deep breath, adjusted the lace that edged her décolletage, and stepped up to the door of Sir Aubrey's supper box.

As long as the means justified the glorious outcome she had in mind, she'd be forgiven. It was only natural Sir Aubrey would wish to reward her bravery in seeing him vindicated, his reputation restored and Lord Debenham branded the villain he really was.

Her family would forgive her for the same reasons. And Araminta would be the beautiful consort at Sir Aubrey side, responsible for his rise from beleaguered politician to one of the leading peers in the land. Only last night Araminta had heard whispers that the health of the ailing, childless uncle to whom he was heir had taken a turn for the worse.

The strains of Haydn drifted across from the orchestra, mingling with the aroma of roasted chestnuts from a nearby brazier. Araminta felt almost giddy with her own boldness but as she raised her hand to knock, her courage almost failed her, which was rare indeed.

Then she thought of his astonishment when she presented him with the letter, and of the kisses he'd rain all over her as he begged her to marry him; and excitement curdled in her belly. She was conscious of a tremendous heat between her legs, similar to the sensations she'd felt when Jem had been so overcome with desire that he'd all but kidnapped her before kissing her so passionately in the tavern. She pushed aside the intruding memory of Lord Debenham's kiss in the hackney carriage shortly afterwards. She couldn't deny the excitement she'd felt at the time, but upon reflection she was glad she'd pursued the safer option: Sir Aubrey.

Quietly, she turned the door knob and slowly opened the door. Her moment had nearly come. Soon, Sir Aubrey and she would realize their shared destiny. Yes, indeed, victory was about to be hers.

With heart beating wildly, she stepped across the threshold. In just a moment she would drop the gauze veil and Sir Aubrey would spring to his feet in a blaze of hungry ardor that she'd so boldly taken steps to be alone with him.

She put her hand to the ribbons that tied the veil in place and her heart beat even more wildly. Her body was on fire. There he was, sprawled upon a sea of cushions, it appeared, his eyes lust-laden as he focused them on her. He'd obviously heard her enter for he swung round, still sprawled amidst the cushions. He didn't even rise though the wicked glint in his eye made up for that.

And then he spoke. Words that stole the breath from her lungs and left her crazy with dismay. Then blood lust.

His voice was a low growl, dangerous with desire. "Hetty? Is that you, my darling? Come! My, my, so this is what you had in store for me."

Chapter Nine

A cool breeze had sprung up. Cosmo rubbed his hands together as he and Lissa decided the final points on how to proceed, beneath an overhanging tree branch upon which two lanterns swung.

"I predict rich pickings, Miss Hazlett," Cosmo remarked happily, encompassing the supper house a few yards away with a sweep of his arm. "Why, they've not even gone to the trouble of putting out the lantern hanging by the entrance. Very accommodating." He chuckled. "You must make detailed sketches of their clothes so their identities might be further verified. Mrs. Crossing's, in particular. Her husband is an exacting man."

It was at this point Lissa realized she could not go ahead with the arrangement. *An exacting man.* Earlier, as she'd watched from the darkness while Mr. Crossing and Cosmo had talked near the rotunda, she'd been struck by Mr. Crossing's belligerent manner. Even from a distance he'd appeared a frightening man, broad-shouldered with a massive head upon a bull-like neck. The way he'd waved his fists around reminded Lissa of two pork knuckles aggressively facing each other off in mid air.

Now she realized that she was about to become party to a situation that may well endanger the anonymous woman in that supper box.

"I can't do it," she whispered, raising her head to look at Cosmo. "Even if she is guilty, it's not right."

Cosmo's mouth dropped open, as if he truly were caught by surprise. "What do you mean, you won't do it? You're as motivated by the riches that will come your way as I am. Besides, I've made a pledge and the pair is only a stone's throw away. You *must* do it. I can't be made to look a fool."

Cosmo put his hands on her shoulders and drew her into the light. He looked more panicked than menacing. "You *will* do it, otherwise I'll tell Mama about your young man. You know you're not allowed followers. I'll tell her he's been making improper advances and that you've encouraged him. Don't think I didn't notice the way you looked at him when he came to visit. And he at you. Something is going on. Well, let me tell you, Mama will happily shred *his* reputation, if you're not so worried about your own. She's very effective at that sort of thing. So do your job and do it well, Miss Hazlett, if you don't want to suffer the consequences."

Lissa shook off his grasp and rose. She hated this man who wielded his power in such a petty, tyrannical fashion. Of course, she could expose him and leave the Lamont household but the exhilaration she'd felt when Cosmo had unexpectedly thrust a sovereign into her hand after dinner had coalesced into a sense of her value and increasing power. He'd never have done such a thing if he'd not realized how reliant he was on her. Between his threats and the unexpected money, she saw that clearly.

So Lissa refrained from her impulse to flounce off into the night. To leave Cosmo, the Lamonts and London meant abandoning this arrangement, her only avenue towards independence.

"Your threats don't frighten me, Master Cosmo, because I know you need me too much," she said calmly. "But you will *continue* to pay me, as agreed, for if you do not, I have no incentive for staying or for keeping our arrangement secret."

This had the desired effect. Of course he was frightened of exposure, though he hid it well enough. Just as Lissa hid her grave misgivings about what she was about to do as they trod the dark stretch of grass in silence.

Perhaps they would be confronted with a scene of perfect innocence. Perhaps the couple had slipped away already, unnoticed. She tried one final gambit. "This wasn't what I agreed to do when I said I would do your sketches," she whispered as they paused by a statue of a small boy. "It's...so sordid. Please, Master Cosmo. Surely you can tell Mr. Crossing you never saw his wife. Just this once?"

"Do you know how much Mr. Crossing has offered?" Cosmo sounded determined. "Miss Hazlett, he has seen the detail in those sketches and tells me only a master could render such an exact likeness in just a few quick strokes. Do you realize how valuable this is? I can garner so many more such commissions. I can make a fortune from this! *We* can make a fortune, but we need to work together."

He gave her a small push and she stumbled forward as he added in her ear, "Console yourself...you're only recording the truth. If Mrs. Crossing is guilty of a misdemeanor, it's *her* fault, isn't it?"

It soon became clear that whatever was happening within the supper box was far from innocent. Lissa leapt back at the plaintive moan of ecstasy that issued clearly from the small wooden structure, while Cosmo dashed forward to investigate where a peephole might afford him a proper view.

He had to return to drag Lissa with him while she tried to block her ears to the sounds of joyful lovemaking within.

Cosmo drew her to the rear of the building. A back curtain was not fully drawn, and through a full inch of exposed window, a tangle of naked limbs could be seen on the banquette by the far wall. A single candle burned on a low table, bathing the room with light.

"How can I possibly draw something like...*that*?" Lissa felt ill with shame as she turned her head away. "Besides, I can't see their faces."

For once, Cosmo looked uncertain. Then a look of greed and prurience crossed his face. "I shall call you when they are finished and...putting themselves to rights. As long as they are identifiable, that should be sufficient. I can elaborate on what I saw, when I hand the sketch to Mr. Crossing."

Lissa lingered, confused, her heart pumping. The gentleman had had his hand up the lady's skirts and she appeared to be...liking it. Of course she knew how animals procreated but she'd never properly considered what human love-making entailed, though she'd certainly never have expected anything like this. The more she thought about it, the more disappointed she became. How could this brutish behavior resemble anything like love?

When she envisaged herself enjoying greater intimacy with Ralph she was swamped with tenderness. Her heart seemed to hitch in her chest during the quick, unexpected occasions she'd hugged him. An overwhelming sense of liking and trust had seeped right through her. She'd wanted to keep hugging him. Dear Lord, she'd have been horrified if he'd done anything remotely like what the man inside was doing to Mrs. Crossing. If indeed it *was* Mrs. Crossing.

But that's what Cosmo was being paid so handsomely to

ascertain, and Lissa was merely required to record what she saw. The truth. Could she make herself feel any better about it if she put it that way?

Soon Cosmo was back at her side, hurrying her back to the supper house, pushing her head toward the opening in the curtains. Now she could see quite clearly what was happening within and make out the distinguishing features of those involved.

The lady, who appeared young and very pretty, was retying her garter at the knee while the gentleman, who Lissa now saw was much younger than she'd believed, was angled behind her, doing up the buttons at the back of her gown.

Cosmo pointed at Lissa's sketchbook which she'd withdrawn from her pockets and obediently she began to sketch. She was able to capture the limpid look of love in the young lady's pale blue eyes. Though they were slightly protuberant, this did not detract from her prettiness. Her lips were moist and full and her flaxen hair curled over one shoulder. Every now and again, her lover would stroke her hand as she tidied her coiffure.

The gesture caught at Lissa's heart. With her sketchbook resting on the window sill, her pencil flew over the parchment. She was unable to willingly do a bad rendition and besides, Cosmo knew she was fully capable.

Just as Lissa finished with a flourish, a gasp made them raise their gazes and focus again on the scene inside.

Perhaps the young man had caught a tendril of hair in the top button of the young lady's dress, for she gave a little yelp and turned her head toward him. Lissa caught the moment they locked gazes and the look they exchanged was one of such tenderness, she nearly dropped her pencil.

Without a word, the young man took the lady's face gently in his hands and kissed her lingeringly on the mouth. The night was silent and quite clearly they could hear him utter the words, "If I can't be with you forever, I will die." The young lady closed her eyes and pulled him down beside her so she could rest her head upon his shoulder. He stroked her cheek and went on, his tone lower but more urgent, "Promise me you'll have courage. That you'll be waiting at the docks for the first Dover crossing of the coming month."

The young lady gave a short sob as she twisted in his arms to look at him. "How can I bear the wait? How can I bear the thought that I will see you again in public but not be able to acknowledge you?"

"Because that is the only way forward. The only way we can be together." He took her shoulders and helped her to rise, looking down at her with tender desperation. "I shall send you a note regarding the tides, but only the one. Otherwise it's too dangerous. You won't lose heart?"

Lissa sent a panicked look at Cosmo who firmly removed the sketchbook from her grasp. He then put his hand on her shoulder to steer her away as the young lady's reply drifted across the silence. "I would take any risk to be with you, my darling William, for each beating from Mr. Crossing only hardens my resolve."

Lissa pulled out of Cosmo's grasp as he drew her with him across the grass towards the rotunda. "You can't give the sketch to Mr. Crossing after what you just heard!" she protested. "Mr. Crossing beats her! You can't blame her for taking a lover. She needs to escape."

"Don't be such a ninny. She's dishonored her husband. Mrs. Crossing belongs to Mr. Crossing, and he can do to her what he likes. If he beats her, it's because she deserves it. I would, if I were her husband and she disobeyed me. I'm only too glad we could aid Mr. Crossing in his quest for justice for he acts quite within the law, and you know it."

Lissa could barely speak for anger. She tugged at Cosmo's arm, as he started to walk on. "Mrs. Crossing is running away because her husband is so cruel to her. Can you not understand that's what she meant? She's in *danger*. You can't risk her safety and future happiness."

"She should have thought of that before." It started as a sneer but was spoiled when Cosmo sniggered, and Lissa was reminded of one of his infantile sisters. "I think I can sting him for four times what he promised, now that I've recorded everything."

***

If Araminta had been able to indulge herself, she'd be sobbing her outrage in the safety of her bedchamber, on her soft feather mattress, with Jane not asking any questions but waiting on her, nevertheless, with warm possets and soothing concoctions. Though perhaps something stronger would be more in order.

She'd certainly not be standing here, feeling as vulnerable as she ever had, with this…dangerous gentleman regarding her with quiet interest.

She drew in a shuddering breath and tried to smile. *Pretend to like what is happening*, she told herself. Pretense was everything.

The truth was, though, that the glittering life that had beckoned to Araminta from a shiny platter heaped high with promise lay in a heap of cinders.

Cinders, like the charcoal remains of the letter she'd taken from Hetty and which she'd tried to use to make Sir Aubrey understand where he must direct his honor. Everything had moved so quickly in the past half hour. Sir Aubrey had thought Araminta was Hetty, and that could not be forgiven. Dear God, he'd taken Araminta's virtue and so what if he'd mistaken her for her sister, dressed as she was in an identical dress and shrouded with a veil as she'd thrown herself upon him? He was more than ready for her when she'd impaled herself upon his pulsing, rock-hard member in her supreme sacrifice for the good of her family.

It was no excuse that he declared he was mortified as he'd struggled out from beneath her. He had raged at her, as if it were her fault, claiming he'd married Hetty by special license not half an hour before.

And then he'd rushed into the night in search of Hetty and Araminta had had no choice but to follow for she had the letter and she meant to use it. There was still time for Sir Aubrey to wriggle out of this foolish, impulsive union with her sister. Why, the marriage would not yet be registered. They could waylay the clergyman. Couldn't he see that anything was possible, now that he knew Araminta loved him?

But Sir Aubrey would not see sense. Not even after they'd discovered Hetty in the clutches of Lord Debenham who was clearly in his cups and posed no danger at all, though Sir Aubrey had taken exception to the broken bottle of arrack that Lord Dabenham had waved in the region of Hetty's throat. Did the stupid man not understand that of course Lord Debenham would not have hurt Hetty? Yet Sir Aubrey had cast all common sense to the wind and refused to succumb to Araminta's warnings. Finally, Araminta had had no choice but to burn the letter which could have restored his good name and which painted Lord Debenham in such a bad light.

Now here she was alone with Lord Debenham. She didn't feel comfortable, it was true, and she was close to distraught at the events of the past hour, but he was her last chance. If she did not make the most of her opportunities, she could find herself facing a third ignominious season or, worse, carrying the child of the man she'd expected to marry, the man she'd thought desired her as she desired him…

The man who'd just married her sister.

Frozen, she stood by the window. Lord Debenham, who should have been looking at her as if she were the most delectable creature, was instead thoughtfully smoking a cheroot as he lounged in a chair with legs crossed at the ankles, resting on the table.

"Aren't you going to thank me?" Her throat felt dry, her words brittle. She tried for an alluring smile.

"For burning that incriminating letter? When you hoped to blackmail Sir Aubrey with it so he'd marry you?" Lord Debenham chuckled. "Now you want to compromise me so *I'll* be forced to marry you?"

Araminta had never been spoken to by a gentleman in such a manner.

"You are a very handsome man, my lord." Yes, she could do this. She could play up to him—and maybe she had to, even if just to prove that she was still irresistible. That Hetty wasn't the one to waltz off with the prize, leaving her older sister languishing, a laughing stock, an ape-leader with no dowry, their father having lost all his money.

She moved forward and boldly draped herself over his lap, careful to hike up her skirts so that he had a good view of exposed thigh. Yes, she had to entice Lord Debenham, because right now she didn't know what else to do.

Predictably, Lord Debenham placed one large, hairy hand on her knee and began to stroke her skin. With her heart in her mouth, Araminta watched. There was both revulsion and wild eroticism at play. He was dangerous and he was attractive. He was also terrifying. But if he made her his wife, she could be one of the great hostesses in the country.

His hand roamed higher. The other dipped into her bodice to fumble for her breast. Araminta wasn't sure what to do now. There was no suggestion of desire or tenderness in his exploitation. As for herself, she felt numb. As if the bruising, sudden, intimate encounter with Sir Aubrey had never happened.

"How tempting you are when you lay yourself on a platter for my enjoyment, Miss Partington." He sighed. "However, I regret that I am not prepared to be tricked into being forced to offer for you. It's dangerous enough that you are alone with me, but I'll not take your virtue. You are a poisoned chalice—and I've already promised you to Roderick."

With a gasp, Araminta leapt off his lap. "How dare you!" she cried. "I wouldn't marry your nephew if he was the last man alive! Besides, he's…in love with my sister."

"Well, your sister has just taken herself out of the race, and the truth is, Roderick has lusted after you like a dog in heat ever since you crossed his orbit. He might not look like he's capable of much, but once he gets over his awe of you, I think you won't be disappointed by his prowess."

Araminta couldn't believe he was speaking to her like this. Did he think he could be so coarse, just because she was alone and unprotected? "I would make his life misery!" she declared. "But it won't come to that because I will never marry him!"

Lord Debenham rose with a smile and headed toward the door. "You may just have to if you come to the end of another season without an offer," he said, opening it to usher her out. "Young Roderick is a very wealthy man, and he stands to inherit a great deal more. An ambitious young lady like you is quite capable of looking past his shortcomings."

Tearfully, Araminta pushed down her skirts and lunged for the cold outdoors. Her nightmare evening was getting worse by the moment.

Lord Debenham chuckled, patting her bottom as she passed. "Now hurry on back to your chaperone, Miss Partington, and don't look so crestfallen. If I weren't expecting a couple of colleagues any moment now I'd have happily tasted the delights you were so keen to offer."

If she'd had the foresight, she'd have picked up the broken bottle of arrack at his feet and wiped that smirk off his face.

Chapter Ten

"Good Lord, is that…Miss *Partington* running out of that supper box? I've met her before and she's a beauty. With a reputation, I might add." Cosmo stopped in his tracks and Lissa looked in the direction he jerked his thumb. In the dim light of a lantern, she saw a figure dressed as a Spanish dancer with no head covering, tear across the lawn and disappear into the throng.

"I…I'm sure it could not have been." Lissa licked dry lips. Hetty had also been dressed as a Spanish dancer but the lithe, fleet-footed creature had not been the sweet, reflective, much plumper younger sister, she felt sure.

She peered again at the supper box. "That's…Lord *Debenham's.*" They were en route to hand the sketch directly to Mr. Crossing but when another gentleman suddenly appeared in their line of vision, Lissa saw her opportunity. "Yes, that's Lord Debenham standing in the doorway of his supper house. And look, there is Lord Smythe! Lord Debenham is inviting him inside. Quick, we must take this opportunity to do the drawing Lady Smythe requested."

It took a couple of moments to persuade Cosmo of the merits of executing both commissions rather than return, first, to find Mr. Crossing and perhaps miss the opportunity of sketching Lord Smythe.

Not that Lissa was keen on the idea of getting closer to Lord Debenham than she had to. The few minutes in his arms on the dance floor had been the most uncomfortable she could remember and the more she heard about him from Ralph, the more terrifying he seemed. While Araminta had made no secret of her interest in Lord Debenham, she'd also told Lissa she was interested in Sir Aubrey. No, the figure fleeing from his supper box surely couldn't have been her, for she'd have been very properly chaperoned this evening.

Wishing she could quell the disquieting flutters of doubt she felt, Lissa quietly followed Cosmo in the direction from which the mystery figure had fled.

The sounds of slightly slurred laughter emanated from within and as they drew closer, Lord Debenham's distinct, ironic drawl punctuated the night air. Even that was enough to make Lissa want to take to her heels and run.

Still, she forced herself to the task, glad of the delay in returning to find Mr. Crossing.

The light was better here than it had been when she'd sketched Mrs. Crossing and her lover. There were three men gathered, the last having turned the lamp up full when he'd arrived a moment or so before. All seemed extremely convivial and Lissa was shocked to see an empty bottle of arrack, broken, its jagged bottom pressed against the leg of one chair. None of the men seemed concerned as they discussed the matter at hand.

"Hurry." Cosmo elbowed her and wordlessly Lissa began to sketch.

Lord Smythe, the eldest of the trio looked to be in his late fifties. His thatch of thick dung-colored hair was in stark contrast to the thinning locks of the youngest, a nervous, reedy-looking man with a bulbous red nose. Lissa was surprised at his presence for despite his foppish rig-out, he spoke like a poor man. His cheeks were sunken, giving him a cadaverous look, and when he laughed, Lissa saw most of his teeth were black stumps. Yet he was richly garbed in a paisley waistcoat and claret-colored wool coat together with black satin pantaloons.

With deft, quick strokes, Lissa recreated the scene: foppish Lord Smythe with his caramel drawl, the wizened, younger man whom Lissa heard Lord Debenham refer to as Buzby. He dominated the conversation until Lord Debenham mounted a strong defense for whatever was being argued. Lissa paid little attention until she heard Buzy's aggressive tones, "And then our esteemed Lord Liverpool will rue the harsh line he's taken with the machine-breakers in the north. If that won't stop the government in their tracks, I don't know what will," before the men started laughing.

She glanced nervously at Cosmo but his expression remained impassive. He'd either not heard, or chosen to pretend he had not.

For Lissa, the implications were terrifying, made more so as the conversation progressed.

Were these men plotting treason?

She was aware of Cosmo craning over her shoulder to see her work and she stepped back, suddenly nervous, giving a small cry as she dropped her sketchbook onto the ground.

Immediately Cosmo was upon her, roughly clapping his hand over her mouth as he dragged her to the back of the structure and into the shadows. Her heart pounded as she heard one of the men mutter something in fright, and then the door was thrown open and Lord Debenham thrust his head out for a cursory look around.

Apparently satisfied, he returned. "Damned squirrels," she heard one of them say before the conversation resumed, this time on a more muted level.

Lissa picked up her sketchbook and hastened deeper into the darkness. She wasn't going to risk being caught by Lord Debenham, knowing what she now did of this evil, terrifying man. The letter that Hetty had obtained from Jem confirmed his involvement in something havey-cavey, though Ralph hadn't told her its full contents or why he'd not taken possession of it. Perhaps Jem no longer had it but was able to relay its contents, having learned in the interim what it had said.

Now Lissa had witnessed His Lordship giving voice to treasonous sentiments, and had sketched him with his associates.

It was a huge relief to be back in the safety of the thoroughfares, where revelers jostled her and men, lightheaded with drink, sang public odes to their consorts. The perfection of the weather seemed to add to the high spirits of the crowd.

Except Lissa didn't feel high spirited at all. Quite the opposite, in fact. For all that Mrs. Crossing might be guilty of terrible wickedness, the genuine and touching way the couple had said farewell to each other spoke to Lissa's purest sentiments.

She decided to destroy the sketch. She didn't care how much Cosmo was being paid for it—or how much she'd make.

"There you are, my lad!"

Their progress about the rotunda was arrested by a broad-shouldered giant with an enormous head topped with lustrous salt-and-pepper curls topping a bullish neck, and extravagant mutton-chop side-whiskers. He clapped Cosmo on the shoulder. Mr. Crossing. His smile was unctuous but the right side of his lip curled up in what resembled a snarl, though Lissa soon decided this was really a smile as he went on, "Raising the breeze, eh? No, you've been working, and on my account, too. So, do I reward you? Have you found the twopenny whore? You have? By God, if she tries to cut the wheedle with me..." His words trailed off but his gesture left Lissa in no doubt that Mrs. Crossing would soon feel her husband's displeasure.

She stared at his hands. They were monstrous, flexing now as if he meant to wrap them around the young lady's throat the moment they were reunited.

Cosmo clicked his fingers at Lissa. "The picture for Mr. Crossing, please." He sent a nervous glance in the direction of his benefactor, adding, "This is my—er, cousin, who sometimes acts as my assistant. She has the artwork."

Impatiently he held out his hand but Lissa stammered, "I...I don't have the picture. I...I sent it back to the house with my maid." She sent Mr. Crossing an apologetic smile. "I had no idea we'd see you this evening, sir, and merely wanted to ensure it was kept safe."

Lissa was ready to be strongly censured. And indeed she was. Cosmo immediately rounded on her, but it would seem her rueful expression was sufficiently ameliorating for Mr. Crossing, who gave her a fatherly pat on the shoulder.

"Tomorrow then. You can present it to me when I'm breakfasting with my wife. That'll surprise her. No need to tear strips off your poor cousin." He smiled at Lissa who was mesmerized by his fat, fishlike lips. She didn't wonder at the risks the very young, sweet Mrs. Crossing would go to escape a close encounter with them.

Snapping back to the present, she saw that Cosmo's benefactor had narrowed his eyes. He made a sucking noise then said in a loud whisper as he pulled Cosmo slightly away, "I trust you did not find her...in a state that would cause embarrassment either to herself or to me." Clearing his throat, he eyed Lissa with some awkwardness. "I would that you had not accompanied Mr. Lamont."

But Cosmo broke in quickly, saying, "Indeed, my cousin remained in the rotunda while I executed your commission. I made sure she did not...er, see...the result of my jottings, which I immediately consigned to a pouch as, like you, I would hate to have caused her distress."

"Distress?" His eyes grew bulbous.

He was about to say more, but Lissa interjected quickly, "I think my cousin is exaggerating, sir. When he pointed your wife out to me, she was deep in conversation with another lady, listening to Mozart." She placed her hand firmly on Cosmo's forearm. "And now, cousin, shall we leave? Mama will be cross if you keep me up too late."

Cosmo rounded on her when they were out of hearing. "Do you not see how you might have brought the price down with your little reassurance? Mr. Crossing was only too ready to believe the worst of Mrs. Crossing's misdemeanors. He will pay well to have evidence of her duplicity."

"I will not be responsible for setting up his bristles," Lissa muttered. In the shadow of a large statue-topped plinth by the edge of the rotunda where the orchestra was playing, she swung round to face him. "Mr. Crossing has the look of a man spoiling for violence at the slightest opportunity, though I think we already know that from what we overheard his wife telling her...friend."

Cosmo gave a snide laugh as he regarded Lissa. "What are you, really?" He shook his head, adding with unusual introspection, "You pretend to the world that you're a demure governess, but you're the first to cut shams the moment you're in a hobble." Reaching forward, he pinched her cheek. "Maybe you and I make a better pair than I thought."

He did not seem to mind that she flinched away from him with a look of horror.

Taking her hand and caging it once more on his sleeve, he bade her continue walking as he went on, conversationally, "Directly after my tailor's visit in the morning, I shall deliver my sketches." Then he stopped, his look cold. "I certainly won't let your conscience prevent me from making a handsome return on this evening's work."

Chapter Eleven

Lissa barely slept that night. Cosmo had taken the sketch from her, forcibly, at the front gate. There was nothing she could do.

For hours she tossed and turned on her lumpy mattress. How could she live with herself if she were responsible for the beating of an unhappy wife? How could she get the sketch back? Was there any possibility of stealing it from Cosmo in the morning, before he could deliver it?

Dawn lightened the room but it was the maid's knock on the door that wakened Lissa from the exhausted sleep into which she'd finally fallen not long before.

After that, there was the usual round of supervising the girls over their breakfast in the schoolroom, followed by the thankless task of trying to enthuse them with some simple demonstrations on the abacus.

Miss Maria sauntered in while Lissa was again explaining the principles of addition to a yawning Harriet. Lissa likened the eldest Lamont girl to a cat. Miss Maria could be very still and quiet but then she loved to pounce, contradicting Lissa at every turn, undermining her authority in front of her sisters.

After ten minutes of this, Lissa sighed. "You are clearly bored, Miss Maria. Perhaps you'd like to take the lesson."

Maria's eyes narrowed, and she was about to offer some no doubt rude rejoinder when she remarked in surprise, "Why, there's a young lady stopped by the fence. Where's her maid? My goodness, that is a fine pelisse she's wearing. Oh, but I do like it."

Lissa would have ignored her had she not then crinkled her nose and said, "Good Lord, she's looking right into our garden. Like she wants someone."

Lissa scrambled up and hurried to the girl's side. "Look after Nellie and Harriet for just a moment, Miss Maria." Under normal circumstances she'd have kept a low profile, but memories of last night's extraordinary series of events and the thought that Araminta might help her, or indeed needed help, were more important.

"Where are you going?" Maria squeaked in outrage as Lissa brushed past her. "To the young lady? What business can you have with such a fine personage? Who is she?"

The fact that Araminta did indeed cut a mighty impressive figure should be sufficient for Maria to let Lissa go without further objection or the need to tell her mother, Lissa thought as she hurried into the garden. Araminta was striking whatever gown she chose to wear, and Maria would be eaten up with curiosity, perhaps jealousy.

"I recognized you at the Masquerade last night," Araminta said without preamble, pursing her lips and clasping her hands on the top of the fence when Lissa appeared. "I recognized you, even in costume, near the orchestra. I hope you weren't spying on me."

"Spying? On *you*?" Lissa's sharp response was quickly replaced by interest that Araminta was looking like Lissa felt. Drained and wan. "Araminta, are you quite well?"

"No, I am not!" the girl snapped. "Have you not heard the news that will soon be all over town, making me a laughingstock?"

Lissa clapped her hand over her mouth and felt the pain of Araminta's public shame. "So that was *you* running from Lord Debenham's supper box?" she gasped.

If possible, Araminta looked even more stricken. "No!" But the strangled cry only confirmed her guilt. Quickly she added, "Hetty has eloped. Can you believe it? Hetty!" She spoke her sister's name as if she were the most loathsome creature on the planet. "And who do you think she's eloped with?"

Araminta answered her own question with another strangled sob. "Yes, with Sir Aubrey! Sir Aubrey led me to believe he would be speaking to Papa to ask for my hand, but he ran off with Hetty last night. Married her by special license and now they're on their way to France. What am I supposed to do? I can't bear being at home. Mama and Papa are utterly horrified, as you can imagine, and it's all anyone is taking about. Hetty is such a selfish girl! Mama is nearly at her time, and now Hetty has gone and done this just when she'll need her most."

This news was even worse than that of Hetty and Sir Aubrey's elopement. "Lady Partington is...about to be confined?" she whispered. "She's having a...?" She couldn't even say the words.

Her poor mother. Lissa had left home more than six months ago and her mother had certainly not known then. Perhaps she still had no idea that the man she regarded as her husband—the man who had abandoned her at the altar more than twenty years before—had fathered a child on his real wife. A baby that would be delivered at almost exactly the same time as hers.

How could Father? Rage bubbled through her veins, making it difficult to concentrate on Araminta's own troubles, until her sister snapped, "I said I shall be a laughingstock and you don't even care!"

Lissa blinked and responded without thinking. "You'll just have to marry Lord Debenham then."

She was taken aback when, with no warning, Araminta covered her face with her hands and burst into tears. What a pitiful sight she looked, with the flowers adorning her gypsy bonnet appearing to droop by her pretty face in sympathy. "I would if I could but he..." She left the sentence hanging then looked up at Lissa with tragic eyes. "Oh, I wish I were a simple governess with not a care in the world. Like you."

"I have more cares than you, Araminta, when I have not a feather to fly with while you have been indulged your whole life. I'd thank you not to make such comparisons without thinking first."

"Well, Papa has lost a lot of money, so I may well have to be a governess if I don't make a decent match before the end of the season."

Lissa felt herself go cold. She had not known this, either. She thought again of her mother's tenuous security. If Lord Partington were indeed floating in the River Tick, he'd not be able to afford to keep up two households. He was hardly generous with his by-blows in the first instance.

"Why did you come here, Araminta? To elicit my help in your matchmaking endeavors?" she asked, not quite understanding her. "I don't see how I can achieve that?"

"My reputation is in ribbons. Hetty has shredded it into tiny little pieces." Araminta rested her head on top of her whitened knuckles and let out another little sob. "Only marriage to Lord Debenham can salvage it, but he is not...in a marrying frame of mind. I don't know why I came here. I don't know you. I wish you didn't exist, in fact. But I am friendless."

To Lissa's concern, Araminta began to cry even harder. Whatever would Miss Maria think? Lord, but her half-sister really was in a bad way.

"I didn't mean what I said before. Marriage to Lord Debenham would not be a good idea," Lissa murmured, shivering at what she'd overheard the previous night.

"And what would you know about Lord Debenham?" Araminta raised her head to glare at her, prompting Lissa to say defensively, "His man of business tells me Lord Debenham is mixed up in some very havey-cavey business. I'd caution you, Araminta—"

"Lord Debenham's man of business? You know him?" Araminta cut in, her eyes widening.

"Yes, and he's told me a great deal about Lord Debenham that—"

"Why, that's capital! Just the sort of information I need you to find out." Araminta rubbed her hands together. "So, if you're friendly with his secretary, he'd tell you all about Lord Debenham and his…weaknesses. Oh, Larissa, you need to tell me what they are. You need to think of any little thing that will aid my cause."

Lissa felt trapped. "I *am*…friendly…with Mr. Tunley but a lowly governess does not get many opportunities to leave her place of employment." Lissa really didn't think aiding Araminta's cause was a good idea. However, perhaps there could be mutual benefits to such an arrangement. She was desperate to speak to Ralph who might be able to advise her with regard to Mrs. Crossing.

"Well, you must find a way for I'm relying on you to tell me everything there is to know." Araminta clapped her hands, her face shining.

"Yes, but how, Araminta? Despite what we talked about before, I still have no respectable clothes and the Lamonts keep me all but under lock and key."

"Fiddlesticks! Why do you need respectable clothes if you're only going to an office to see a man who works for Lord Debenham?" Araminta looked truly perplexed. "It's not as if you need a ball gown for a day visit. You will go now, won't you?"

"All right, not a ball gown or an evening gown, but I *do* need an afternoon gown, since our father has not seen fit to provide me with a wardrobe beyond what a lowly governess would wear and if I appear at Mr. Tunley's office wearing this, I'll be turned away." The fact that her father had not provided Lissa and Kitty with a decent wardrobe had always rankled with Lissa. She did not mention that in a fit of resentment towards her nobly born half-sisters, she'd refused to take the several fine gowns with which her father had presented her before her London trip, as she'd known they were Araminta's castoffs from two seasons ago.

She'd since regretted such stubborn pride. "Give me two of your last season's gowns, *including* a ball gown. That can be your return on the information I provide. I can make them over. I'm good with a needle."

As she walked back up to the house, she saw Maria's nose still pressed against the window, and when she let herself back into the schoolroom, her eldest charge rushed forward with a look of imperious anger. "You'd better tell me what you were discussing with that young lady or I shall tell Mama," she threatened.

But Lissa had a plan. She might not be devious and totally self-absorbed like Araminta, but she had a strong streak of self-preserving cunning, so she knew exactly what she had to say.

"Only if you promise that what I tell you is strictly secret between you and me," she said in a tone to convey great gravitas once she'd settled the girls.

Miss Maria eagerly took the bait, and when Lissa had drawn her to the two seats across from the unlit fire at the far end of the room, she said in a low voice, "The young lady is a viscount's daughter—I shall not tell you who—but if you had observed her more closely, you'd have seen the resemblance between us, which has been remarked upon in public circles. She has sought me out as she wishes me to help her secure a most desirable match since, as you know, I have connections with Lord Debenham and his man of business. Both these men are friendly with …er…*an*other gentleman, whose friendship the young lady wishes to build upon."

She was, naturally, not about to reveal that Lord Debenham was the focus of Araminta's interest.

Miss Maria's mouth dropped open. "But how can you help? You're just a governess." She said the word with such derision that even Lissa felt her hopes plummet.

Regaining her enthusiasm, she responded robustly, "But a governess with good connections, and a face and figure that already have people wondering if this viscount's daughter and I are cousins. Her maid will bring around several gowns for me to make over so I can aid her in her enterprise."

"But you're employed here." Miss Maria was looking increasingly stricken.

"Yes, and that's where I'll need your help, Miss Maria." Lissa hoped the excited suggestiveness of her tone would bolster Miss Maria's enthusiasm, for it seemed she was too unimaginative to wonder at the benefits for all of them. "You want to make a good match, and surely you would be looking higher than a clerk. With your pretty face and figure, you could really rise in the world. If my good offices have been elicited by a viscount's daughter whose fine gowns will enable me to attend certain society events, surely I can in turn help you to meet a…better class of potential husband."

With it put so simplistically and so compellingly, Miss Maria was like clay in her hands. "Oh yes," she whispered, shifting excitedly in her seat. "Mama says I'm pretty enough to snare an earl…if I could only be introduced to one."

"Well, I shall introduce you to lots of titled gentlemen." Ironically, Lissa could indeed see the plump and pretty, dark-haired Miss Maria being introduced with some success into such lofty echelons, but the only person she herself was interested in was Ralph.

Ralph was her next quest. A quest that needed Miss Maria's assistance.

She pondered her alternatives as she rose. A small lie was needed to achieve success. "I know how much you would love to attend Lady Smythe's ball on Thursday, Miss Maria. I can arrange that, but only if I can get away to visit Lord Debenham's man of business this afternoon. I'll need you to look after your sisters and you must promise not to tell anyone that I've gone out. Or where I've gone—and especially don't tell your brother. I can't tell you the reason but I can promise that there will be no invitation to the ball on Thursday if you cannot agree to this."

Not surprisingly, Miss Maria eagerly gave her assent, and without wasting a moment, Lissa changed into her Sunday best and departed the household to visit Ralph.

He was astonished to see her, and hurried round from behind his desk to take her hands and kiss them, for they were alone in the small office where he worked not far from the Inns of Court.

"My angel! Miss Hazlett, what brings you here?" He grinned then added jokingly, "I'm afraid we can't elope yet. I've still not made enough to keep us both. But if you can remain patient—"

"Oh Mr. Tunley!" She cut him off. "I can be as patient as I have to be. But I'm here on important business." And she proceeded to confide in him the events of her evening at Vauxhall while his expression grew ever more astonished.

"So now I must urgently warn Mrs. Crossing that she's about to be revealed. Her husband looks a cruel and unsympathetic man, and when he sees the sketch that Master Cosmo intends to deliver to him shortly, and which I have drawn, he will beat her, if not worse. She'll never be able to run away with the man she truly loves."

Ralph patted her down onto a red velvet upholstered chair and knelt at her side. "Hush, my love, you are overset. We must think on the problem calmly so that we can discover a solution."

Lissa was an independent soul. She'd had to be, since her parents were so involved with one another to the exclusion of their children, so it was a novelty to have anyone take a real concern in her affairs. Ralph's tender ministrations inspired in her a fierce determination to make something of what she felt could be realized between them.

If they only had the means.

Finally he rose and began to pace, stopping on the edge of the Persian carpet to lean against the desk. Reaching for the sketch Lissa had shown him of Lord Debenham in company with Lord Smythe and another gentleman in the supper room at Vauxhall, he held it up to the light. "Indeed, that's my employer to a tee." He nodded slowly, his expression admiring. "Look at that cruel mouth. Not only is it physically and anatomically correct, but you've managed to imbue him with his signature arrogant, cynical air. As for those other gentlemen, I've seen them make clandestine visits to the office. Always thought they were too smoky by half. You truly are a gifted artist, Miss Hazlett."

"Well, my gift is about cause great and unintended harm! Please, Ralph, you do agree the matter is serious? But before I go on, may I say that I think we are familiar enough with one another, surely, for you to call me Larissa…though I prefer Lissa."

"And you shall call me Ralph." His gentle smile became a grin. "My, but we have come a long way since our auspicious introduction…Lissa, and I am determined that we shall travel far together, but for that, I shall need luck and ingenuity." He became brisk. "Enough of daydreaming. You have an immediate problem, though I believe I have a bigger one in Lord Debenham."

"Yes, Ralph, but I came here for help regarding Mrs. Crossing. I fear it will go very badly for her. Her husband is not a nice man."

"But, short of murder, he is entitled to discipline his wife as he sees fit, and if he is confronted with evidence that she has been behaving in what you suggest was an unwifely manner, then the law—and indeed, public opinion—will side with him."

"You surely don't think that justifies—"

Ralph held up his hand to cut off her protest. "It doesn't matter what I think. I'm stating facts. And unless you have managed to steal the sketch from Master Cosmo, I don't see that we can do anything except forewarn your lady in potential distress."

Lissa felt very downcast. Miserably, she said, "Master Cosmo has informed Mr. Crossing that he will hand over the sketch this afternoon."

"Do you know where Mr. Crossing lives?"

Lissa shook her head. "All I know is that they'll both be at Lady Smythe's ball on Thursday, only then it'll be too late." She sighed. "Master Cosmo was angling for an invitation. Originally he'd proposed handing over the sketch then." She twisted her hands and shifted in her seat. "And I've gone a bit beyond myself in promising things I can't deliver. The only reason Miss Maria, who is Cosmo's sister, has agreed to keep my coming here secret is because I promised her that I would somehow get her an invitation, if not to Lady Smythe's ball, then to others where she might meet prospective suitors who are more in line with her lofty ambitions."

"You mean suitors more elevated than lowly clerks or men of business to much greater personages."

"Oh Ralph, how can you say that?" Lissa leapt up and gripped Ralph's hand, squeezing it and fearing she'd mortally offended him—until he burst out laughing at the same time as he wrapped his arms about her. "No, don't pull away. It's very nice and we are for now quite undisturbed, though I daresay it's not proper at all that you're here unchaperoned."

"Indeed it is not and I shouldn't be anywhere but looking after two very trying little girls. But Ralph, I have done a terrible disservice to Mrs. Crossing. What am I to do?"

He was thoughtful as he stroked her hair, still holding her

against his chest. "The best plan, as you say, is to secure invitations to Lady Smythe's ball for you, Master Cosmo and Miss Maria. You can use that enticement to Master Cosmo to hold off handing over the sketch and also to win over Miss Maria, so that she'll happily be complicit in enabling you to see me whenever the urge presents itself. At least for the next few days. I've no doubt your Master Cosmo would be unable to resist rubbing shoulders with those whose hallowed ranks he wishes to join. Tell Master Cosmo to send a note round to Mr. Crossing to say he'll hand over the sketch at Lady Smythe's ball. Then as soon as you arrive at the ball, you must try and find Mrs. Crossing to warn her. It doesn't help her much, but forewarned is forearmed. If she fears for her safety so much and is planning to elope with her lover, as you suggest, she might get a message to him, asking for his help." He shrugged. "Not that I know the first thing about the circumstances, though I hate the idea of any woman suffering violence at the hands of someone who has the advantage of strength and brutality. However, she is guilty. There's no justifying infidelity."

Lissa thought of her own parents, and of the new babe Lady Partington was soon to deliver. Perhaps it would be a son, her father's longed-for heir. Meanwhile Lissa's new sibling would be another Hazlett bastard. Both her parents were guilty of infidelity and she was the product.

"Oh, Lissa, my dearest heart, I never meant to hurt you with my thoughtless reference." Ralph, realizing his faux pas, squeezed her tightly and kissed the top of her head.

"I know you didn't and I don't blame you for it." Lissa sighed as she raised her face to his. "It's true that my life has been blighted through the infidelity of my parents. But I'm not going to think of that. All I know is that I need to live with my conscience, which means I can't be the reason harm comes to Mrs. Crossing, regardless of her crime." She hadn't realized her fists were clenched until Ralph gently uncurled them. Frustrated, she added on a sigh, "But listen to me run on. How am I to secure these invitations to Lady Smythe's ball? Everything you say is wonderful, but these are not the circles in which I mix. Nor do I believe Araminta is in a position to ask Lady Smythe." Not with her sister having caused such a recent scandal, she thought.

"But they are the circles in which my brother mixes." Ralph shrugged at her surprise as he put her away from him, still holding her hands. "He would organize it without a problem, my sweet. I just need to ask him."

"Your brother? Could he?"

"Yes, Teddy, the eldest of my five older brothers, will probably be in attendance in any case. He could, and he would, secure an invitation if I requested it of him. Now, tell me again the names of this extensive guest list we must submit to Lady Smythe. I cannot possibly be expected to remember the proper name of Miss Mary or whoever she is when my senses are so entirely filled with the vision of loveliness before me."

In a dreamlike state, Lissa returned to the Lamont household, where a very cross Miss Maria met her at the doorway to the nursery.

"You've been gone an age and Nellie and Harriet have been positive demons. I can't bear to spend another moment alone with them."

Lissa did not bother to remark that she regularly felt the same way but she was able to quickly ameliorate Miss Maria's ill temper when she told her about the invitation to Lady Smythe's ball that would be forthcoming.

Chapter Twelve

Araminta had no wish to attend Lady Smythe's ball. For the first time in her life she wanted only to bury her head beneath her feather down pillow and block out the world.

Friends whom Araminta didn't know she had called in unexpectedly to discuss Hetty's scandalous behavior, rather than the fetching effect created by the mixture of fake and real foliage in Araminta's new bonnet she'd picked up that morning from the milliner.

Mrs. Bradbury's sympathetic horror at Hetty's scandalous behavior was barely tolerable, but it took all of Araminta's willpower during afternoon tea not to hurl a plate of neenish tarts at Miss Potter's smug, "Whoever would have thought the younger Miss Partington would waltz off with a husband first? I suppose beauty doesn't count for everything, after all."

So now here she was, at Lady Smythe's grand affair, grimly fielding the inevitable opinions of the gossipers who wished to include her in their speculations as to how Hetty had waltzed off with such a dashing, dangerous gentleman.

Watching a shy but eminently eligible young blade head in her direction then clearly reconsider and address the plain miss to her right was like salt in a wound. Araminta felt like stamping her foot but tempered her anger so that she had the requisite well-bred smile for Lord Debenham when he suddenly emerged in front of her.

Once again fear and fascination warred within her. Why had she elicited Lissa's help in discovering ways in which to win from him a marriage offer when she knew he was dangerous? The truth was, there was something decidedly exciting about that. She also knew a great deal more than he would like since she'd seen that letter, which put her in quite a nice bargaining position. If only she'd not burned it, she could have used it to encourage Lord Debenham to marry her, but then he might have considered that blackmail. Still, with the letter no longer in existence there was no stain on his character and for that he ought to want to reward her.

"Miss Partington looks uncommonly lonely all of a sudden. Not so full of fire and fun as on the last occasion we met, eh?"

Araminta was determined not to drop her gaze and show either shame or fear. "How delightful to see you, Lord Debenham." Nevertheless, she felt ill at the sight of his nephew, Roderick Woking, who materialized beside him. "And you, sir," she added, nodding.

"Poor Roderick was distraught when he heard your sister had been so ill used by that rascal, Sir Aubrey." Lord Debenham's reptilian smile reflected no sympathy for either Roderick or Araminta.

Mr. Woking moved restlessly beside him before he squared his receding chin. "Does she not realize her new husband will be made to forfeit everything when he's convicted of his Spencean activities?" His rapid words were accompanied by a nervous hand wring before he ran his fingers through his sparse hair several times. "Yes, he will be brought to justice, and when he's charged with treason, his estates will be forfeited to the crown. She should have thought of that."

"Now, Roderick, common sense is not a trait that is observed when passion is in the ascendant. Miss Henrietta was obviously seduced by Sir Aubrey's honeyed words, but she will rue the day. Fortunately her elder sister has more sense." He bowed before Araminta. "Now, my dear nephew is enormously desirous of asking you to dance, though I fear we will find your dance card filled."

No other young man had asked Araminta to stand up with him this evening, and the fear that Hetty had ruined her chances for a match this season made her want to weep.

Before she could snatch her dance card away, Lord Debenham had raised it, remarking, "Oh, indeed that is not the case. Well, perhaps you would do Roderick the honor of accompanying him onto the dance floor for this set. Regrettably I must leave you, as I have secured Miss Smythe for the next dance."

With the greatest reluctance, Araminta allowed herself to be drawn onto the dance floor and into the limpid hold of Mr. Woking, as the dance was a waltz.

She tried to keep a semblance of a smile in place, for she could not show her aversion. But it was hard. The young man's breath was like the breeze of death against her cheek. It made her want to gag but instead she kept her head held high and called upon all her reserves of stoicism. But as she glanced about the room and saw other young ladies with far more desirable dance partners, including—to her surprise—her own half-sister who was in the arms of a rather handsome young man she'd not noticed before, she felt like casting good manners to the wind and simply fleeing from this awful place.

Everybody was talking about Hetty and making speculations about what her sister's scandalous actions would mean for Araminta. The only reason no gentleman had asked Araminta to dance was because of horrible, hateful Hetty, and to be perfectly honest, if Hetty walked into the room right now, Araminta would have called her to account in front of everyone.

She hadn't realized Mr. Woking had spoken until he squeezed her hand and repeated his question with a concerned look. "My dear Miss Partington, I can see you are distracted, and I can well understand why, in view of the shame you must feel on your sister's account."

Araminta sent him a baleful look. "You cannot possibly understand, Mr. Woking. How dare you even presume to understand the anguish I am feeling at this very moment?"

Her voice had risen and she realized she'd have to temper her hysteria in view of the interested look her half-sister, who happened to be very near, had just sent her. Goodness, but how had Larissa managed to acquire an invitation—and who was that very charming, gentleman with the flyaway hair and warm blue eyes leading her around the dance floor?

Right now, Araminta felt that charm and boyishness were a good deal more preferable than dangerous good looks. Not to mention lovelorn swains with clammy hands and breath like the grave. She swung back to Mr. Woking, feeling very vulnerable right now. "My sister set out to ruin me," she said, her voice wavering. "To humiliate me. And she has succeeded."

"I believe you have everyone's deepest sympathies, Miss Partington," said her dance partner with unctuous civility. "I believe it's their delicate sensibilities which account for the fact you are finding yourself less...popular than usual. Indeed, I would have stayed away too for the very same reasons, had not my uncle told me I should be kind to you."

He cleared his throat and added, hurriedly. "That is to say, you are hardly a charitable case, Miss Partington. Oh no, I did not mean it in that way."

"How did you mean it, then?" Araminta glared at him, stepping back with relief now that the waltz was at an end. She shook her head and held up her hand as he began to speak. "Pray, do not trouble yourself to answer. I have no interest, and I wish to be returned to Mrs. Monks."

She ignored his heartfelt gaze as she rejoined the redoubtable widow, and was hardly soothed to see Lissa looking more striking than she could have imagined in the apple green and cream ball gown Araminta had discarded the season before.

Larissa, catching Araminta's eye, acknowledged her across the room with a nod and, Araminta was certain, a narrowing of the eyes. Was she, like everyone else, thinking Araminta diminished on account of Hetty's shocking behavior? Had she noticed that Araminta was not surrounded by admirers as she usually was? The idea was insufferable.

Still focusing on the handsome young man at Larissa's side, she swept over to greet her and to gain an introduction. "You have done a fine job making my old dress look less last year," she said with a smile intended to be friendly and disingenuous. It was decidedly galling to see her gown looked better after its rejuvenation than it had when Araminta had worn it new. Well, if their papa lost all his money, Araminta could employ Lissa to be her dressmaker for a fraction of what she paid to have her new gowns made, she decided.

Araminta's interest in Mr. Ralph Tunley took on a keener edge when she learned he was Lord Debenham's secretary, the young man in whom Larissa had confessed her interest. And when their circle was joined by a dashing brown-haired gentleman who greeted Mr. Tunley with easy familiarity before introducing himself as Lord Ludbridge, Mr. Tunley's eldest brother, Araminta was in silent transports. Especially when he gazed upon her with such blatant admiration that had not an edge of pity or censure for the fact that her sister's scandalous elopement had all but consigned Araminta's marriage aspirations to the fireplace.

This was her gift from heaven. It was a sign that she need not cry herself to sleep every night on account of Hetty's betrayal.

Here were two charming, eligible young men she'd never met, right before her. True, the youngest was penniless despite his excellent lineage and therefore not a prospect in the immediate sense. However, there were six brothers, at least a handful of them unmarried, she quickly gathered, and the eldest, titled one, was smiling at her warmly.

Yes, her star was again in the ascendant.

***

When Lord Ludbridge—or Teddy, as Ralph affectionately called him—had excused himself to dance with Araminta, Lissa gazed with surprised wonder at her companion.

"You never told me, Ralph," she whispered, fiddling with her fan.

"I told you I'm as poor as a church_mouse, and that's the truth." He grinned. "I didn't think it relevant to add that my eldest brother has a title and a daily battle to ameliorate the damage our grandfather wrought upon the family fortunes, due to his fondness for the gaming table."

Lissa shook her head. "That doesn't matter. Whether you're drowning in the River Tick is nothing compared to birthright. So you're Lord Ludbridge's younger brother, and I am...stained and beyond redemption." She tried to sound forceful when really she felt like crying. "For my own self-preservation, I can't see you again after tonight, Ralph."

"No, Lissa!" He clutched her hand, dropping it quickly as he glanced about the room.

But the throng of people seemed too occupied by each other to notice the young couple on the edge of the dance floor.

"Lissa, I know what you're saying, and it doesn't matter to me that—"

"That my parents aren't married?" She couldn't look at him, though she stared, stricken, about her. "Why has the room not gone silent? Why have I not been struck by lightning and told to leave?" she wondered aloud.

"Because no one knows and they won't care. Besides, *I* don't care a jot, and once my mother meets you, she won't be able to help but love you." Ralph's soothing voice eased her feelings a little though she knew it was not true. He indicated their fellow revelers. "You are not the only one, my love. Look at Miss Claremont over there. Yes, quite respectable and set to make a fine marriage, despite the fact she has been left two sizeable inheritances by two different men claiming to be her father."

Lissa put her hand to her mouth. "Or because of it," she said with a wry smile. "I have not a feather to fly with and no father listed on my birth certificate. No, Ralph, there is no future between us."

Araminta chose that moment to waltz by in Teddy's arms, smiling her most engaging smile, and Lissa was assailed by an unexpected wave of grief. Her half-sister had the lineage to be entirely eligible for Ralph's brother. With her beauty, she could navigate that path if she chose, though Lissa wasn't sure if she should warn Ralph that Araminta had a less charming side.

And then she heard Mr. Crossing's name and remembered why she was here.

Ralph patted her shoulder at the obvious panic in her voice when she reminded him of her mission. "Lady Smythe will have seen her if she's arrived. She invited her. Ah, there is the good lady. Allow me to introduce you to her for, of course, you were added to the guest list at Teddy's behest."

It was clear why Lord Debenham employed Ralph, for he was a charming diplomat, Lissa soon realized. The boyish charm was a façade that put his quarry quite at ease as they supplied him with the information he sought. Lissa had thought him shy and diffident but, it seemed, that was only with her. And it was a ruse, besides.

"Why, there she is, and looking as pretty a picture as the day she married." Lady Smythe pointed across the room to a petite young lady who resembled a piece of Dresden china in an exquisitely embroidered gown of pale blue net over a white satin underdress. The tiny pearls sewn into the swathes that trimmed the hem were reflected in her flaxen hair, which was swept into a high topknot with tendrils curling down her neck.

Lissa had captured her prettiness in the sketch she'd done of her, though at the time, Mrs. Crossing had been tousled and anxious-looking with a high color. Now she looked the epitome of serenity beside her florid-looking husband, who towered menacingly over her. Lady Smythe murmured the word "doting" but Lissa thought "possessive" was a more appropriate adverb.

"Newlyweds?" Lissa asked innocently.

"You might think it, the way her husband never lets her out

of his sight, but they were married in the spring four years ago, in fact." Lady Smythe was still smiling at the harmonious-looking Crossings when Lissa and Ralph made their excuses and left.

"How are we going to get them apart?" Lissa asked, suddenly panicked when she saw Cosmo advancing upon her.

"Leave it to me." With a nod, Ralph went smoothly up to Mr. Crossing and engaged him in conversation.

Lissa did not wait to hear what he was saying, and she certainly didn't want Cosmo to notice her engaging Mrs. Crossing before he reached her. Fortuitously, Miss Maria Lamont chose that moment to tug at her brother's arm, and Lissa swept up to her quarry, almost hissing, "Mrs. Crossing? Yes, I thought so. I have an urgent message for you. Do you have a moment?"

The flare of terror in the young lady's eyes was very real as she glanced at her husband. But he was so engrossed in conversation with Ralph, he did not notice her follow Lissa into a darkened corner of the room.

"A message? What message?" She fiddled convulsively with her fan, and Lissa replied in a rush, "There is a picture of you and a…gentleman at Vauxhall Gardens. A sketch that was commissioned. I wanted to warn you before it was handed to your husband."

"What…do you mean?"

For a moment, Lissa feared the young lady would faint clean away. She'd never seen anyone so white before. "You know what I mean. In the supper box at Vauxhall Gardens. Your husband commissioned someone to follow you and sketch who you were with." There was no time to mince words. "That sketch is to be handed to your husband tonight."

Mrs. Crossing put her hands to her face and her shoulders began to shake. Lissa quickly moved in front of her to block her obvious distress from appearing too public.

"Oh, dear Lord, no. He'll kill me," she whispered. "I knew he would one day. I should never have imagined I'd get away."

"Please, all is not lost!" Lissa gripped her wrist. "There may be a way."

"But the sketch reveals my companion? Yes? And it is a good sketch? Recognizable?"

"It's a good sketch," Lissa agreed. "The truth is, I was forced to do it. I have it with me but I'm playing for time because I want to help you. I didn't realize the...situation in which we'd find you. Anyway, I hoped you had a brother, someone with whom it was plausible you were with that evening. If you described him—or someone else—I could try and amend the sketch before I hand it to the man who insists that it will be given to your husband during the ball."

"I have a brother," she said shakily. "He is distinguished by his red hair. Wild red hair. Yes! Could that work? No, but the sketch will be charcoal."

"Thin? Portly? Tell me. Quickly!" Lissa could see Mr. Crossing detach himself from Ralph. He was now making his way across to his wife, who saw him too, and Lissa had to remind her in a low voice not to lose her courage.

"Rake-thin," she whispered, already turning with a shaking smile for her husband. "Square jaw, and he has a favorite waistcoat embroidered in half-moons. He's an eccentric, to be sure," she added in a rush.

Lissa excused herself as Mr. Crossing arrived. Quickly she made her way to Ralph's side. "I need a red crayon or pencil. Now!" she whispered. "Oh Ralph, if I ever needed something from you, it's this."

Ralph's initial surprise turned to fondness. "If only all your desires were so easily acceded to. Come, I shall ask Lady Smythe, and as I see Master Cosmo coming in our direction, I shall have a word in Teddy's ear. Ah, I say, wonderful timing. Here he is. Teddy, can you waylay that gentleman there and ask questions later?"

"Gosh, but you do have an amenable brother," Lissa remarked as she followed Ralph to the supper table where Lady Smythe had stationed herself with a garrulous old dowager.

"Teddy is far too kind for his own good, and quite fair game. I'm only surprised he's reached eight and twenty without getting himself hobbled. Faithful chap, though. Never got over his first love." He clicked his tongue. "Sad, sad affair. I'll tell you about it someday. Still, he has a remarkably stoic and cheerful nature, so you'd never guess at his heartache. But then sentimentality runs in the family, as you can tell.

"And here is Lady Smythe, only, much as I would wish you to cleave to me like glue I think it's dangerous, and I should release you into the care of your chaperone for a moment while I elicit the necessary tools."

Reluctantly, Lissa returned to the matron into whose care she'd been supposedly placed to preserve appearances for tonight's entertainment. She'd arranged to meet Ralph in the corridor outside the ballroom, later.

True to his word, he was waiting for her with a red crayon, which he handed to her, together with a piece of charcoal and a larger folded piece of paper, saying, "I know you didn't ask me for both, but I thought they could be useful, if not necessary. Once you've amended the sketch, you can seal it in this parchment. I've brought wax for the task, since I thought you'd not want Mr. Lamont to see how you'd changed things. "

"You have saved the day, Mr. Ralph Tunley," Lissa declared on a sigh of relief. "And now I must send you away, because we cannot be seen together like this."

And because it was too tempting to throw her arms about him and show her true gratitude in a most unseemly manner.

***

Araminta had never expected to enjoy the evening so much. It had given her a marvelous sense of superiority to dismiss Mr. Woking in such a belittling manner. He was quite repulsive, and the idea that Lord Debenham imagined she'd throw herself away on such an inferior piece, even if Mr. Woking was his nephew, was insulting in the extreme.

Now here she was, in the arms of the most handsome gentleman in the room, making them quite the most head-turning couple as they waltzed around the dance floor.

Not only was Lord Ludbridge handsome, he was also titled and, it appeared, charmingly pliant. He'd fetched her lemonade after their first dance and then promptly invited her for a second twirl.

"I cannot believe that your brother is secretary to Lord Debenham," Araminta remarked as they navigated a couple who lacked their finesse. "It is the most remarkable of coincidences, for I recently became acquainted with your brother. A most charming young man."

"Far too charming for the work he's doing." Lord Ludbridge lowered his head to speak with greater intimacy to Araminta. His sweet breath stirred the tendrils of dark hair that fell from her elaborate, feathered coiffure, and her heart thundered with anticipation and the keenest desire. Goodness, this didn't happen often. Not since she'd sized up Sir Aubrey as a likely prospect before Hetty had stolen him. She decided not to think of her exciting, bruising encounter with Jem, or the danger-edged kiss she'd shared with Lord Debenham. These men were, as of right now, consigned to the past.

Strange that meeting Lord Ludbridge seemed to have entirely dispelled her despair over losing Sir Aubrey to Hetty. It only confirmed that the irresistible man with whom she was dancing must assuredly be her destiny.

"What do you mean, My Lord?" She smiled up at him, hoping to elicit more about Lord Debenham's proclivities or the nature of the work young Mr. Tunley was required to do on his account. Just because Araminta no longer wished to marry Lord Debenham didn't mean it wouldn't be to her advantage to know as much as she could about him.

She felt like stroking the darling man's cheek, the way he was looking at her with such transparent admiration. Lord Ludbridge was quite charming. She'd need to find out more about his personal finances, though from first appearances he was plump enough in the pocket to satisfy Araminta when the alternatives were so very dire.

He looked about to say something then buttoned his lips. "My brother is far too tenderhearted to work for a man who has less of a charitable streak than he should have, given his circumstances. There, I've said nothing out of turn, even if you know Lord Debenham personally."

Araminta blushed and dropped her eyes. But no, surely this young man knew nothing at all about her. He'd have no idea she once weighed up the advantages of making Lord Debenham her husband, and he'd surely have no notion of what had happened in the supper house at Vauxhall with Sir Aubrey.

She blanked her mind to the humiliation. She would never again make such a mistake. That, too, was in the past, never to be revisited. From now on she would look only to the future, and the future was right here, at her fingertips.

She squeezed Lord Ludbridge's hand lightly and, surprised perhaps at what he might perceive as forwardness, he glanced down at her. Adopting her most artful, mischievous smile, she said, "I have met the gentleman but two dances were quite enough. I had to run to his nephew to save me, for I believe Lord Debenham has quite a fearsome reputation."

Lord Ludbridge gave her hand a little squeeze in response and, to Araminta's surprise, he actually colored as he realized what he'd done. "I am surprised that a young lady as innocent as you would even know he had a reputation," he remarked.

"Promise me that if you see him coming in my direction this evening, you'll cut in and ask me for the next dance." Araminta adopted a look that was part appealing and wholly enchanting. She knew this by the way he looked at her with such a heart-melting smile.

"I would be only too happy to aid you in such a manner, Miss Partington."

As he led her off the dance floor, Araminta was about to murmur her appreciation in terms that made clear her enormous gratitude, only he was buttonholed at that moment by his brother.

She just made out the indistinct words, "Teddy, can you waylay that gentleman there and ask questions later?"

Araminta looked in the direction Mr. Tunley was pointing. She could see Larissa's employer, young Mr. Lamont, crossing the room, his sights set on her half-sister. Araminta's lip curled.

Social climbing upstart, she thought, before deciding he'd make a good match for Larissa, after all. He considered himself so above Miss Hazlett, the family's governess, but little did he know Larissa came from stock far better than his own.

Perhaps it would be kind to think of helping her sister. It would be a charitable thing to do. And Mr. Cosmo Lamont would be a perfectly suitable suitor. Larissa certainly couldn't continue gallivanting with Mr. Tunley, for she'd soon have her heart broken, and a good sister like Araminta must do what she could to help her nearest and dearest. Mr. Tunley would be filled with aversion if he knew Larissa was…

Araminta could barely articulate the word to herself, but blankets came to mind, with herself firmly on one side—the good side—while poor Larissa flailed on the other.

She smiled sweetly at Mr. Tunley and nodded at Mr. Lamont as Mrs. Monks responded to her summons and came to lead her away, as any good chaperone would her gently nurtured debutante charge.

And her heart thrilled at the charm and gratitude she read in His Lordship's answering smile before he began an earnest conversation with Larissa's soon-to-be suitor, Mr. Lamont.

**

From a distance, Lissa could see that Ralph, reliable as ever, was where he'd promised he'd be. Perhaps the corridor hadn't been such a wise choice, for he was quite conspicuous, but everything had been organized so hurriedly and besides, this would only take a moment.

"It's done, and should, I believe, answer the purpose. I'm sorry I can't show you, for I've sealed it, but now I'm ready to hand the two sketches to Mr. Lamont."

She shivered and Ralph gave her a comforting pat. "I really should stop taking such liberties. When are we going to spend time together that is a little less fraught than these clandestine meetings? Now, have courage, my dearest, you are quite the heroine."

Lissa glowed with pleasure. "I hope Lady Smythe is pleased with the sketch I've done of her husband. See, I've taken him out of the original picture of the three gentlemen I sketched in the supper house, and drawn him on his own. What do you think?"

She held up the two pictures and Ralph grinned his admiration. "I'm more interested in your rendition of Lord Debenham. You have captured the very essence of my employer's black heart beneath the self-satisfied sneer. Well done. I could identify Lord Debenham at a glance now, even if I'd never met him before. And Lord Smythe and that other reprobate who looks mightily out of place are truly well done. You are a fine artist. Lady Smythe will be in transports and your Master Cosmo is going to find himself a very busy young man, with a flurry of commissions coming his way."

Lissa, about to respond, instead gave a gasp as she was jostled by a passing gentleman she'd not noticed advancing down the corridor toward them.

"I beg your pardon, miss," he apologized as he bent to retrieve the sketch that had fluttered to the floor. He was about to hand it back to her when the smile on his face was wiped away by shock. "Good Lord, where did you get this?" he demanded, before again apologizing, this time for the expletive.

Lissa's chaperone for the evening appeared in the doorway, but Lissa was too concerned by the stranger's reaction to respond to her summons.

He still had not relinquished the sketch. "Forgive me my

manners. Allow me to introduce myself." He bowed. "Sir Archibald Ledger. I had not thought it possible to have such a compelling picture of these three men in company together. The detail is superb, the rendition quite…extraordinary. Might I ask the name of the artist?"

Ralph glanced at Larissa, who said hesitantly, "I believe the artist wishes to remain anonymous." She held out the sketch she'd done of Lord Smythe alone. "There is perhaps better detail in this one." If Sir Archibald wished to commission her directly, she would not be averse. "Lady Smythe wished for a rendition of her husband and asked the…er…sketcher to follow him while at Vauxhall Gardens to capture him during an unguarded moment, so she could present the sketch to him later as a surprise."

She was getting into her stride now, perfecting her spiel so she could perhaps gain an extra commission. Vulgar though it was for a lady to think of money like this, a future with Ralph would only be possible if they had more of it. "Perhaps you are interested in having a sketch done of your wife?"

The way he snorted, seemingly in derision, shocked Lissa. "Not possible. At least, not for a while yet. Lady Julia was recently delivered of a healthy ten-pounder at my estate."

"Congratulations," Lissa murmured. It seemed the only appropriate thing to say. "I trust all went well."

"Yes, yes," he went on dismissively. "Now, the sketch. I'd like to buy it from you—or the artist. I assume the sketch from which the commissioned subject was extracted is no longer necessary, if the main purpose was to capture Lord Smythe's likeness. What say, five pounds?"

"Five pounds!" cried Lissa. The sum was exorbitant. It was more than she'd earn in three months as a governess. "You're welcome to it for that price, sir."

Her astonishment was compounded as he promptly handed over the money without demur.

"Extraordinary," he muttered as he took his leave. "I cannot believe how fortuitous this has been."

He left Ralph and Lissa staring at one another before Lissa burst into nervous giggles. She held up the money and stared wonderingly at it. "Oh Ralph," she whispered, "I've never had so much in my life."

Gently, he stroked her cheek. "If that's all it takes to fill your eyes with such glee, my job is going to be easy. That is, if I ever find a loose five pounds lying around."

***

Even though Nellie and Harriet were as difficult as ever the following morning, Lissa smiled to herself as she tidied the schoolroom, thinking of Ralph and when she'd next see him.

When they'd farewelled one another in a darkened corner of the ballroom with Lissa's chaperone looking on, she and Ralph had been ridiculously proud of themselves. Mrs. Crossing had been saved and Lissa had made a fortune, all within an evening.

She was still smiling when she glanced up at the sound of footsteps on the stairs. Cosmo appeared, greeting his sisters morosely before ushering Lissa into a corner.

"How the devil am I going to arrange my next commission?" he complained. "Lady Baxter. She wants to sit for me. Yes, *sit* for me!"

"It doesn't sound terribly complicated. You're a passable sketcher, Master Cosmo. I'm sure you can please her with whatever you produce."

"I hope that's not another way of suggesting you will not do as I bid you."

"There may be more inducement to helping you if I ever saw the money you keep promising me."

"Lud, you are vexing! What about that sovereign I gave you?"

"That's not a third of what you've received for the three sketches for which I know you've been paid."

"I told you I had a couple of small but very pressing bills to pay and that as soon as I was flush, I would be in a position to give you your share. Besides, I paid you for the first sketch. Are you so addle-headed that you don't understand I need to paint Lady Baxter so I can do the very thing you want me to?"

Lissa turned her head from his venom and the very vulgar manner in which he couched his words. Stepping away, she bent to fold a pile of small garments on a table nearby. "I trust your sister enjoyed herself on Thursday night."

"The trouble with Maria is, the moment she gets something, she wants more." He kicked the chair in front him. "Now she's threatening to drag me off to listen to some fiendishly dull musical soiree next week because a certain gentlemen in whom she's interested will be going."

"Perhaps I could accompany her." Anything that would get Lissa into society, where she could contrive to meet Ralph.

"And why would the governess be invited to such an event?"

Lissa shrugged as she straightened the sleeve of a linen shirt. "It just occurred to me that if Lady Baxter happened to be amongst the audience—since she most likely is on account of her love of music—and were quietly seated somewhere I could observe her, your difficulties might be over. But then, you're quite right, why would I deserve to go out any more than I do?"

But he was not listening. "Lud, you could be right. If Lady Baxter *is* there, it would be an ideal opportunity. I shall ask Maria to find out. She was saying it seemed every second person at Lady Smythe's was going."

Chapter Thirteen

Araminta gave herself a final considered appraisal in the looking glass at her dressing table and tried to temper her tears of frustration. Home? She couldn't believe her father was demanding that she return.

"Do you think he'll miss me, Jane?" she asked, turning her tragic gaze upon her maid who was hoisting up two carpet bags from the Aubusson carpet to take down to the carriage.

"Who, miss? Lord Debenham? He were mighty put out that you didn't thank him for his flowers."

"Of course, I don't mean Lord Debenham! I mean Lord Ludbridge. I've not told Mama about him yet because I wanted it to be a surprise."

"You're forever giving your family surprises, miss," Jane muttered, heading for the door. "What surprise is this one?"

Araminta followed her. "I'd wanted Mama to be surprised and delighted when I told her about Lord Ludbridge's marriage proposal but now it's all spoiled for I'll have to tell her all about him during the week I'm back home."

"You didn't mention he'd proposed, Miss."

"Don't be so silly, Jane. He hasn't yet, but he will. I just wouldn't want to make the same mistake I did over Sir Aubrey."

"No, Miss, I'll wager you wouldn't."

Araminta grabbed her maid's shoulder and hauled her back into the room just as she'd reached the passage. "What can you mean, Jane?" she demanded, as close to slapping the girl's face as she'd ever been. "You know, I don't like your tone." She closed her eyes briefly as she fought for forbearance. Perhaps it wouldn't be wise to make this an issue. Smiling quickly, as if she'd never been angry, she went on, "I made the mistake of telling Mama about Sir Aubrey too early on in the piece. I don't want to make the same mistake regarding Lord Tunbridge."

Since Lady Smythe's ball the previous week, Lord Tunbridge had sent numerous notes to the house, and she'd danced with him at Almack's. Then suddenly, her father had recalled her home, insisting she provide her mother with care and assistance during Lady Partington's lying-in. Araminta didn't know of any other debutante subjected to such parental thoughtlessness. As if Araminta could be of assistance. She didn't know the first thing about babies.

Immediately she'd written him a letter, telling him she was very relieved that the birth two nights before had gone well but that she did not feel she could contribute what was necessary for the felicitation of mother and infant. This had resulted in a short, acidic response. Araminta was to leave London the following day or her father would come and fetch her back to The Grange, where she'd remain for the rest of the season.

So now Araminta was being rattled about in a carriage, returning to the estate for which her father had reminded her she'd been prepared to make the ultimate sacrifice in order to be its mistress: marry the heir presumptive, her late bacon-brained cousin Edgar.

Fortunately, Edgar had tragically drowned in an accident involving Lady Julia Ledger, but it was sobering to recall how close Araminta had come to ruining her life. Especially now that she had such glittering opportunities at her fingertips. The thought of Lord Ludbridge made her heart swell. How clear he'd made his disappointment when she'd told him she'd have to leave London for a while.

Her father's summons left her feeling cheated, and she was struck by the urge to take her anger out on someone. She had half a mind to let Lady Julia's husband, Sir Archie Ledger, in on a few secrets about the wickedness his young wife had got up to when the pair of them had attended the fateful weekend house party at The Grange all those months before, which had resulted in Edgar's death. However, she'd given away the idea after failing to come up with how such a revelation would directly benefit herself.

Recently she'd heard that the "lovely Lady Julia" had been delivered of a girl.

Everyone, she thought, was having babies or eloping. Her last sight of Larissa had been of her half-sister staring moon-eyed at Mr.

Tunley. Well, now it was Araminta's turn.

If anyone deserved a good match, it was Araminta.

"Mother!" she cried as Mary, the housemaid, opened the door of her mother's bedchamber. For the moment she truly was overjoyed to see her darling, lovely mother lying against the plumped-up pillows, smiling at her over the downy head of a light-haired infant. "I've missed you!" In that moment, she realized she really had.

She took a seat at her mother's side and reached over to kiss her on the forehead. "So this is my new sister."

"Would you like to hold her?"

Araminta shook her head. "Perhaps later. She smells a little, and she has a very screwed-up little face, doesn't she? Like...she's just tasted vinegar."

"She looks very much like you as an infant." Her mother smiled down at the sleeping baby, wrapped in a small white woolen blanket. "She will improve. Hetty, on the other hand, was a complete cherub. The prettiest baby I ever saw."

Araminta bristled. "Obviously infancy is no gauge of how a child will blossom."

"Now, let's not be snide. Hetty looked radiant the last time I laid eyes on her. And even if she has scandalized your papa by eloping with a man with a reputation, I could not be happier for her." Lady Partington put her hand out to Araminta, who took it reluctantly. "Please don't be cross with your sister."

"How could I not? She ruined my chances of a good match this season. It was mortifying attending Lady Smythe's ball, when barely anyone asked me to stand up. They were all whispering behind their hands about the scandalous Miss Henrietta Partington, who eloped with a man rumored to have been involved in a plot to bring down the government. I could wring that girl's neck."

"Araminta, please. What's done is done, and Hetty is happy at last. That's all I've ever wanted for her." Her mother squeezed her hand before removing it to tuck the blankets more securely around the child as it stirred. "And very soon, I predict, you will make a match that will please you as much as it will us. With your beauty and your ambitions, not to mention your dowry, I have no doubt it will be a glittering one, too."

Araminta let her mother's words wash over her as she stared out of the window. At least her mother still had faith in Araminta's abilities, even if she was talking Hetty up undeservedly.

"Your papa and I received a letter from your sister last week, in which she voiced concern over your interest in Lord Debenham. She warned us to be vigilant, as she said he was not a gentleman you should associate with, no matter what the inducement, and that she had this on good authority from her new husband. Well, your father decided then and there that you must come home so that he could talk to you."

Araminta straightened. "I do not think Henrietta is in a position to dispense marital advice to me," she said, crisply.

"My dear, no need to take that tone. Hetty is merely concerned for your happiness."

"Hetty is gloating now that she has precedence over me for the first time. She's always wanted to tell me what to do, and now that she's married, she thinks she can!"

"But there must be truth in her concerns, surely? I know nothing about Lord Debenham but if your sister thinks you should stay away, especially if it's on Sir Aubrey's advice, then, of course, I must bring the matter up with you." Her voice changed and she looked with great sympathy at her daughter. "I know you had ambitions regarding Sir Aubrey, and I know you're cross with Hetty for marrying him, but please don't do anything rash, Araminta."

"How dare anyone imagine I'd do anything...rash!" Araminta had to take several deep breaths to rein in her outrage. She smoothed the folds of her jonquil travelling dress over her knees and gazed out of the window at the sweeping lawns of the gated park. There was a time when to be mistress of The Grange seemed the epitome of success. How much her ideas had changed. "Always I am mindful of the consequences of my actions...unlike Hetty!" She exhaled on a sigh. "But you can set your mind at rest on account of Lord Debenham. It's true that for a very short while I considered him a likely prospect, since he'd made his interest for me so very clear. However, there is another young man I met at Lady Smythe's ball several weeks ago who is clearly taken with me, Mama, and I do like him tremendously."

She smiled as she recalled the way Lord Ludbridge had looked into her eyes as he'd raised her gloved hand to kiss her fingertips the first night when they'd said goodnight. He'd been smitten from the very first glance, he'd told her more than once, since then.

And then Araminta had been dragged back to the country. Lord Ludbridge's note and the bouquet of flowers he'd sent her on the morning of her departure had reassured her of his desire to see her the moment she returned, so perhaps leaving the city so soon after Hetty's scandal was not such a terrible thing. It might make him more inclined to make her an offer, sooner.

"Who is this young man?" Her mother looked indulgently at her, clearly pleased at such news.

"Lord Ludbridge. Have you heard of him?"

"Only good things." Her mother's smile broadened. "That he is a fine-natured fellow—as are all his brothers—and he's been working hard to restore the fortunes of the estate, after his grandfather had gambled so much away. Apparently after his late father fell ill, he left much of the handling of daily matters to his eldest son who has acquitted himself well."

Frowning, she added, "I hear he's not in London much and that he prefers the country. I don't know if that would suit you, Araminta. And I believe there would be...pecuniary restraints." She cleared her throat. "I know your ambitions extend to more—"

"I have changed greatly, Mother, and am no longer as I was before I went to London for my second season," Araminta assured her. She wasn't best pleased to learn that Lord Ludbridge was not as plump in the pocket as she'd supposed or hoped, but he was very handsome, charming and clearly taken with her, and Araminta was not going to end her season without an offer. If she had to marry someone with less money, then he must at least be easy to manage.

"I'm glad to hear that, Araminta. I'd hoped you would...soften a little. I want you to be happy and I believe that if you place more emphasis on what your heart is telling you, rather than pursuing only your stated ambitions, you will find the contentment that I have."

The child was waking, whimpering, its little mouth making sucking motions, its eyes still closed. Araminta was horrified when her mother put it to her breast and, although it shut the little beast up, she felt it most undignified.

Her mother smiled when she caught Araminta's look. "I gave both of you to a wet nurse, and your father feels I ought to do that now, but really, this is the easiest way to settle the child. I know it's frowned upon but I've decided I don't much care what others think. Oh, Stephen, Araminta has returned."

Araminta turned as her cousin entered the room after a brief knock.

He smiled warmly as he advanced. "Cousin Araminta, the last time I saw you was at Vauxhall, which was not too long ago. But my, how things have changed since, eh?"

Araminta felt herself burn with color. He surely was not referring to the Sir Aubrey disaster, though the way he was gazing at her mother suggested he would not care. A strange and vague unease manifested itself, and she rose.

"I had not realized you'd left London, Cousin Stephen."

"I came straight back when I heard news of young Celia's birth."

"Celia?"

"That's what we've called her," her mother said, and Araminta stared as Stephen occupied the chair she'd just vacated and reached across to stroke the head of the suckling child. Certainly it was not immediately apparent that's what the child was doing, but that Cousin Stephen was in her mother's bedchamber while her mother was feeding the child seemed quite wrong. Hesitantly she took a couple of steps toward the door. "I must dress for dinner."

Her mother and Cousin Stephen raised their heads as if they'd forgotten her, and her mother smiled again. "I'm so delighted at your news, Araminta," she said. "It is my greatest hope that you will discover happiness like your sister. And then you, too, will know the joys of motherhood."

Almost immediately her mother was completely absorbed by the tiny usurper, whom she was now handing over to Cousin Stephen to hold, and Araminta was forgotten.

Angrily, Araminta opened the door into the passage and was assailed by the smell of the roast dinner that was being prepared in the kitchen basement.

Generally she loved saddle of beef, but unexpectedly she found the smell thoroughly unpleasant. In fact, she felt quite ill. She was glad to reach her bedchamber and avail herself of the damp cloth that Jane handed her, but all she could think about was the look on Cousin Stephen's face as he'd held the child.

Entranced.

It didn't make sense, but it was how she intended Lord Ludbridge would look at her when she'd worked her magic on him.

Chapter Fourteen

It was another ten days before Lissa was able to leave the Lamont household again. Maria was struck down with a chill, immediately followed by Cosmo.

Only when the pair had recovered their good health was talk revived about sketching Lady Baxter. After some judicious enquiries, it was established that she would indeed be attending the weekly musical soiree hosted by Lady Milton. Immediately, Lissa dispatched a note to Ralph telling her where he could find her, if he so chose.

As Lissa took a seat beside her charge and observed those arriving to take up one of dozens of little gilded seats in front of a piano, a large harp and an even larger potted fern, she recognized many of those from Lady Smythe's, including Lord Debenham, as well as Mr. and Mrs. Crossing, who looked surprisingly harmonious.

She'd placed her reticule on the seat next to her but slyly removed it when Ralph slid into place as the harpist and piano player—twins, she could tell at a glance—began to tune up.

Surreptitiously, he clasped her hand for the briefest moment before confessing, "I thought I wouldn't survive for the need to see you. Could you really not have found a moment to slip away? I can only think you can live far more comfortably without me than I without you."

His words brought both pain and pleasure. "I was on call nursing Miss Maria and Master Cosmo for every moment I wasn't teaching Nellie and Harriet. Oh, but Ralph, it was ghastly." On the pretext of dropping something on the floor at her feet, she bent down and, when Cosmo did the same, she whispered, "I thought Cosmo couldn't be more awful but apparently, when he's fighting fit, he's at his absolute *best*."

Ralph chuckled, before remarking in a tone of surprise, "There's my brother…with Miss *Partington*."

Lissa turned to him with raised eyebrows. "It looks as if she's his guest." She felt sick saying the words.

"Now there's a turnabout. I don't think Teddy's invited a young lady anywhere since Miss Bella broke his heart. You do know that I believe you far and away the prettiest of the two of you."

"That's a very kind thing to say, Ralph, but Miss Partington has been praised for being a beauty her whole life." Before she could receive a response, she had to turn back at a question from Miss Maria.

Lissa had to be grateful to the young lady, at least for this outing. Miss Maria had simply informed her mother that she would be taking Lissa to a musical soiree, and as Miss Maria was infinitely more forceful than her highly strung mama, who spent most of the day on a chaise longue, there proved to be no difficulty.

If only everything could be achieved so easily, thought Lissa as she glanced across at Araminta, who was chatting animatedly with Lord Ludbridge. Lissa had never seen her sister look so beautiful. Araminta glowed, and it appeared Lord Ludbridge was entranced as he gazed back at her, despite the fact, it seemed, he was unable to get a word in.

"My brother looks as smitten as I," Ralph murmured, adding hurriedly in an even lower voice, "with the other sister, of course. For five years he's pined for his lost Bella, our neighbor with whom we'd grown up. For the past two I've told him he can't burn a flame to her forever. A surprise that the two young ladies who've engaged his interest couldn't look more different."

"How did Miss Bella break his heart?" Lissa asked the question more to deflect him from his extravagant praise of Araminta. She was deeply dismayed at the idea of Araminta setting her cap at Ralph's brother. How would Lissa compare as a prospect for Ralph in consequence? The truth would be revealed, and a situation could not possibly be allowed whereby two sisters—one of aristocratic stock with a handsome dowry, the other illegitimate and penniless—could marry two brothers like Ralph and Lord Ludbridge.

She swallowed down her sadness. Marrying Ralph was what she wanted more than anything, yet how could it ever be possible?

"I think I mentioned once that Miss Bella's father leased a house near our estate. He worked for the East India Company and she and my brother were once inseparable. He was going to marry her. Then one day, Miss Bella just disappeared."

Lissa, who'd been staring at Araminta, jerked her head back to look at Ralph. "What do you mean, just disappeared?"

"Just that. Teddy went to London. He intended to choose a betrothal ring and to make arrangements so he could ask Miss Bella to marry him when he returned. But he got back to discover their house empty and the family gone. He could never discover where. It was as if they'd never existed."

"I've never heard anything so extraordinary. And she never wrote to say where they'd gone? There was no forwarding address?"

"Nothing. Teddy tried everything to elicit information. It was the strangest thing. Now, five years later, Miss Araminta looks to be the one to at last mend his broken heart."

***

Araminta was very pleased with the intensity of Lord Ludbridge's gaze. Even after that simpering harp player, Miss Shrew—or whatever her name was, though she certainly resembled a shrew with that unfortunate nose—started her infernal strumming, which everyone else seemed to think divine, he couldn't take his eyes off her.

He really was the most charming young man she'd met in two seasons. He was tall and well made with a strong jaw and a delicate mouth. It seemed everyone liked Lord Ludbridge, too.

Going back to see her Mama had not been the tragedy she'd thought it for it was clear how much His Lovely Lordship had missed her. As for herself, she could not wait to kiss that mouth. In fact, before the week was out, she would do it. The time had come to get matters moving.

Lord Ludbridge offered her his arm when the assembly rose for refreshments. With a coy glance, Araminta murmured her thanks and was rewarded with a most gratifying smile. Her heart fluttered with pleasure and she gave his arm a little squeeze. Yes, he really was a most handsome and agreeable gentleman. Titled and rich enough. Indeed, Lord Ludbridge was the answer to all her difficulties.

"Ralph, good to see you!"

Araminta turned at Lord Ludbridge's warm tones and was horrified to find herself confronting her escort's brother in company with her half-sister. Mortifying was that their hostess, Lady Milton, who materialized from behind the harpist, immediately exclaimed over the resemblance between the girls.

Mr. Tunley had already opened his mouth but Araminta interrupted quickly. "There is no family connection. I am Lord Partington's daughter and Miss Hazlett is—"

"My grandfather was a country solicitor from Hampshire," Larissa murmured.

"Hampshire? I know that part of the world. And your father?"

Araminta felt as panicked as Larissa looked but Mr. Tunley changed the subject, smoothly. "I am impressed by our entertainers tonight. You have put together an excellent program, Lady Milton."

For a moment, Araminta thought he'd saved them from any further uncomfortable questions, but the panic she'd felt must have gone deeper than she'd thought, for all of a sudden she felt the room closing in on her. She flicked open her fan and began a vigorous attempt to circulate the air but the heat of the dozens of bodies was too oppressive for such meager measures.

"Excuse me—" she began before she grasped at Lord Ludbridge's arm, her legs buckled and darkness closed in.

***

Aramina came to on a royal-blue velvet chaise longue in Lady Milton's sitting room surrounded by her hostess, her chaperone and—as good a reason as if she could have come up with the idea of fainting, herself—Lord Ludbridge.

"What happened?" Despite feeling thick-headed and dazed, she was delighted at the expression of concern on Lord Ludbridge's face.

"My dearest Miss Partington, it would seem the close air was too much for you. How do you feel now?" Lord Ludbridge, who was kneeling on the red and gold carpet at her side, gently patted her hand.

She fluttered her eyelashes and he cleared his throat and released her hand, Araminta coloring prettily. At least, that was the effect she was confident she achieved, for he looked suitably entranced.

After a sly exchange of smiles, Miss Monks and Lady Milton excused themselves and discreetly took a turn about the room, stopping to chat in confidential voices by the window at the far end, which allowed Araminta and His Lordship a little privacy.

"I think I can sit up now," Araminta told him uncertainly, adopting the frailness of an invalid. He immediately snaked an arm about her shoulders to help her into a comfortable sitting position.

"Goodness, I can't imagine what came over me. You are very good to have looked after me so well. What a kind man you are. I'm sure you must be the kindest of all your brothers."

Indeed, he did seem a very kind man, and a very kind man who was clearly entranced by her was a very pleasant lifelong prospect.

"Ralph is known as the tenderhearted one of us all." Lord Ludbridge appeared bashful as he said this.

"Surely not as tenderhearted as you, my lord." She was about to expand upon this theme when she had a flash of inspiration. With a sigh, she added, "I'm so sorry he's forced to work for that wicked Lord Debenham, about whom all those terrible rumors are swirling. I noticed that your brother was at the recital with Miss Hazlett. I do wish he'd warn Miss Hazlett about his employer."

"Miss Hazlett?" Lord Ludbridge looked confused. "I cannot imagine why some imagine the young lady resembles you. I've never met one to rival your beauty."

Araminta smiled coyly. "You are too kind, Lord Ludbridge. But I'm worried that your brother is showing perhaps undesirable interest in Miss Hazlett. I saw her spying on Lord Debenham at Vauxhall Gardens the other night."

"*Spying* on him? What can you mean?"

Araminta adopted a look of uncertainty. "I…I'm not sure. At first, I assumed she must have been spying. She was quite alone, peeping through the window of the supper house he was occupying. Of course, I didn't know it was him until I was returning with my cousin and sister, and saw Miss Hazlett running down the path. I was afraid for her and about to go to her assistance, when I saw Lord Debenham appear in the doorway. He watched her go and then went inside again."

Araminta shook her head as if the thought distressed her. "I wasn't sure what I should do or if I should even say something, but you are such a kind, sensible, reasonable man, Lord Ludbridge, perhaps you could have a word with your brother."

Lord Ludbridge was clearly shocked. "Surely you were mistaken, Miss Partington."

"Indeed I was not. I greatly fear that Miss Hazlett has an unhealthy fascination for Lord Debenham. After all, she was alone and completely without a chaperone. I'd hate to think she'd set her sights on someone so unsuitable. And clearly your brother is…fond of her."

***

Araminta was congratulating herself on her inspiration when she arrived home midafternoon and waltzed into her bedchamber. Jane, who was laying out her clothes for later that afternoon, glanced up to ask her if the pale white and jonquil sarsnet evening gown would be to her satisfaction, but Araminta ignored her to close the door, loudly.

"I do wish the smell of dinner was not so overwhelming in this house. It never used to be," she complained. "Oh, and you'll never guess what happened at Lady Milton's. I fainted quite away and Lord Ludbridge played the knight errant. I hadn't planned it at all but it could not have worked better."

"You fainted, miss? Why, you've never fainted in your life before."

Araminta lowered herself onto the stool at her dressing table and untied her bonnet. "No, I haven't, have I? Well, it didn't matter. It was quite fortuitous, for Lord Ludbridge was most concerned and has made his interest plain. I shall want a new trimming on my white silk for Lady Amelia Sedgewick's ball the day after tomorrow. Do brush my hair for me, Jane. I feel a little odd and I need some soothing. My stomach is not behaving and I think it's because of all this excitement."

Obediently, Jane ceased her current task of tidying the bottles on her mistress's dressing table to attend to Araminta. She picked up the boar-bristle brush and looked at its figured silver back thoughtfully. "I used to soothe my dear mama with long, even brush strokes when she was not herself. Mama had such lovely hair. Fair and fine. She were strong and robust like you, miss, and not one for having fainting spells, or feeling bilious either except…"

After removing the last of Araminta's hair pins, she began to draw the brush through her mistress's long, loosened hair.

Araminta, who was feeling unaccountably tired, rested her chin on her hands and closed her eyes. "I do hate the way you don't finish your sentences, Jane. It's as if you think I have the energy or inclination to finish them for you. It's quite rude."

"I beg your pardon, Miss."

"Well, finish your story, then. What was your mama's malady? Perhaps mine is the same and I may learn from it, for I must say, I've not been feeling myself the past few days."

"Just that mama only fainted and threw up into the chamber pot when she was breeding, miss. I thought I shouldn't say some'at that would sound coarse, Miss, though breedin's the most natural thing in the world when a pair gets married and starts to 'ave bairns. I should know, bein' the eldest and bringing up a dozen, for mama would keep havin' em."

"Yes, that was coarse, Jane, and I wish you hadn't said it," Araminta replied, although not as crossly as she might have, as Jane dutifully continued to brush out her tresses.

Breeding? She nibbled her bottom lip as she considered Jane's words. Breeding only occurred to married people or those beyond the pale, like Larissa's mother. It didn't happen to well-intentioned, virtuous young ladies like herself.

"Turn your head, miss. Why, you are awful pale!"

Jane's anxious tone broke into Araminta's growing fear. No, it couldn't have happened to her. Those hideous few seconds when Araminta had thrown herself upon Sir Aubrey, thinking he was about to ask her to marry him, could not have resulted in her worst nightmare.

It could *not* be happening to her.

Araminta's encounter had been so very brief and so very unromantic, followed by a humiliation of such proportions she'd had to exorcise the memory of that night from her brain as best she could.

But as a waft of cooking aroma filtered in through the door and her stomach protested to such an extent she had to leap up from her chair and make her way to the chamber pot to be ill once again, she could not discount the possibility.

In fact, the more she thought about the very tiny changes in her body, and the realization that her courses were more than a week late, she had to contemplate the possibility that she, Miss Araminta Partington, was indeed breeding.

And that for the first time in her life she was not equipped with a cunning plan. No, she had not the first idea how she was going to extricate herself from this profoundly horrifying situation.

Chapter Fifteen

With no more entertainments to look forward to, or commissions to execute, Lissa slipped, with resignation, back into her old routine. Three days had passed since Lady Milton's musical afternoon and she'd heard nothing from Ralph.

While her disappointment was acute, she wondered if dull, dreary days were better than being on tenterhooks with regard to the various threats that had hitherto beleaguered her: Cosmo's uncertain temper, Lord Debenham's villainy, Araminta's escapades.

Maybe she should simply accept that attending to the demands of spoiled children was her lot in life.

Of course, such prosaic intentions flew out of the window when she received a parcel which, when opened in the privacy of her tiny bedchamber, revealed a very lovely gown that Araminta was apparently gifting to her.

"I have arranged an invitation for you to attend Lady Grenville's ball tonight," she'd written, "and as I realize you may have nothing suitable to wear, and I know how much you want to impress your Mr. Tunley, I wanted to show my appreciation with a new gown."

Lissa thought it best not to wonder at her motivations. Araminta wanted something but, no doubt, she'd reveal all in good time. But, of course, Lissa could not keep from speculating. Probably, she thought with sinking heart, Araminta was seeking information about Lord Ludbridge now that she'd apparently transferred her interest to him after giving up on Lord Debenham.

Lissa put on the gown and twirled in front of the tiny looking glass in the nursery and the lovely gown of palest green flared about her ankles. She liked the fashions for figured work around the hems and the fact that skirts were fuller this year. The dainty puffed sleeves were tiny and trimmed with small embroidered leaves. What made it most unusual was the crimson sash embroidered with the same leaves.

To Lissa's surprise, the dress was rather large about the middle, and seemed more Hetty's size than Araminta's—which perhaps was the reason Araminta was gifting it to Lissa.

"What are you doing?"

She swung round at the accusatory tone to find Miss Maria advancing through the gloom of the nursery, where the girls were quietly drawing, looking suspiciously at her. "Where did you get that dress?"

"It was…a gift."

Miss Maria marched up to give it a closer inspection. Lissa saw the gleam of envy in her eye as she fingered the embroidery. "You should be attending to my sisters," she said, grimly, as she straightened, "not twirling around as if you're about to go to the next grand ball." Immediately she brightened, smiling as if she expected Lissa to share in her excitement. "You'll never guess, Miss Hazlett, but I have been invited to attend Lady Grenville's soiree tonight. Yes, imagine it! A proper invitation has been delivered for *me*, Miss Maria Lamont, to attend Lady Grenville's soiree, and I shall be accompanied by Cosmo."

Lissa, standing on a bare piece of wooden floor in the center of the room, saw the two little girls raise their heads at their sister's lofty tone while her spirits plummeted. Ralph, it appeared, would also be attending the ball, and Araminta had arranged for Lissa to go. But how was that possible, now?

Tentatively she said, "I've also received an invitation. And this new dress."

"What are you about, Miss Hazlett?"

Lissa turned as Mrs. Lamont arrived in the schoolroom, wheezing after her battle with the stairs. "You're wearing Miss Maria's new gown. How can you imagine you'll deport yourself at the same entertainment tonight as the young lady of the household? That dress was delivered to this house, meaning it was intended for my Maria."

"No, it was a gift." Lissa was on the point of producing the card that had accompanied it when she remembered its reference to her friendship with Ralph.

"I don't think so, Miss Hazlett. And I suggest you remember your place. You will be looking after the girls, in the schoolroom, where you belong. Miss Maria has now been accepted into the ranks of the fashionable, and with her charming face and figure, she will make a fine match."

She put a proprietorial arm about her daughter's shoulders. "Indeed you will, my dear."

Mrs. Lamont turned to Lissa. "Miss Hazlett, take off that dress immediately and change into something suitable for walking. I want you to take Harriet and Nellie for some fresh air as soon as you're ready. Leave the gown on the bed for Maria to take back to her bedchamber."

***

What could she do? Lissa wandered the pavements with a small girl's hand in each of hers. Miss Maria was a usurper but Mrs. Lamont had complete power as her employer.

Of course, Lissa could not have imagined she could keep up this double life. She could not further her friendship with Ralph. Their love was doomed. She missed him greatly, and several days seemed such a long time. Perhaps she'd never see him again. She wondered what he was doing and if he'd be at the soiree tonight.

The little girls tugged at her hand. Lissa had been requested to make it a quick walk as nursery tea was nearly upon them but the girls were keen to go into the park.

Why not? The longer she was away from the Lamont household the happier she'd be.

They were all crossing the road when she recognized Lord Debenham's valet, Jem, limping toward her. After sending the girls ahead through the gates, she turned to greet him and was struck by the crooked twist to his once-perfect nose and the number of purple and yellow bruises, now fading, across his cheek.

"Good day to you, Miss Hazlett. You look well. What of your friend, Miss Partington? Me master, Lord Debenham—as you well know—were speakin' of her only the uvver day."

"Indeed?" Lissa glanced across to ensure the little girls were behaving themselves. They were sitting on the grass and playing with what looked like a fallen bird's nest. She returned her attention to Jem. There was something meaningful in the way he couched his words.

He lifted his cap to run his hands through his corn-colored hair and Lissa was struck by the jagged scar that sliced his scalp, as if someone had taken a sword to his head. Had Jem suffered *so* badly for his involvement in the letter, which Araminta had used to try to blackmail Sir Aubrey into marriage before she'd burned it?

"Strange coincidence, then, that me sweetheart, Jane, what's maid to your friend Miss Partington, told me sumfink interesting about a dress wot she says Miss Partington sent to you this afternoon."

"Well, it seems everyone knows everyone's business," Lissa remarked, ready to move on. The fact that she wasn't going to be wearing the dress after all was hard to take with fortitude. She didn't need Jem to be crowing over his superior knowledge of her life.

"You can sound haughty, Miss, and I don't care a scrap. But as there were summat shady going to be taking place tonight, I thought you might jest consider it worth a shilling for me to warn you."

Lissa's mouth dropped open. "Are you..." She stopped, horrified. "Is this blackmail?"

"Dunno, Miss. I didn't reckon you 'ad secrets like that Miss Partington, but if you do, then maybe it's blackmail, or maybe it's jest that your friend has plans you don't know about yet, but that it might be worth two shillings to 'ave forewarning of." He took a deep breath. "That's if you gets me meaning."

"Miss Partington wouldn't wish me harm." Lissa tried to sound dignified. "I've been too..." She'd been going to say "helpful" before deciding "useful" was a more apt word.

"Well, if that were in the past only you weren't useful now, I wouldn't be too confident of her loyalty, miss. There ain't no loyalty amongst rogues and thieves, I can tell you."

"How dare you be so insulting?" She felt suddenly angry toward Jem, highly indignant that an inferior would speak like that, though it was true she was mistrustful of her half-sister.

Jem looked at her expectantly. "Well, Miss?"

"I don't have any money with me," she said tightly. "And if it's something I really should know about, then a gentleman would tell me."

Jem shrugged then gave a half grin. "You're right, Miss Hazlett. Tell yer wot. I'll do you a favor and I won't ask fer no money. Jest don't wear the green dress and yer'll be right as rain, no tales told and no one in any tricky situations."

He offered her a quick bow and strode off, quickly turning the corner and disappearing before Lissa could catch up with him to call him back.

Hurriedly she collected the little girls and walked them home, just as Miss Maria appeared on the stairs dressed in the embroidered green dress, her dark hair elaborately coiffured, her mother's jewelry adorning her throat.

"Ah, Miss Hazlett, Mama will be glad to see you back." She sounded very grand and grown up as she tugged at her mauve elbow-length gloves. "She's cross that you've made the girls late for nursery tea. I placated her."

Offering Lissa an overindulgent smile, she took another step down the stairs. "I was going to wear my oyster sarsnet but this is far superior, don't you think? I'm sorry you thought it was for you—"

"Miss Maria, you cannot wear that gown tonight."

Miss Maria sent her a mutinous look before she clearly chose to her ignore her. "Do you not think this could have been made for me? Clearly it was," she said, airily.

"But it was *not*, and Miss Maria, I fear there's trouble brewing. I don't know what, but I believe it would be unwise if you…insisted on wearing it."

"Is that a threat?" Miss Maria looked ugly when she was crossed. "Ah, Cosmo, the governess insists I cannot wear this dress to attend Lady Grenville's soiree. That trouble is brewing, she says." She gave a simpering laugh as she turned to look over her shoulder at her brother, who had just started down the stairs. "Should I trust her?"

Lissa, who hadn't exactly expected support, despite Cosmo's reliance upon her artistic talents, was, nevertheless, taken aback by his vituperative look.

"As much as you should trust a fox to look after your ducklings," he said in a low voice, passing close enough to hiss in Lissa's ear, "Mr. Crossing, who has made no mention of the work I delivered until I chanced to meet him in the street, told me he was delighted by the sketch. Delighted!"

His nostrils twitched and Lissa faltered at the vitriol in his voice as he added, "So delighted, there was no suggestion of an added payment for further investigative sketching. For more than a week I've tried to contact him. Now, finally, it's to hear that never was there a happier husband to have received proof that his wife had not been lying to him. Yes, the *redheaded* gentleman in the picture was apparently his wife's *brother!*"

He extended his hand as if he were going to pinch Lissa's shoulder then drew back at the last minute at the sound of his mother calling to her children, and her footsteps sounding louder in the corridor.

"Maria, there you are, and what a picture you look! Cosmo, are you ready to escort your sister? Miss Hazlett, you should be in the nursery looking after the children."

Lissa decided it would be futile to reiterate her concern over Miss Maria's insistence on wearing a gown that was apparently going to cause ructions.

Perhaps Jem had been lying in the hopes of earning a couple of shillings, though Lissa doubted it, and as soon as she reached the schoolroom, she promptly dispatched a note to Ralph, outlining as briefly as she could Jem's warning.

All evening she worked restlessly at her mending after Clara had put the children to bed. She'd hoped Ralph might respond but he didn't. When the clock struck eleven she realized he would not.

Despondent, she went to bed.

***

Araminta needed something hopeful to concentrate upon, otherwise she would go quite insane. The idea that she, Araminta Partington, could possibly have found herself in the unfortunate position she had was unthinkable. More than she could bear, in fact, and right at this moment, she'd never hated Hetty so much.

It was her sister's fault that Araminta was...

She couldn't even put it into words. No debutante could afford to be in such an intolerable situation, which meant Araminta simply had to swap her status as debutante for respectably married woman. And all within a couple of short weeks. Yes, that was apparently the time frame she was looking at, according to Jane, whom she'd taken into her confidence only because Jane knew everything there was to know about such things, and she could offer advice. Araminta had not the first idea about matters like this.

All she knew was that she had to put a wedding band on her left hand within a timely four weeks of the unfortunate incident that had precipitated this disaster.

That left her with a frighteningly short window of opportunity but Araminta felt confident of ultimate success. She had to. If she couldn't quite get the wedding band slipped onto her finger, then she had to orchestrate a situation in which what had happened with Sir Aubrey, also happened with the man who would soon be her husband.

That, of course, would be Lord Ludbridge.

The arrival of a dress that had been made for the treacherous Hetty—who no longer needed it, because she'd eloped—had, at first, enraged her. It was only as she'd paced her bedchamber, running her hands up and down her stomach and willing whatever was in there to miraculously disappear, that inspiration had struck. The painful reminder of past disappointments could in fact work to her advantage. All that was needed were a few artful tugs of the strings in the background.

To this end, while mingling with the throng at Lady Grenville's soiree, meekly and quietly at her chaperone, Mrs. Monks' side, she gained the attention of one of the waiters and handed him the folded note she had prepared back at home.

"Deliver this to that young lady in green that you see in the far corner by the window," she told him, pointing to a distant figure half obscured by the throng. The cut of her evening dress with its red sash was entirely distinctive. "The lady with the dark hair."

Within moments, she'd dispatched a second message via another waiter, this time to Lord Debenham.

Turning back around, she received a jolt of surprise and delight to see Lord Ludbridge appear before her. He looked so boyishly pleased that she was here this evening, and immediately began to compliment her on her gown until she giggled and tapped him on the shoulder with her fan.

"You'll quite turn my head," she told him. "And unless you plan to give me ideas you have no intention of giving me, you'd better stop now."

Instantly he sobered, and took her hand to give it a brief squeeze before he dropped it with a look of embarrassment as he glanced about the room. "Then I won't stop. Will you walk with me in the garden? There are lanterns along all the paths and we won't be alone. Ask Mrs. Monks. I'm sure she'll agree."

Araminta quickly gained her chaperone's assent and happily placed her gloved hand in the crook of Lord Ludbridge's arm. Half an hour in the garden alone with the handsome viscount sounded almost too good to be true. He would tell her how much he admired her and make her feel happy, like she deserved, not frightened and wretched. And as long as she ensured Lord

Ludbridge was in the library at 11 p.m. at least one of the complications in her life might be eliminated.

**

Ralph, meanwhile, was madly trying to find clean, fresh linen in which to present himself at the entertainment he'd had no intention of attending until five minutes before. The invitation would have been irresistible, had he known Miss Hazlett would be there, but he'd sadly faced the fact that London's social whirl would always remain on the perimeter of the real drudgery of their lives.

Ralph had to work for his living, and long days performing often unpleasant tasks left him with little energy, although this might have been different had he been remunerated sufficiently. He often imagined taking the divine Miss Hazlett on lazy boating trips upon the river, or surprising her with presents that would elicit such bursts of excited gratitude that he'd feel her smooth young arms twine impulsively about his neck.

Of course, that would be a very dangerous thing. He realized that the more he had to do with her, the greater his susceptibility to falling completely and irrevocably in love. This would make his daily toil even worse, due to the added torment of knowing how impossible it was for them to be together.

But the hasty, last-minute request from his beloved Lissa was impossible to refuse. She'd assumed he would be attending Lady Grenville's soiree and had asked simply for him to keep in his sights a young lady in a green dress with a red sash embroidered with flowers.

The message had been short and cryptic. Perhaps she was someone whom her dreadful employer had been asked to sketch. Ralph had no idea who this young lady was, but if Lissa had asked him to discreetly follow her, he would not fail in the enterprise. She would have a very good reason for asking him anything, he knew.

Having finally found linen, clean and crisp enough to do service tonight without declaring him the pauper he was, Ralph was admitted into the midst of the well-dressed throng—where he was immediately confronted with a dark-haired young lady in a green gown embroidered with flowers, the very description Lissa had given him.

Why, he wondered, had Lissa not said it was Miss Maria she wished him to keep within his sights? And there was her brother, Master Cosmo looking the Pinkest of the Pinks with his fashionably tight-fitting trousers, high pointed collar and Titus coiffure. Ralph ran his fingers thoughtfully through his own thatch of hair and immediately dismissed the idea of attempting something the least bit fashionable with it. He'd never aspired to the dandy set, or even desired to be a Nonesuch like his brother.

Not wishing to be observed, Ralph quickly entered into conversation with Admiral Cannington, who was clearly delighted to have an audience for his latest adventures in the West Indies, where he'd apparently distinguished himself and made a fortune to boot.

Meanwhile, he noticed Miss Maria kept looking over her shoulder, as if she were being observed. Or searching for someone. Yes, that's what debutantes did, didn't they? Sized up the quarry because, after all, the whole reason they were here was to find a husband.

Perhaps Lissa was worried that the young lady had fixed her interest on someone unsuitable. Well, Ralph would ensure she didn't do anything rash.

Therefore, even as Ralph indulged in the excellent champagne that was circulating and enjoyed, more than he'd expected, his conversations with a variety of guests, his protective instincts were on alert when he noticed the young lady receive a discreet note from a waiter.

He saw her eyes widen as she took it, and her quick furtive look across the room, before her gaze settled upon a rather portly, fair-haired young man in military attire talking to a middle-aged woman in a purple toque. The young man seemed to feel her eyes upon him, for he turned to look over his shoulder, smiling when he intercepted Miss Maria's gaze.

She colored and looked away, while Ralph felt both somewhat of a voyeur but also the importance of the task entrusted to him. For some reason, Lissa was concerned, and she needed Ralph to ensure this young lady didn't get herself into trouble. Perhaps this portly, unassuming young man was the unsuitable object of her interest.

"Baby brother, I didn't expect to see you here tonight. Not the kind of entertainment you usually frequent."

Ralph looked up into the smiling face of his eldest sibling and clapped him on the arm before he greeted his companion, Miss Partington, with polite restraint. He wasn't sure what he felt about this young woman, who did indeed resemble the woman he loved but who elicited such very different emotions. He certainly felt no warmth in her gaze, though she smiled and said how delightful it was to see him.

Ralph wondered at Teddy's interest in Miss Partington, which was a little awkward, in view of Ralph's interest in her half-sister. Perhaps Miss Partington felt similarly uncomfortable. It would not be unreasonable.

Of course, it was only natural Teddy would wish to take a wife at his age. Ralph just wished he'd not set his sights on Miss Araminta Partington. Nevertheless, he engaged her in pleasant conversation and she declared how much she loved riding, which quickly resulted in an eager invitation from Teddy to take her in his high-perch phaeton the following day. Ralph was surprised she elected to go before luncheon when she'd been warned there was a greater chance of morning rain.

And then Teddy and Miss Partington disappeared into the garden, and Ralph continued to chat to all number of people until the clock struck eleven, at which point he noticed the young lady in green nervously whispering something to her brother before hurrying toward the door that led into a passage beyond. He felt uncomfortable following her, and in fact nearly failed in his task when he was waylaid by the garrulous Mrs. Gargery, but after a minute or so he extricated himself and carried on, just in time to hear the click of what he knew to be the library door farther up the corridor.

About to go in, he hesitated. Perhaps she had a secret assignation with the portly young man, in which case it was no business of his to interrupt, despite Lissa's request.

However, Lissa's brief note had conveyed more concern than anything else for the wearer of this particular green dress. For a moment he marveled at her talent for intrigue, which was just what Ralph had always aspired to in his position. The longer he worked for Lord Debenham, the more unsavory dealings he uncovered, though not as yet anything that would put His Lordship in the dock. Debenham was too canny for that. Like most cruel men, he'd learned to cover his tracks.

Ralph put his ear to the door and, to his amazement, discerned his employer's iron-clad yet silky tones. He could not interrupt but if Lord Debenham was alone with innocent Miss

Maria, he needed to stay near in case he was required to render immediate assistance.

"So, you have enticed me here, madam. What? Because you *esteem* me? No, you plan to blackmail me, don't you? You look very young for intrigue, yet the deadliest are the unlikeliest. Well, what are your demands?"

Should he intervene? What *was* Miss Maria about? Ralph remained frozen on the spot while he digested the silence, menacing and pregnant with possibility until broken again by Lord Debenham sounding even angrier. "Speak up, you puling little fool. Who sent you? Won't tell me? Lost your nerve, have you? By God, but you have chosen the wrong man for your foolish and naïve carryings-on."

The sound of his heavy footsteps was followed by a short, shrill cry, and then the door burst open and Miss Maria hurled herself into the passage, tripping over her skirt and falling to her knees.

Ralph helped her up but the girl was clearly too distraught and in a hurry to leave to look him in the eye, much less recognize Ralph. Not even pausing to say thank you once she was back on her feet, she tore past him and disappeared into the ballroom.

Ralph was hardly going to enter the library right now. In fact, he knew it was time to make tracks to be well out of sight, should his employer choose to follow the unfortunate young lady, though he considered this unlikely. He was about to turn back to the ballroom when his surprise at recent events was compounded by the clear, surprised tones of another young lady who sounded remarkably like Miss Araminta Partington.

"Good evening, Lord Partington, how are you this evening? I hope we didn't interrupt anything."

His suspicion was confirmed when Ralph heard His Lordship greet Miss Partington by name before addressing Ralph's own brother. Clearly Miss Partington and Teddy had entered the library through the garden.

Ralph decided he'd remained long enough at Lady Grenville's soiree. He wished he could stop by the Lamont household and contrive a secret meeting with the divine Miss Hazlett. He needed to warn her that for some reason her half-sister had intended a secret meeting between Lissa and Lord Debenham. He shuddered, relieved that it had all fallen flat, but glad he had evidence of the young woman's duplicity. Ralph had worked too long for a villain not to recognize others of his ilk.

But it wasn't possible to speak to Miss Hazlett tonight. Once he returned, he had to satisfy himself with writing a lengthy description of what he'd heard through the closed door, which he dispatched to a street urchin who must have run his hardest for his money. For Ralph was just preparing for bed when he received a surprising answer from his lady love.

Wearily he slid beneath the covers, holding the hastily scribbled note to his chest. For the moment, it was the closest he would get to her.

Chapter Sixteen

It was little wonder Nellie and Harriet could not concentrate on Lissa's lesson on the great rivers of the world when Miss Maria's wails and the remonstrances of her mother could be heard two floors away.

That Miss Maria's evening had not been a success was borne up by Ralph's detailed missive the night before. Now Lissa was bursting with impatience to learn every detail. She was therefore astonished to be summoned by the housemaid, who told her she had a visitor in the drawing room.

The reason she was not banished elsewhere was clearly because the rest of the family was determined to hear whatever her mystery caller had to say.

When she saw it was Ralph, she affected cool politeness though her heart raced up her throat and threatened to turn her into a gibbering fool. However, her worst fears regarding her ability to manage the situation were not realized, and she decided she must be getting rather good at this intrigue lark.

"Mr. Tunley, how nice to see you again," she greeted him. "Do you have a message from Lord Debenham perhaps?"

"Lord Debenham is paying his respects?" Mrs. Lamont asked with a mixture of fear and hope. This elicited a muffled wail from Miss Maria, who was sitting unusually hunch-shouldered upon the chaise longue.

Ralph smiled. "I'm afraid not. Please excuse me for speaking plainly, Mrs. Lamont. I find myself in an awkward situation, for my employer is a man who does not mince words, and I certainly would not choose to pass on this message."

Lissa bit her lip and stared between Ralph and the Lamont family, who were gazing at him in almost terrified expectation. When none of them spoke, Ralph went on. "Lord Debenham respectfully requests that his gifts should be enjoyed by the intended recipients. I refer, in this instance, to a certain green dress."

He did not get any further, for at this, Miss Maria threw herself forward and onto her knees, covering her head with her arms as she wailed, "I never knew! I never knew it wasn't for me!"

"Yes, you did," Lissa said crisply. She looked enquiringly at Ralph. "Was there any other message from Lord Debenham?"

He responded with commendable aplomb. "Indeed there is, however, he was adamant that it was for your ears only, Miss Hazlett." He turned to the three Lamonts, who were now all staring at him with fear in their eyes. "I trust you'll grant Miss Hazlett a few moments of privacy?"

Lissa burst out laughing when they'd gained the conservatory and closed the door behind them. "Oh my Lord, I was so concerned for Miss Maria and what would happen, and while such an encounter with Lord Debenham was very terrible for one so young, it did serve her right. It certainly confirms any suspicions that for reasons known only to herself, Araminta wished to entice me into Lord Debenham's orbit." She shivered. "I'm sorry, Ralph, I do not like your employer."

"And I'm afraid I don't care overly for your sister. She wanted to discredit you, that is quite clear, only she was not terribly cunning about it. But how can I tell Teddy when he is happy for the first time in years? Teddy told me Miss Partington had passed on the information that she'd seen you spying on Lord Debenhan, all alone, in his supper box in Vauxhall Gardens. When that did not quell my interest, I suspect she devised this neat little device."

Lissa gasped. "*Spying?* She told him that?" But then, the truth was that Lissa had indeed been spying on Lord Debenham." She had to let that go. But the other? "Yes, the gown was clearly Hetty's, for it was too big for Araminta. I believe she entertained herself with this grand subterfuge in order to make it appear I was consorting with Lord Debenham, and ensuring our encounter was witnessed by your brother." Unable to help herself, she smiled. "Poor Miss Maria, she must have been terrified. I find Lord Debenham frightening enough, but I can't begin to imagine what Miss Maria felt when she became the butt of his anger."

"I certainly do." Ralph's grin quickly faded. "Sadly, I can't leave his employ until a plum job as second attaché for some British diplomatist falls into my lap."

Lissa's heart flipped. Agitated, she tore off the palm frond she was playing with. "Oh Ralph, you don't mean it," she said, crestfallen. "A diplomat? Why, then you'll be travelling all over the world. We will never be able to—" She bit off the words that would be too forward to utter. Even if Ralph had so often alluded to a shared future, it had always been half jestingly.

"I've always wanted to be a diplomatist, but I want you to be my wife more," he said seriously, taking Lissa's hands.

"Why, Ralph, that is… I really don't know what to say."

"I don't know why, since you've heard me voice the sentiment often."

"But never seriously."

"My dear girl, if I were in a position to make you a serious offer, I'd go down on one knee this very moment." He brought her hands up to his lips. "But I'll not elicit an avowal of your return affections and deny you an opportunity to accept a rich, handsome suitor who can offer you now, what I cannot."

"Ralph, don't—"

For once the quirk that made his mouth seem always to be laughing at himself or something else was not in evidence. He looked as sad as she felt. "It's true, Lissa, that I want what's best for you. I will not see you save yourself for me when I have no idea how long it will take me to become elevated in the world sufficiently to take a wife."

"I've lived on very little my whole life. I don't need a carriage or a—"

"Hush, dear girl, I know very well your wants are modest." Beneath the drooping fronds of the tallest fern, he cradled her against him and rested his chin on her hair while he stroked her cheek. "But the truth is, I can barely keep myself. Occasionally I get a family handout but I cannot rely on those. My self-respect demands that I am able to offer you at least a modicum of comfort."

She sighed and closed her eyes. "Very well, then. The fact that you want me will be enough. I won't insist on anything that will make you uncomfortable."

He laughed and kissed her forehead as he turned her in his arms, putting his hands on her shoulders, ready to let her go. "What a perfect angel you are. So unlike that half-sister of yours. My poor brother doesn't know what he is letting himself in for."

"Hush." Lissa put her fingers to her lips. "Let's not talk of Araminta."

"I won't say another word on the subject except that I predict interesting times ahead. My brother received a most extraordinary missive yesterday that I hope might change matters considerably, despite certain complications."

"Oh, Ralph, what?"

He shook his head and buttoned his lips together even as he smiled. "A true diplomatist does not speak of such things until they have come to pass."

"But you just said you—"

"Loved you? Actually, I didn't say those words, which was really quite remiss of me, because in fact I do love you. Quite sincerely...and I could go further. Quite passionately, only I dare not dwell on the extent of those dangerous depths when my feelings are immaterial if I'm unable to act upon them."

"Oh Ralph, what a ridiculous speech. If you love me, you can say it properly. I like to hear it." She reached forward and kissed him quickly on the lips. "There. In my employer's conservatory. How much greater proof do you need that my feelings match yours?"

He raked his fingers through his hair as he closed his eyes and rocked back on his heels with a deep sigh. "Yes, I love you, Miss Hazlett. And now I must go before I am quite wild with desire." Opening his eyes, he gathered her quickly in his arms, kissed her forehead, then set her away from him as he turned toward the door.

His expression was full of the greatest tenderness as he looked over his shoulder. "One day I will say those words to you in a way that makes you feel full of joy, not despair, as I feel. Good day to you, my most precious Lissa. I do not know when we will see each other again."

Lissa sighed. "Nor do I. Master Cosmo is so angry with me for changing the picture of Mrs. Crossing when he thought he would get so much more for evidence that would ruin the man's poor wife."

"Yes, the last time I saw Mr. and Mrs. Crossing together they looked very cozy in one another's company."

"Well, if I were to have been the means of ruining such good relations, then it was the least I could do." She grinned. "However, I was more concerned about saving Mrs. Crossing. Her husband is not a nice man."

"He's not," Ralph agreed. "I've heard this corroborated in various quarters. Well, my dear, let us hope Cosmo needs you for a lucrative commission soon. Soon, I must leave for Little Nipping but I shall be gone only one night. When I return, I shall do my best to orchestrate an invitation for you on behalf of my employer. Then I shall whip out my cravat, execute my most artful knot and we can pretend that idling our time away in the pursuit of leisure is what we do, everyday."

***

"I fear it does look like rain." Araminta felt quite pleased about this as she gazed at the overcast sky.

Cousin Stephen had accompanied her to Rotten Row, where Lord Ludbridge would shortly collect her. After that, the two of them would take a bowl through the streets to the outskirts of the city, where Lord Ludbridge would introduce her to—she couldn't believe this part—his mother. Yes, his mother! He'd sent a note round the previous evening to make the final arrangements.

Now Cousin Stephen was levelling at her that censorious look that made her want to slap him. "I trust you will behave, Araminta."

"Behave, Cousin Stephen? I'm sure that is rather rich coming from you, of all people." She dropped her eyes and slanted a sly look up at him. "I declare, I was never more shocked than the day I followed you to the river and found you—"

"Dear God, that is not something to bring up in public!" he exclaimed. "You were…spying on me."

She raised her eyes heavenward in mock forbearance, glad to have embarrassed him. At the time to which she referred, less than a year before, she'd been desperate to snare Cousin Stephen for her own husband. The sight of him lying, naked, on the river bank—in fact, more than simply naked but indulging in some very unrespectable self-pleasuring—had been wickedly erotic. Her pride had been sorely dented when he'd so roundly rejected her and sent her on her way after she'd made herself known.

These days, her once dashing Cousin Stephen was more like a boring uncle, the way he doted on Araminta's mother and the new baby, eschewing all pleasure-loving when he could have been a handsome consort for the occasions Araminta wasn't dancing with someone else. Now Cousin Stephen was spending a few days in town on business but rather than stay for any of the entertainments on offer, he planned to return to The Grange before the end of the week.

"Besides," she added, full of self-righteous indignation, "I think that when compared to my scandalous sister, I should be thoroughly commended for my wise choice of potential husband. Mama will love Lord Ludbridge, do you not think?"

Cousin Stephen's smile softened. "I believe she will. So you are confident, then, of his affections and you truly anticipate success? It's not very long ago that you were pining for Sir Aubrey."

"You make it sound like some coarse competition," Araminta huffed before her lips curved up into a satisfied grin. "Yes, Lord Ludbridge is smitten. And to think that he is taking me to meet his mother after we will have spent twenty minutes alone in an open high-topped phaeton. What could go wrong? I am very confident that he returns my affections, Cousin Stephen."

"And do you return Lord Ludbridge's affection, equally? I mean, it's not just because it's nearly the end of your second season?"

"Goodness, how many times must I repeat myself? I'm hoping to make him my husband, didn't I say? Then it doesn't matter if Papa loses all his money. At least I won't have to work as a dowdy governess like—"

She pressed her lips together. Her half-sister was a complication she would rather not have as part of the family. "Oh look!" She clapped her hands together as she hurried forward. "Here he comes. Goodness, what a fine pair of high-steppers." Araminta knew it was a clever move to admire Lord Ludbridge's two proud bay mares. These things were important to Corinthians like His Lordship; only His Lordship wasn't vain like so many who bore the moniker.

"I'm glad you like them, Miss Partington. Here, let me help you up."

She grasped his hand, laughing as he swung her up over the wheel and deposited her onto the seat beside him. "Goodbye, Cousin Stephen. You mustn't worry too much."

"Miss Partington's in safe hands, I assure you," Lord Ludbridge called out as he flicked the ribbons and the equipage flew forward, catching Araminta by surprise as she was dislodged, falling back against Lord Ludbridge's chest. Already things were going well, she thought as he apologized, for she'd only had to make a small adjustment to the trajectory of her landing.

And now he was snuggling her against his side, first holding the reins in both hands and then relinquishing one hand so he could snake it about her shoulders. She raised her head to smile at him, murmuring loudly enough so he could hear above the noise, "Oh, this is nice."

"Very nice," he agreed. "My dear mama is very much looking forward to meeting you."

"I fear she may disapprove," Araminta replied, making a moue, holding back the feathers of her leghorn bonnet that were being blown about by the wind.

"Disapprove? Why?"

"Because of the scandal involving my sister. I was afraid no one would want to be associated with me after Hetty simply abandoned all her morals and ran away with a man everyone knows is…well, you know what I mean, Lord Ludbridge."

"I cannot hold you responsible for your sister's actions." He looked discomforted as he admitted, "It's true that Mama was concerned but she is a fair woman. When she meets you, she will love you for the kind and virtuous young lady you are, Miss Partington."

"Oh, I do hope so." Impulsively Araminta rested her head on his shoulder and her hand upon his heart, before drawing back quickly, as if remembering herself. "Forgive me, Lord Ludbridge," she cried, biting her lip. "You make me forget myself. I do not think I have ever met such a lovely man as you."

He colored as he stared at her a moment before having to return his attention to the road. "You are truly adorable," he muttered, patting her arm, clearly quite distracted.

Araminta glanced at the sky once more, wishing it would rain so they would have the excuse of having to find shelter somewhere. But they arrived quite dry at the estate by the river which, Araminta soon learned, was the dowager's favorite abode as she did not care for the large, draughty home in the highlands or the antiquated Queen Anne house in Essex.

Her Ladyship greeted her with formal reserve at the bottom of the steps of a large, square, stately building. "I am pleased to meet you at last, Miss Partington. My son has spoken about you in glowing terms, though I believe you've known one another for but a short time."

"One does not always need a long time to know one's heart, Mother," Lord Ludbridge said, thrilling Araminta with his words, though his mother's response suggested this might be a topic they'd been over before.

Once seated in the drawing room, Araminta pretended interest in a stuffed fox in a glass jar upon a nearby table. "Did you used to follow the hunt, my lady?"

"I remain an excellent horsewoman, Miss Partingon, and am not yet too old for the sport."

"I beg your pardon, of course I did not mean to insinuate you were. I'm very partial to riding, too. Especially to hunting."

The dowager leaned back in her chair by the fireplace. "It does not surprise me to hear it, Miss Araminta. You have that look about you."

Lord Ludbridge intervened quickly. "Perhaps we should have refreshments now so that I can show Miss Partington around. Rain is threatening."

Over a dish of tea and cucumber sandwiches, the dowager Lady Ludbridge mentioned her five other sons and the fine marriages some of them had made. "Alas, there is not much left for a sixth son, and so I fear poor Ralph will have to wait awhile before he's in a position to take a wife."

This was pleasing news to Araminta, who said, to shore up opposition to any attempts Mr. Tunley might be making to mitigate his single state, "He is a charming young man." She turned to Lord Ludbridge. "No wonder Miss Hazlett is taken by him, though I suspect her efforts to entice Lord Debenham will bear more fruit."

The dowager sipped her tea. "Lord Debenham? What does he have to do with this?"

Lord Ludbridge looked uncomfortable before smiling at Araminta. "Lord Debenham is a rather different kettle of fish, and not, I believe, someone who could be compared to my brother. I really cannot see that any young lady who found a man of Ralph's character pleasing to her would be similarly interested in Lord Debenham—"

"Oh, I'm not suggesting there's a remote resemblance between the respective characters of your darling brother and his employer. I simply fear Miss Hazlett is using Mr. Tunley as a useful conduit to get the attention of Lord Debenham. Why, she all but admitted it to me, when I saw her leave his supper room at

Vauxhall Gardens several weeks ago."

"My, but you are forthcoming," the dowager said, as if this were hardly a good thing.

Lord Ludbridge rose quickly. "Miss Partington, perhaps you'd care for a walk?"

"That would be lovely." Araminta offered her future mother-in-law her sweetest smile as she followed Lord Ludbridge into the lobby. She did not care for the dowager, but that was a problem easily solved. Once she and Teddy were married they'd send the old woman to her majestic Scottish castle or the quaint Queen Anne estate, where she could not interfere with the way Araminta intended to manage things.

She squeezed his arm and offered him an adoring look as he gazed down at her. In fact, she really was feeling most indulgent toward him, so there was no feigning the arrangement of her facial muscles.

"I am so happy to know you, Lord Ludbridge," she murmured as he led her into the garden and onto a gravel path that traversed a formal arrangement of shrubs and flowerbeds, while well-tended grass swept down to the river. She shaded her eyes and imagined grand entertainments with guests being transported from the city by barge up to their front door. It was too exciting for words.

"And I, you, Miss Partington. I...I have never met a more lovely girl, in fact." He seemed lost for words after that, as he continued to stroll with her toward a copse of enormous elm trees a short distance away.

"Oh!" Araminta cried as a drop of rain landed upon her chest, quickly followed by more.

"We must hurry!" Lord Ludbridge seized her hand and together they ran across the last stretch of grass to seek shelter beneath the thick branches of an elm tree. Araminta was breathing heavily, but laughing from the exertion, and in a fit of abandon, she threw her arms about His Lordship's neck and drew down his head to kiss him deeply.

She felt him stiffen momentarily with surprise, but he was quickly kissing her back, sweeping her into his strong embrace and thrilling her with the hardness of his chest and the growing, incendiary passion of his response.

"Darling girl," he murmured between kisses as his hands ran

over her back, skimming the top of her bottom, going no farther but creating the most alarming force of desire deep within Araminta's groin.

She pressed herself harder against him, cupping his face as if that could intensify the kiss, wishing they were in a position whereby they could divest their garments and indulge in a mad coupling that would satisfy Araminta on every level.

"Oh, my dear lord," she gasped as she dropped her hands and suddenly found they were upon his rump. Such a hard, manly rump that she could not wait to feel in all its nakedness. This preliminary lead-up to what she would soon be able to enjoy for the rest of her life was almost more than she could bear.

"Miss Partington!" he gasped at last, drawing back and placing his hands on her shoulders as if he did not trust himself. "Forgive me. I have behaved in a most ungentlemanly manner. I have entirely forgotten myself." His breath came rapidly and, appearing distraught, he raked his hands through his hair. "I must atone."

"You need not, please, my lord. I was…I was equally to blame." She averted her eyes to look at the dripping leaves as if she were ashamed of herself. "I do not know what came over me, except…that I wanted this as much as you." She ended on a whisper as he gathered her in his arms.

Araminta wilted against him. This was heavenly. Everything she ever could have dreamed of. Lord Ludbridge was utterly divine. She could not imagine a husband more to her taste. And he was entirely smitten. Entirely!

"Did you? Did you really?"

"Oh, yes!" She raised her head to kiss him again but he shook his head, his look regretful as he put a gentle hand on her shoulder to hold her away.

"Miss Partington, this isn't the right place, I know that. But I will find the right place, very soon." He paused, as if uncertain whether to go on, then said in a rush, "I want to ask you a most important question. A question that will have very great ramifications for you and me for the rest of our lives."

Dear Lord, the moment was upon her, even sooner than she had anticipated. "What are you saying, Lord Ludbridge?" she prompted, her heart beating wildly.

He shook his head. "Not yet, Miss Partington, not yet—"

No! She held out her hands imploringly. He had all but asked her the question upon which hinged her whole future. How could he withhold something so very important at the very last moment?

"Please understand me. I am not in a position right at this moment to say what my heart is pleading for me to say, but I do want you to know of my feelings."

"Why can you not say it now?" She felt like crying with frustration.

"First there is something very important I must do. Do not look so sad." He tilted her chin up with his forefinger and kissed her tenderly on the lips. "It can wait one more day. I should not have said what I did but you make me forget myself. You see, this is not the first time I've said it, is it? I am utterly mad for you, my darling girl."

He offered his arm and reluctantly Araminta laid her hand upon it as they turned back toward the house. A gentle sun now bathed the damp lawn in a faded yellow light, warming his face as he smiled down at her.

"Tomorrow, I will see you. Tomorrow, I will ask you what I hope is the question you anticipate. And that you will give me the answer I wish to hear."

Chapter Seventeen

Ralph was glad he would only be in Little Nipping for one night. Every couple of months he made the journey with Debenham who went to oversee his landholdings. On this occasion, Ralph had gone up ahead in a hired chaise. His Lordship was due to ride up later in the day.

Now, hunched over his desk in the overseer's office, Ralph dipped his quill into the inkwell for more hated letter-writing. He was glad he did not have to put his own name to half of his employer's correspondence, but increasingly he detested being a party to Debenham's business dealings. The time had almost come when, despite several salary increases, he could no longer do this.

Generally, Lord Debenham left him to his own devices, satisfying himself with terse enquiries as to Ralph's progress or tossing a sheaf of correspondence upon his desk with instructions on how he should expedite certain matters on his irregular visits.

But this afternoon, Lord Debenham strode into Ralph's office, slammed the door behind him, paused, waiting for Ralph to acknowledge him, and when he did not, brought his fist down hard upon the surface close to where Ralph was working. The vibration caused a spattering of ink and Ralph jerked his head up in surprise.

"Don't you glower at me!" His Lordship cried. "Not when I'm travel-stained and weary but fearing I may have to ride poste-haste home. First of all, what's this business you've engaged in with my tenants that threatens to stall the eviction process?"

For a moment, Ralph was at a loss. "The notices have all been served, my lord." Bad business all over, he thought. God, he hated this work.

"You sent a shilling to Rogers, and now he's blessing me for my kindness. It's got the wind up the rest of them, who are no longer convinced their Lucifer of a landlord has no mercy in him. Which of course he has not. Now all of them are dragging their heels because they're under the illusion I have some soft spot that might be tapped!"

Ralph held up his hand so he could voice his protest. "My lord, I met Rogers last year, and his family, personally. How could I not do something? The youngest child is dying and needs medicine. A shilling was, I think—"

"I don't pay you to think. I pay you to carry out my orders! Rogers believes I sent the money. But more to the point, what do you know about a sketch drawn of me at Vauxhall Gardens, which I neither commissioned nor authorized? Tell me that!"

Ralph was so taken aback at the turn in the conversation he didn't know what to say? "A sketch?" he finally managed, hoping his dry throat didn't give him away.

"Are you deaf? Yes, a sketch, that's what I said. A sketch of me with two miscreants I'd liefer not be associated with. It's all a lie, of course. Someone's out to tar me with the same brush as two felonious suspects with Spencean leanings. Not something I'd be involved with, that's to be sure. And now I've been depicted in their midst. A party to their plotting is what it's meant to look like! Yes, well, you look suitably horrified, that's good. But what are you going to do about it?"

Ralph carefully laid down his quill and leaned back in his chair. Lord Debenham was frequently bullying, all too often demanding and unreasonable, but this was the first time Ralph detected real fear in his employer's face. He shook his head. "I'm afraid this is the first I've heard of any sketch."

"Then tell me who has made a name for depicting a face so full of character there is no one who does not instantly recognize the subject?"

Ralph hoped he did not betray himself by the waves of fear that made him glad he was sitting down. He dropped his eyes as he reached for his quill, simply for something to occupy his shaking hand. "I cannot say, my lord."

"There's a name. I agreed that the fellow could do a drawing of me at some garden party. A piece of vanity. A bit of fun at the time. And it was an excellent sketch, I grant you. But I don't recall his name, though he was quite the dandy. You surely remember it?" he insisted. "You've been about more than usual for you. Tell me where I can locate him so I can make him admit he falsified the drawing, that he was bribed by my enemies. By God, I'll make him sorry!"

Ralph furrowed his brow as he forced himself not to react with either defensiveness or fear. "I do recall this artist who is making his name doing commissions," he said slowly. "Though I had not heard of a sketch commissioned of yourself, my lord."

"Well, one has been commissioned, and I need to find out who executed it and who ordered it!"

Ralph wasn't about to mention Sir Archibald Ledger, who'd bought the sketch for such a huge sum. Of course he should have known there was more to the transaction than appeared to be the case.

Lord Debenham pounced. "You do know. Who is it?"

Quickly, Ralph tried to consider a range of ramifications for various answers. Of course, if Debenham discovered he'd deliberately withheld information it would be bad for him. And if Ralph did not tell him, Debenham would easily find out the information, elsewhere. With a sigh, he supplied an answer that would best serve Lissa's interests.

***

Lissa was staring from the window in the nursery when, to her astonishment, she saw Lord Debenham's carriage pull up at the front door and His Lordship, himself, march up the stairs.

She thought her legs were going to buckle beneath her. "I must...get something for the girls," she said lamely to the nursery maid. "I'll be gone but a minute."

Quietly she crept down the back stairs. If Lord Debenham were after her, she'd be called into the drawing room. Was it about the sketch? Sir Archibald Ledger's willingness to pay her such a huge sum should have alerted her to the fact there was more to it than a skillful drawing.

In just a couple of minutes, she heard his loud voice booming through the drawing room door as she was hurrying down the passage, past that room, hoping to make it into the garden. Lissa couldn't help herself. It wasn't eavesdropping. It was self-preservation. Tiptoeing to the door, she put her ear to the keyhole.

Mr. Cosmo Lamont, the famed sketcher, had apparently drawn Lord Debenham without his permission. His Lordship hadn't seen the sketch but he'd heard that he'd been placed in company with two villains. A false rendition. He'd learned the news, of all places, in a tavern en route to the country and had returned immediately to London.

Clearly, Miss Maria Lamont was a party to this villainy, enticing His Lordship into the library at a specified time during last week's ball, no doubt to blackmail him over the sketch before her courage had failed her. Were the two working together? Upstarts! Social climbers! To whom had Mr. Lamont sold the sketch? If Mr. Lamont didn't divulge this information, Lord Debenham was going to call upon the full force of the law.

Quaking as she listened to this thunderous diatribe, Lissa wondered if she would hear Cosmo admitting that he couldn't sketch a right ear, much less render a human being recognizable. The thought that she might be exposed and have to suffer the wrath of her darling Ralph's employer was too terrifying.

The arrival in the passage of Mrs. Lamont saw Lissa scurrying back to the schoolroom before she could hear the end of the diatribe, but shortly after Lord Debenham stormed out of the house, Cosmo's boots sounded upon the stairs.

"What have you told others about our secret arrangement?" he demanded, throwing open the nursery door. As Clara had just led his sisters downstairs, Lissa was alone. "Were the terms not crystal clear?" In a rage, he paced back and forth, nearly tripping over a small chair and kicking a rag doll into the corner. "We agreed I would get the commissions and, in return, you would deport yourself in society like the lady you've always wanted to be. How much simpler could it be? Clearly, you have gone above and beyond yourself!"

Lissa bridled at the way he sneered this. With an effort to control her anger, she reminded him, "And I would get a third, which, I might add, has not been forthcoming to date, Master Cosmo. Not all of it, by a long stretch. And no, I've said nothing to anyone."

Perhaps it wasn't wise to challenge him so directly. The room was gloomy and isolated and Cosmo could be unpredictable.

He took a menacing step forward, his brow rumpled like an angry bulldog. Lissa glanced nervously at the way he flexed his fingers, as if he really did wish to place them on her person and do her harm.

"So you have taken your revenge, is that it, Miss Hazlett? You think I am not a man of my word?" His nostrils twitched and the whites of his teeth were revealed by the curl of his lip. "You were so impatient for your money that you told lies so that Lord Debenham would threaten me, and you assumed I'd be so terrified I'd hand over the money you believe you're owed."

"I've told Lord Debenham *nothing*, nor have I told anyone else about our arrangement," Lissa reassured him, assessing her escape route. Cosmo was right when he accused her of not trusting him. "I do not know why he thinks he's been drawn without his knowledge. No one has commissioned a picture of him."

She clapped her hand to her mouth to stop mentioning the sketch in which he'd appeared with Lord Smythe and Buzby for this was clearly what had angered him. No, whatever happened, she could tell neither Lord Debenham nor Cosmo that this sketch had earned her five pounds after it had attracted such interest from Sir Archie Ledger.

Lissa angled herself toward the doorway but Master Cosmo pinched her shoulder and drew her roughly toward him.

"You are a liar, Miss Hazlett, but if you don't want to find yourself walking the pavements without a character, you are going to do something for me."

***

Araminta's nausea was as regular as clockwork. She'd feel ill mid-afternoon but as soon as she'd thrown up the contents of her stomach half an hour later, she'd be absolutely fine. Her breasts felt tender and she was more tired than usual, but neither had too much of an effect on her general mood which, right now, was ebullient.

She was going to be Lady Ludbridge, mistress of three estates and the cosseted wife of a sweet, handsome, very manageable viscount. She hoped the child she bore would be a girl. It would be only fair to Teddy, to present her new husband with a daughter rather than the desired heir, but regardless, her future was assured.

She had never been so happy.

Jane was busy brushing the hem of her walking dress, which she'd just taken off, in preparation for the gown she'd wear tonight.

Ah yes, the gown that had to be just perfect for her assignation with Teddy. Her grand seduction. The bodice could not be too tight, so that he might be enticed to slip his hand inside. She was glad skirts were fuller this year. That would aid the plans she had made.

"Stop doing that, Jane, and help me with my dress," she said once she'd dabbed at her face with a cold flannel. "And don't look at me like that."

"Like what?"

Increasingly, Araminta found Jane's feigned innocence and her tight-lipped attitude beyond irritating. Much as she would love to get rid of the girl, she needed her. In fact, she'd need her until her wedding, when Araminta would find some means of passing her on. It was never wise to have a person who knew too much cluttering up the place.

"Like you disapprove of me. Yes, I know what you're thinking but you'd not do anything differently if you were in my position."

Araminta thought she heard the girl mutter something along the lines that she wouldn't have got herself in Araminta's position, but she pretended she didn't hear. She was in too good a mood to let Jane spoil her wonderful contemplations about the future. Jane was just jealous.

"What do you think about these earrings?" Araminta sat down at her dressing table and tried on a pair of tiny pearl drop earrings.

"Very nice, miss."

"They don't bring out the emerald light in my eyes as well as these others but they are more demure. I think that is the look I should strive for."

"Yes, miss."

"For goodness' sake, will you stop being so wretchedly censorious, Jane!"

Araminta swung round on her seat and glared at her maid, who had just dropped the hairbrush and was rising.

"Sorry, Miss." Jane blanched visibly at her mistress's fury, which made Araminta feel far more charitable toward her. "I bin meaning to ask. Did the young lady like Miss Hetty's green dress?"

Araminta frowned, irritated at the memory of that night, which hadn't at all gone to plan. Teddy should have witnessed Lissa secretly closeted in the library with the dangerous Lord Debenham, but her stupid half-sister had for some unknown reason lent the gown to her employer's social-climbing daughter.

"She didn't wear it, after all. Now will you stop asking how other people enjoyed things and start worrying about whether I'm likely to enjoy tonight with a maid as inept as you dropping everything and being impertinent. Time is galloping and you haven't started on my hair!"

Excitement at her tryst was gaining hold. In truth, it was difficult to imagine anything else but the magical feeling of being in the arms of a man who truly adored her, a man who would lavish upon her beautiful clothes, her own carriage, three houses full of servants.

What's more, a man whose naked body she'd thoroughly enjoy curling against as wicked, wanton happenings took place beneath fine linen sheets—though tonight the only thing missing would be the linen sheets.

For some reason she was suddenly visited by an image of Sir Aubrey's enormous pulsing member, but she quickly banished it. That had not been an encounter she should dwell on for her own peace of mind, though it had provided some useful information on what men's bodies did when they were in the throes of desire. She'd not known about that before.

Well, she'd had sensations when pressed against eager young men, including Jem, but had never seen anything quite so blatant as Sir Aubrey's impressive erection. She hoped Lord Ludbridge were similarly well-endowed.

Jane hadn't responded to her setdown but now she finished doing up the last pearl button at the back of Araminta's gown and stood back to assess her handiwork.

"You look lovely, miss. And I can hear the carriage coming round the front for you. What time will you be back this evening, Miss?"

"Good heavens, how do I know what time I'll be?" Araminta flew to the window, her heart beating wildly as she saw the carriage that had just collected Mrs. Monks, her chaperone for the night.

What a pity Papa wasn't in residence otherwise Teddy could have asked him for Araminta's hand directly, this evening. Instead, he'd be asking Araminta in the summer house at Lord Billingsly's estate, where they were going to be watching fireworks being set off from a barge moored in the middle of the river. There would also be an outdoor buffet and other refreshments laid out in festooned tents, and entertainments and champagne. Lots of it.

Shivers of excitement ran through her as she thought of what would happen next. Earlier, Araminta had sent Jane off on the pretext of selling a basket of fish to Lord Billingsly's cook. Afterwards, Jane had navigated His Lordship's estate, so Araminta knew the exact locations of the most suitable trysting spots. She now knew where she had to lead Teddy, and at what time.

"Mrs. Monks is waiting for you in the vestibule," Cousin Stephen told her. "Enjoy the fireworks. And Araminta...?"

She stopped her preening in front of the mirror above the fireplace in the drawing room to glance at him. "What?"

"Do behave yourself."

"Good heavens, Cousin Stephen, I think it would have been more charitable of you to have suggested I enjoy myself." She took his arm as he led her outside to the carriage and breathed in the balmy evening air with rapture. "And I *am* going to enjoy myself. You may depend upon it."

***

It was a perfect evening for such an entertainment. An evening full of promise.

Araminta wrapped her embroidered mantle about her. The tiny beads sparkled, reflecting the stars twinkling in the sky and the hope in Araminta's heart.

She smiled and, turning, caught Teddy's lovelorn look. Oh, but tonight was the beginning of a lifetime of fulfilled hopes and dreams. She had the perfect man by her side: besotted and rich.

Mrs. Monks was ever the millstone, but she knew that this was the night Araminta would get her proposal. Mrs. Monks would allow more than the usual latitude and it was useful that she knew enough of the other gossipy old matrons to be entertained.

"Shall we walk a little?" Teddy enquired. They were now on the banks of the river, surrounded by milling guests, festooned tents offering all manner of refreshments, jugglers, dancing bears and musicians. When he saw her glance about her, he added quickly, "I certainly don't wish to be accused of taking liberties. Perhaps you would rather remain with the crowd."

She could tell how impatient he was to whisk her away, alone, but perhaps a little mingling might be in order. It was always a good idea to whip up a gentleman's desire to the maximum.

"A glass of champagne would be lovely," she suggested.

A table near the water's edge was tended by several bewigged footmen. They were filling champagne coupes borne by a dozen or more of their kind, scurrying along the path that skirted the river. Knots of revelers were laughing or gazing at the sky, watching the preparations that were taking place on the barge a hundred yards away.

Araminta graciously accepted the champagne Teddy offered her and, together with Mrs. Monks, they entered a tent festooned with multicolored chiffon scarves and lanterns hung about on poles. A pair of acrobats was performing in the center of the area. One leapt from the shoulders of his partner, somersaulting in the air before landing in a well-choreographed tumble before swapping positions.

Araminta stared, entranced by their gleaming, muscled torsos. She liked what a real man looked like beneath his linen. She overheard Mrs. Monks mutter something about the unseemliness of such a spectacle and Teddy tugged her arm, as if he felt that she should not be exposed to such rampant masculinity. With a backward look, she reluctantly followed.

"Oh dear! Why...Miss Partington!"

Appearing out of the darkness, a gentleman had inadvertently knocked her arm, causing her to spill her champagne over the front of her pelisse. When she saw it was Mr. Woking, she had to try hard to keep the acid out of her tone, if only for Lord Ludbridge's sake.

But when she saw that her beloved's attention had been caught by their hostess, Araminta sent Mr. Woking a narrow look as she pointedly dabbed at the moisture.

His dark eyes were nervous in his pallid face. "How will you forgive me?" Nervously he ran his hand over his weak, receding chin. "My deepest apologies, Miss Partingon!"

"Oh, do stop it, Mr. Woking. You were very clumsy but there's an end to it and now I must move on. Why don't you go and talk to Miss Harcourt over there? I cannot but notice the interested looks she is sending you."

She quickly got rid of him as she cleaved to Lord Ludbridge's side, encouraging him to take another coupe of champagne, which, she noted, he drank rather quickly.

"The fireworks begin in an hour," he murmured, putting his head close, his breath tickling her hair. "I'm told the best view will be from the top of that rise over there." He pointed in a direction quite distant from the spot at which Araminta intended to enjoy the fireworks.

"How lovely," she replied. "Shall we walk now? I'd like to see the lights on the bridge. I've never done that before."

"Certainly. Where is Mrs. Monks?"

"Perhaps we needn't take Mrs. Monks."

He looked a little scandalized at this, hesitating as he said, "Our departure will be observed, and I would hate to cause whispers, Miss Partington."

"I...I thought you had something important to say to me, Lord Ludbridge," she said a little breathlessly. "Should Mrs. Monks hear it too?"

"Indeed not, but I had in retrospect wondered if tonight was quite the right time."

No! He could not bow out now. Taking a measured breath, Araminta smiled tentatively. "Of course you're right, my lord. We can't have tongues wagging. I'll go and ask Mrs. Monks, who is talking to the dowager Duchess Dalrymple."

She hurried over to the elderly women, and soon had Mrs. Monks alone. "Lord Ludbridge wishes to take a walk. Please will you accompany us?" She paused, weighing up how to couch her request. "He wishes to ask me something...important, but I doubt he will do so with you in attendance. I will therefore give you a sign. When I remark that the sky is full of stars tonight, I would have you say you are not feeling at all the thing and that you wish to leave; that you are confident in leaving me safely in His Lordship's company for just a short time."

With this agreed to, Araminta bore her reliable chaperone back to the cluster of guests of which Lord Ludbridge was a part. He greeted Araminta with a smile, a flourishing bow and his arm, which she took with shaking fingers.

Soon. Soon she would be the happiest girl in the world.

Lord Ludbridge took up a lantern and leisurely they strolled along the path that rose gently above the river toward a high vantage point, Araminta chatting as if she had no idea of the momentous question she intended he would ask. When they reached a fork in the path, one option rising to a distant spot just out of sight, the other in full view of all the revelers by the river's edge, Araminta stopped and gazed upward. "Oh my, but the sky is full of stars tonight," she murmured.

Like a well-trained pug, Mrs. Monks quickly fulfilled her part in the arrangement and within a few moments, Araminta was alone with His Lordship. Pretending she did not notice his concerned look, she pointed up the hill, tugging his hand as she said, "Oh, do let's see if we can see the fireworks from there."

In less than a minute they were at the top of the rise, where they discovered, nestled in a dip but with magnificent views of the river, a small rotunda.

"It's like a tiny fairy castle!" Araminta exclaimed. "How utterly darling. Come, Lord Ludbridge! Come and let's see inside!"

He was reluctant to go so far from the crowds but Araminta had already darted ahead.

Thrusting open the door, she gasped. "How beautiful." Reverently she touched the silk cushions arranged on the banquette and around the walls. "What do you suppose this little bower is used for? I can imagine someone coming here to write great compositions. I know Lady Marks is very fond of music. Perhaps she comes here."

Mullioned windows overlooked the river and a large bowl of fruit was set on a table in the center of the room.

Lord Ludbridge hung his lantern on a hook by the doorway as he gazed around. He too seemed equally entranced by Araminta's discovery. When next he looked down, Araminta was standing so close, staring through the windows, that he bumped against her and, startled, she gasped.

"I was lost in another world," she declared. "I feel like I've entered some magical fairy palace. Look, the fireworks have just begun, and we can see them from here."

As she spoke, a cascade of colored embers burst in the sky, sending trails in all directions, which floated like sparling gossamer until they disappeared into the river. Araminta clapped her hands in delight and, seemingly unconsciously, rested against Lord Ludbridge's side.

She felt his hand caress the side of her face, and looked up to see him smiling tentatively.

"My Lord?"

Then his mouth was on hers, drawing her into a kiss of exquisite rapture that threatened to send her into that other world of bliss, while another burst of fireworks dazzled the sky.

The multicolored effect was so spectacular they broke the kiss at the same time. Lord Ludbridge turned and gazed at Araminta as if lost in the wonder of the moment.

"Yes, My Lord?' she murmured, though he'd not spoken.

He seemed mesmerized, cupping her face as he whispered, "Miss Partington, will you do me the great honor of becoming my wife?"

A deep satisfaction reverberated to the depths of her very soul.

At last. Her moment had come.

Lord Ludbridge had gone down on one knee and was now gazing up at her as if hanging on her answer. Tears pricked her eyes and she did not stem their flow when they brimmed over. Reverently she bent to touch her lips to his forehead. Her joy was almost overwhelming. "Darling Teddy, I can think of nothing I want more in this world," she murmured, her heart thundering. She cupped his face and gently drew him to his feet and into another kiss, a prelude to a more passionate coupling.

No, it would not end with a simple proposal. And what joy that she could throw herself with such genuine rapture into what lay ahead. Her desire was gaining hold as he deepened the kiss. She'd never wanted a man like this before and she couldn't wait. To her chagrin, despite his ardor, he was showing magnificent restraint. She shifted a little in his arms, turning slightly and standing on tiptoe, so he would be unable to resist the temptation of her breasts swelling above her bodice when he felt her so exposed.

Lord Ludbridge kissed her like a drowning man but it was beyond irritating that he did not avail himself of the opportunity she was affording him.

"Darling Teddy, I've wanted this from the moment I first met you," she murmured against his lips. With a judicious shifting of her person, she managed to orchestrate his hands coming into contact with her flesh, wriggling then giving a little hop and a jerk so that his fingers were beneath the fabric.

"Oh, Teddy!" she gasped as she put her hand upon his, guiding it over her bare breast, beneath her bodice, while tendrils of want spiraled through her. Her nipples were crying out for attention but he reacted as if in shock as he withdrew his hand. Clearly, he intended going no farther, though he continued to rain kisses upon her face and throat.

At last, Araminta managed to draw him away from the center of the room to the banquette, and to slide down upon it so that he was half on top of her, kissing her all the while.

Her womb was on fire. She wanted him. Needed him. Oh, dear God, she needed him now. Jane had told her that she would have to secure a marriage proposal, followed up with a joyful coupling by the end of this week, if there was any chance that the child she was carrying could be passed off as another's. Even then, there would be questions if the child were large and went full term, Jane had warned her. However, Araminta chose to forget this bit.

"My lovely girl, my sweet Araminta," His Lordship murmured against her mouth, as Araminta now guided his hand to her thigh. She'd rucked her skirt high and wore no impeding pantalettes. No, there was a clear path to where he surely wanted to go, now that the marriage proposal was out of the way. To where she *needed* him to go.

She felt the bulge of his erection against her stomach and the evidence of his arousal only deepened hers. She was conscious of the wetness between the juncture of her legs and she could barely wait for what would come next.

To her dismay, Lord Ludbridge suddenly broke the kiss and sat up, causing her to fall a little clumsily against the wall and seat.

"Miss Partington. Araminta," he said, breathlessly, as he helped her assume a more demure position beside him. "We are not married yet. We cannot do this."

"But we *will* be married. Soon, my lord." She didn't want to sound as desperate as she was. "You…you are not taking liberties. I want this as much as you do. I…I have never been kissed by a man before. It's as if you've set me on fire." She slid onto his lap and twined her arms about his neck once more, murmuring against his cheek, "Please kiss me again, Lord Ludbridge. Teddy." She drew her head back and smiled coyly. "Now that we're about to be married."

Tenderly he looked down into her face. "Yes, but we may not be married for a couple of months."

She thought she'd misheard him but when she studied his face she saw his regret. A deafening roar sounded in her head as she repeated, uncertainly, "A couple of months?"

He nodded. "You see, dear heart, there is something very important I must do first." He took her hands and began to explain, speaking gently, smiling, as if it were only natural she would understand the reason for the delay.

Araminta stared while the silent screams of protest grew more deafening. He seemed not to notice for he went on in the same measured tone, "I had a dear friend once, a long time ago. Five years ago, in fact. Mother mentioned her to you—"

"You are in love with another?" Shocked, she pulled away but he captured her in his arms with a gentle, reassuring laugh, and rested his cheek against hers. "I was, but not anymore, for I love you only, dearest. However, listen to me, and then you'll understand."

Araminta was quite convinced that even if he were about to rescue his baby sister from Bluebeard himself, she'd not understand. She had no choice, however, but to hear him out.

"It's been five years since my old friend, Bella, disappeared, and since then, I've felt I've existed in a desert. I truly believed I would never again experience feeling in this old heart of mine." Lord Ludbridge touched his chest. She could hear the smile in his voice, which did nothing to soften her own heart. "Then you came into my life. With your beauty and spirit and passion, I realized I could love again, at last."

"But you are going away to be…with this old love? Teddy, I don't understand it!" She tried not to cry.

"Not to be with her, but to save her. You see, I made a vow to protect her, and although I no longer love her, I owe her this. Only two nights ago, I received an unexpected message after all these years. Her situation is not at all as I'd come to believe. It is very terrible in fact, but I have the means to extricate her from her dreadful life. And so that is what I must do. Ah, Araminta, please do not cry."

"But you cannot leave me. You cannot ask me to be your wife and then leave me for two months!"

Tenderly he kissed away her tears. "My precious love, I have to live with my conscience, and though my heart is here with you, I am honor-bound to make this journey."

"Journey? Where?"

"Across the Aegean. I know it all sounds unbelievable and wild but the truth is, I've discovered my old friend is being held a prisoner and about to be forced into marriage against her will. Only now has she finally got a message out that reached me. She needs my help."

"But can't someone else help her?"

Lord Ludbridge looked censorious for a split-second, before his expression softened. "I know this is difficult for you to understand, especially in the wake of my marriage offer. But Bella is my childhood friend. I am the one person she is able to trust. Please allow me the time I need to salvage my conscience. After that, you will be my entire focus in life. When I return, we will make arrangements for our wedding to take place in just the three weeks required for calling the banns, though you are at liberty to announce to whomever you choose that I have vowed to wed you on my return. I will write to you every day. I promise."

Araminta couldn't believe it.

He rose, though she'd snaked her hand up his arm to try to elicit another bout of passion. It seemed, though, that he had made up his mind to put aside all possibility of carnal delights.

Her brain was in a desperate whirl. She had to make him change his mind. At least before he left. "When are you going?"

"I leave on the dawn crossing tomorrow."

"So soon!"

"The sooner I leave, the sooner I'll be back." He smiled as if this would please her, drawing her toward the door, toward the destruction of her dreams, her best-laid plans. "Bella is in terrible trouble. I may not in fact be in time to avert the disaster that threatens to destroy her life. I know this sounds very dramatic, but please be assured that all my loyalties lie with you, Araminta…my only true love."

At the door, he drew her up against him, and rested her head against his chest. "I have to behave as honor dictates." Softly, he stroked her hair. "I have found you. It seems incredible to me, but you have saved me. Now we can look forward to a long and wonderful life together. You have made me the happiest man, and I thank you for that." His voice was thick with emotion. "But first I must do what is right. This other long-distant part of my life will not interfere with our happiness but the only way I can live with my conscience is if I set to rights what I have been asked to do. And what it is in my power to do."

"So you leave…in the morning?"

"Yes. But my love, I have sent a letter to your father, requesting that I might visit him upon my return. I've also brought my journey forward by several days in order to reduce the time I will be away. I felt that was preferable."

"Oh no, I'd have rather have had another couple of days together. I…can't bear it, Teddy. I'll die without you!"

He chuckled and hugged her closer against him, shaking his head at her attempts to claw him into another passionate kiss. "Too dangerous, my precious," he whispered. "And we have been away long enough. Come, let us return to the merry throng, where we can announce our news."

"Perhaps my father should give his consent first." She felt dead inside, her words wooden, yet her brain was in a whirl as to how she could manage this death knell to her hopes and dreams. So he would leave in the morning? She couldn't let him just go like this without...

He took her hand and drew her outside. "Of course, you are right. My goodness, look at those fireworks. I shall always remember this as the happiest night of my life. The night you consented to be my wife."

Araminta nodded, tears threatening at the back of her eyes, her throat nearly closed up with the bitter taste of impending doom.

As a shower of sparks lit up the sky, she felt as if she too were about to burst into a million tiny fragments.

Chapter Eighteen

Once again, Lissa rattled the doorknob of her attic bedchamber and called for help. Through the grubby glass, she could see the attic rooms of many of the four-square houses about her but no frightened faces pressed to any of them. No faces at all.

The servants could hear her, she was certain. The attic was only one floor up from the nursery and two floors up from the family's bedchambers. Perhaps the children had been removed so they'd not remark upon her surely audible cries. Perhaps the servants had been cautioned not to make contact.

Perhaps she'd be imprisoned here forever.

She heard the clock chime 9 p.m. Then ten.

Cosmo had left her three hours since, triumphantly bearing the sketch she'd tried to hide from him. A lie. An evil lie and if only she could get a message to Ralph, those in high places would know it too. Cosmo had laughed when he'd come upon her portfolio of work, a sketchbook filled with likenesses of various personages.

"Oh my, just look at those feathers drooping down to tickle that turkey neck. It's Lady Smythe to a tee," he'd remarked, becoming conversational when he'd discovered this resource that gave him such an edge. "You never told me about these."

Lissa just sat hunched on a chair by the window. "They were for practice only," she muttered. "I never intended that anyone should see them."

"Indeed, you could hardly have induced Her Ladyship to pay for something that so cruelly exposed her dubious claims to beauty. Such clever caricatures, I will give you that." He'd continued to turn the pages, shaking his head and frowning as he'd assessed each sketch. It was only when he turned to the final page and beheld the sketch she'd done of Sir Aubrey in company with Lord Smythe that he nodded approvingly.

"You appear to have caught them in earnest conversation. Or perhaps in the midst of plotting the government's downfall, they look so serious." Without asking, he neatly tore the page from the sketchbook. "Thank you, Miss Hazlett. I think this will please Lord Debenham. At least it'll get me off the hook."

"And what about me?"

He looked pained at this. "I really don't know what to do about you, Miss Hazlett. Wicked governesses are not within my realms of experience or expertise. I think I shall have to ask Lord Debenham when I hand him this."

So here she was, alone and vulnerable. Seemingly friendless. Cosmo was taking the sketch of Sir Aubrey to Lord Debenham himself, and then what would happen? If Lord Smythe were indeed a traitor, perhaps his close ties to Sir Aubrey, as evidenced by her drawing, would be enough to convict them both in the court of public opinion, failing more substantive evidence. If only Araminta had not burned the letter that revealed the truth.

It was long since the dinner hour but no one had brought her refreshment, other than a jug of water, which had been left on a chest of drawers at the time of her incarceration.

She was desperately hungry, yet terrified when several taps sounded at the door.

"Miss Hazlett, I have a message for you." Without waiting for a response before she left, the maid passed her a plate with a single slice of pie, beside which was a folded note. Lissa recognized Cosmo's hand-writing. Her legs were shaking so much she had to sit down to read it.

"Change into travelling clothes. Lord Debenham will fetch you."

She swallowed but it did not help the dryness at the back of her throat. At the same time her palms felt clammy and the back of her neck prickled with fear.

So she was to be kidnapped and discredited. Or would she be disposed of in some more permanent manner? After all, if Lord Debenham thought she'd seen what was in the letter, who knew what he might do?

In an attempt to keep her terror at bay, she began to pace until finally she collapsed upon her bed, pulling the thin gray coverlet up around her shoulders. Travelling clothes? As if she had a wardrobe that encompassed a variety of changes. The drab cotton gown she wore would have to do service for whatever was in store.

Lissa had known deprivation. The small home in the village by the bridge, which she'd shared with her mother and sister and brother before she'd been sent away to become a governess, had not been commodious or luxurious. Yet it was where her father chose to spend most of his time, cocooned with her mother, the two of them living in a world of their own, which took little account of their growing brood of illegitimate children.

She'd never been close to her mother, or her father; home had not been a place of warmth, but, oh, how she longed to feel the warmth that only Ralph had ever made her feel.

She exhaled on a sob, then straightened at the sound of raindrops.

She hoped it poured, and that Master Cosmo and his sketch were drenched. He was a cruel, spoilt boy, and his sister was no better. Miss Maria had marched up the stairs, shrieking at her through the door that Lissa obviously planned to ruin Maria's chances of a good match. Of course, the girl's encounter with Lord Debenham had terrified her but if she hadn't purloined the green dress that was meant for Lissa she wouldn't have found herself in such a frightening situation. It was a sad reflection on Miss Maria's character that she insisted that evil machinations on Lissa's part were behind the unfortunate encounters both she and her brother had had with His Lordship.

The rain appeared to have subsided, though another smattering of raindrops sounded an odd note. Lissa stood up and peered through the window, but her view was limited to mostly rooftops. By standing on the bed, however, and looking down she could just manage to see onto the street.

After a minute or so she heard a single "ping" against the window. Picking up the candlestick that flickered on the chest of drawers, she held it to her face. Somebody, she suspected, was down in the street.

Her body quivered with hope and excitement.

That somebody might just be Ralph.

In a growing fever of hopeful anticipation, she waited.

She was expecting the sound of footsteps in the passage. After all, the only way to gain entry to her room was via an internal staircase. So it was to her horror, after a noisy flutter of wings and squawking drew her to the window, that she saw illuminated in the faint gaslight cast from a nearby attic window her ever-faithful and trusty Ralph Tunley climbing the drainpipe two stories down.

With a cry of fear, she banged on the window, shaking her head furiously as if that might do any good when he was already more up than down.

He raised his head and grinned at her horrified fury, kissing his fingertips and blowing his appreciation toward her. He was probably too far away for her to hear him but he clearly did not wish to make any noise, for he indicated his intended movements by pointing toward what she could only assume was a window he could enter. Her window was too tiny and besides, her room was locked.

But there were people in the house. Servants and the Lamont family themselves. Lissa quaked at the potential for discovery. The Lamonts had no mercy. They'd claim he was a burglar and throw him down the stairs. He might break his neck or end up in Newgate Prison. Lord Debenham was not likely to vouch for him.

No, Ralph had gone out on a limb in all senses of the word, and he'd done it for her. Lissa. No one had ever striven to such an extent on her behalf. No one had ever really taken much notice of her, ever, but it was not the fact Ralph was the only man who could melt her heart that made him so special. No, Ralph was truly a remarkable young man in his own right.

Her thoughts were still travelling along these lines when she heard the key turn slowly in the lock. Suddenly the door was thrust open and there stood Ralph, grinning as if he was presenting her with a box of chocolates and a bouquet of flowers, rather than offering her freedom.

She flew into his arms and kissed him roundly on the lips, drew back to grin right at him, then kissed him again. All without a sound.

He looked remarkably pleased by the attention and then, without a word, he took her hand, put his finger to his lips, and quietly led her down the stairs.

Her hopes were confirmed that there was no one about on the nursery floor.

The next floor down, where the bedrooms were, ought to be empty too. It was this floor where Ralph had made his entry, for Lissa could feel the breeze from an open window. Now she realized that it was toward this very window Ralph was drawing her, and she froze with horror.

There was a tremendous drop to the pavement. How would she navigate the descent in her skirts? She tried to resist but he was insistent, albeit without making a sound.

"Trust me," he whispered in her ear when they drew closer.

"I have secured a rope. Just hold on to me and let me do the work. We can't go down the stairs. There is no way we'll not be seen."

As the window was already half open, there wasn't the fear of it making a sound. The rope was securely tied from the bannister a few feet into the room, and further secured to the window handles themselves, but the drop looked outrageously high. Her breath started to come in rasping gasps until Ralph turned and, in the dark, held her close against him. For several seconds they simply stood, taking in the warmth and comfort of each other, holding hands, eyes closed.

"Trust me, Lissa. If one of us falls, we both fall. But it is the only way out of a perilous situation. You must believe me."

She nodded, sick with fear. "Before I go out of the window, will you kiss me properly, Ralph? Just in case I break my head on the cobblestones and never get another chance again."

He didn't answer, just tipped her face upward and brought his mouth gently down upon hers, kissing her sweetly at first, and then thoroughly, and, finally, with resounding passion.

They were both trembling when they drew apart and Ralph whispered, almost matter-of-factly, "Take your skirts in one hand as I help you onto the window ledge and keep steady until I join you there. Then put your arms around my waist, hold as tightly as you can…and just trust me."

**

"Is everything all right, Miss? Were the fireworks grand? You're back earlier than I'd 'spected." Jane, who was polishing the silver bottles on her mistress's dressing table, looked up nervously as Araminta entered the room.

Without a word, Araminta brought one arm across the entire surface and sent powder bottles, perfume vials, hairbrushes and jewelry boxes crashing to the floor.

Then she threw herself onto her bed and burst into noisy tears.

"Oh, Miss, I take it things didn't go to plan," said Jane, going down on her knees to start to clean up the mess before changing her mind and putting a tentatively soothing hand upon Araminta's back.

"No, they did not!" Araminta shrieked, beating her fists upon the counterpane.

"So, His Lordship didn't ask you to marry him, then?"

"Yes he did!" Araminta rolled onto her back and glared at Jane. "He asked me to marry him and then said he had to go away on important business for two months! Two *months*! Where does that leave me? In an impossible situation, I don't need to tell you. I might as well throw myself in the river, except the water's far too cold and I'm hardly about to copy bacon-brained Edgar. There must be another way."

"Poison?"

"I mean to get *out of this mess*, you stupid girl!" Araminta screamed. Feverishly, she began to bite her fingernails before realizing the damage she was doing to an important asset. "Oh, Jane, don't look like you're related to a mule. Come up with a plan, for dear Lord's sake!"

Jane took a seat by the bed. "Well, Miss, you could always go and see him and suggest you marry earlier or that you elope. I know it's not respectable—"

Aramaminta was ready to clutch at anything right now. "Well, Hetty eloped it, didn't she? And no one seems to be condemning her for her deplorable behavior." She sat up, thinking. "So you think I should go now, do you?"

"Now?" Jane frowned. "No, of course not now. It's the middle of the night. But...later on."

"What do you mean, later on? He's leaving in a ship for some distant land at dawn. So, of course I must go and talk sense into him tonight. Excellent plan. Quick, Jane, we must waste no time! I don't know why I didn't entreat him more artfully than I did. I was simply too shocked and horrified by what he was telling me."

"But, Miss, how can we simply go out on the streets in the middle of the night?"

"We put on long dark cloaks and cover our hair and faces and we slip out of the door. Have you no imagination, Jane? No common sense? Now, where's that lovely crimson-lined black cloak of mine? Or should I wear the ermine-edged? Yes, that will do, in case he suggests we elope this very minute."

"And what would I do then, Miss?"

"Go with me, of course. I can't possibly elope without a maid."

"But I can't leave Jem without telling 'im."

"You'd have to, because I'd need you. Now stop this nonsense, Jane, and do as I say. Yes, that's the one. And I'll take some of my jewelry. One never knows when one might need pin money, but oh, Jane, he's even richer than I'd thought. Why, that down-at-heel baby brother of his, the secretary to dreadful, awful Lord Debenham, made me think Lord Ludbridge was one of these titled chaps with not a feather to fly with. But you know, his mother was dressed in the first stare, not last season at all. And I'd do anything to have a ruby necklace like the one she was wearing."

"You certainly would, Miss."

"Now, stop dithering, Jane. Are you ready?"

***

Ensconced in a hackney cab outside Lord Ludbridge's townhouse, Araminta was feeling immeasurably reassured by the success of her new plan as Jane made her way down the stairs to the servants' entrance to knock upon the kitchen door. Jane would glean the necessary information, Araminta's desperate note to Lord Ludbridge would be passed on and all would be well.

The moon was high in the sky and Araminta thought again of the burst of fireworks that had first thrilled her, just hours ago, before her world had come crashing down. Soon she'd be experiencing fireworks again, but of a different kind. Fireworks that would culminate in success, not disappointment.

She shifted impatiently on the uncomfortable leather seat.

Araminta's last clandestine encounter in a hired hackney cab with Lord Debenham had had her weighing up her options between him and Sir Aubrey as she'd suggested His Lordship might like to make it worth her while to give him the letter. But now, only Lord Ludbridge would do.

Lord Ludbridge was wonderful and kind…and he was manageable and rich enough. Araminta thought she'd acquired a great deal of wisdom in just a few short months to be happy making such compromises. Her mother would have been proud of her.

She put her face to the window. Where was Jane? Probably gossiping with the scullery maid, and completely forgetting that her mistress's life and happiness were hanging by a veritable thread.

A few minutes later, she heard the quick tapping of Jane's shoes upon the cobbles and then Jane hauled herself into the dark space opposite her.

"Well?" Araminta demanded. "Shall I go to him now? Or in the morning? You took so long, I can only imagine you were waiting for an answer to my letter."

"Oh miss, your letter ain't going to get to His Lordship in time."

"What do you mean, in time?"

"I mean His Lordship left more 'n an hour ago on horseback. He took his valet with him and together they rode through the moonlight to catch the boat to Dover.

"Then we must follow them!"

"It's impossible, miss. They're on horseback. They'll cover three times as much ground as we would in the same time. Besides, we'd need to hire a chaise and I don't know how we'd do that. No, it simply can't be done." Jane's voice trembled. "I'm afraid, miss, there's nothing for it. You'll have to make another plan."

She rapped on the roof for the jarvey to pick up his reins and get moving, partly so the occupants of Lord Ludbridge's London townhouse would not hear her mistress's hearty wails, which did not subside for a full five minutes.

They were three blocks from home when Araminta finally raised her head, wiped her cheeks and, with a gasp, pressed her nose once more to the window.

"I say, Jane, stop the carriage this instant! Is that Mr. Woking I see walking along the pavement?"

Chapter Nineteen

Jane had been highly reluctant to let Araminta step out of the carriage and into the street, alone, in the middle of the night while she continued around the corner.

Indeed, for Araminta, the idea of stepping out onto a deserted street without company would have been unthinkable a few hours ago. No, a few moments ago, even. Jane had wailed that Araminta was grasping at straws. Right now, Araminta was grasping for anything or anyone, and Mr. Woking might just answer.

"Please, sir! A terrible accident has happened!" she cried, appearing in front of him with her face lowered, her hood covering her head. "The carriage conveying me and my chaperone has bolted. Please help me!"

"Good god, madam! And you are alone?"

Araminta huddled into herself and gave a little sob. "Entirely sir! I don't know what to do." She paused, raised her face as she let her hood fall from her head, and uttered in shocked tones, "Mr. Woking!"

"Miss Partington!" he cried at the same time, before looking desperately around. "You really have no chaperone?" he asked, sounding even more aghast.

"Yes, and I've hurt my foot. Please help me." She put out both her hands in a gesture of the utmost entreaty and limped several steps, before losing her balance and falling into his arms.

He held her while he looked around again, wildly. There was no carriage in sight, no sign of anyone. "I...I don't know what to do," he said lamely. "My residence is right here but I can hardly take you there, Miss Partington."

"Yes, you can. It is this one? I need to sit down and see if my ankle is injured. Just for a moment. Can you not do this one thing for me?" She tried to keep the acid from her tone as she gazed soulfully into his face while maintaining her firm grip on his wrist.

Yet still he glanced about him, furtively, as if he were terrified and about to refuse. Araminta began walking him toward the portico steps. If he needed her to lead him on to do anything that required some backbone, she'd have an easy time with him in the future, she thought, grasping for consolation at what she being forced to do.

When the butler opened the door with a mild grunt of surprise, Araminta kept her head well down and covered by her cloak while Mr. Woking nervously explained that he was rendering a friend assistance; that medicinal brandy was required, and perhaps a doctor, but that Doderidge could retire for the night.

A couple of lamps burned low in the drawing room where he led her, easing Araminta onto a sofa before fetching them both a glass of brandy. The room was furnished in sparse, masculine style, not to Araminta's taste, but the brandy was another matter, and after two in quick succession she felt much more up to the task ahead of her.

"Is there bruising or swelling around my ankle, Mr. Woking?" she asked in a small, timid voice, extending her leg. "It is painful but not so very that I think it necessary to call a doctor." She took a shuddering breath. "I don't know what has become of my chaperone but I thank the good Lord I was lucky enough to be rescued by you."

He hovered uncertainly in the center of the room, his wits clearly addled, for he did not blush at her praise as he might have done otherwise. Indeed, he seemed positively doltish as he continued to shy away from the tremendous opportunities she was clearly offering him. "You want me to look at your ankle?"

"That's right." She smiled her most disingenuous smile as she raised her skirt to just above her slipper. "I don't know why, but there was something comforting about seeing it was you, Mr. Woking. I mean, because we know one another so well. It made me feel…safe. Yes, put your hand around it and see if you feel any bones sticking out. I'd hate anything to snap if I put pressure on it when I try to stand."

Obediently Mr. Woking went onto his haunches and gently grasped Araminta's ankle. He began to run his hands over the contours, almost reverently, and Araminta reached forward and put her hand gently on the top of his head. He looked up in surprise.

"I have never given you credit for being such a fine gentleman," she murmured.

His eyes widened and his stupid mouth dropped open. Gritting her teeth, Araminta forced a tender smile. "You were always so kind to Hetty, who then repaid us with such unexpected, scandalous behavior. She didn't deserve you but you are so worthy, Mr. Woking."

"Worthy? Of what, Miss Partington?" His eyes were even wider now as Araminta leaned closer. It seemed that unconsciously his hands had strayed a little higher toward her knee. Araminta tried to keep from shuddering; tried to keep from her mind the rapture of just hours before, which she could never relive. Her life was in ruins, or it would be unless she could find a father for her child.

"Of love, Mr. Woking," she murmured, closing the gap between their faces and touching her lips to his wet, flaccid mouth.

He might be a ninny but it seemed he came alive to all possibilities at such a touch. With a low groan, Mr. Woking's arms wrapped around Araminta's shoulders and before she knew it, he'd joined her on the sofa.

Dear God, it was a nightmare, the feel of his slimy tongue plunging into her mouth, but she had to keep up the charade. Somehow it felt less personal if she could get him to concentrate on doing what she needed him to do, away from her face.

He was still slightly in his cups, she realized. He'd been stumbling along the pavement though apparently very much aware of the dangers to her reputation during their initial encounter, but now it seemed such reservations were put to rest by her encouragement. The bodice whose cut she was so keen to ensure could comfortably fit Lord Ludbridge's hand was now tugged and mauled to accommodate Mr. Woking's eager, seeking, hairy hand, and her fuller skirts, smoothed and pressed with such care with thoughts of Lord Ludbridge's advances proving the prelude to a glorious marriage proposal, were now nearly ripped from the high bodice by Mr. Woking in his haste to do what Araminta needed but despised him for.

Still, with time running out for Araminta, the dreadful, unwelcome but necessary deed had to be done. So she suffered his mouth on hers, his seeking clammy hands mauling her breasts, her thighs.

Wordlessly, she helped him with the buttons that secured the front fall of his breeches so that his member sprang forth, joyfully. Araminta closed her eyes. What choice did she have when ruin was her only alternative?

With a little judicious help, she angled herself so that he had access to her cavern of delight with as few preliminaries as possible, gritting her teeth once again as he entered her. He grunted, and after a few quick thrusts, finished the act, rolling onto his back with a groan of pure pleasure.

Araminta tried not to cry as she lay beside him, staring at the ceiling. This was not how tonight was supposed to end. She swiveled her eyes to the right, expecting to be faced with Mr. Woking's limpid gaze, but his lids were closed and he was snoring softly.

She jabbed him sharply in the ribs and he opened his eyes, giving her a shocked look as if he'd not truly expected to see her beside him. Well, she wished it was all just a bad dream, too.

When his gaze travelled down the length of her dress, which was rucked up to her thighs, he appeared to gather his wits. Leaping up, he grasped Araminta's wrists and helped her to her feet.

"Miss Partinton, what have I done? Dear Lord, what has just happened?" he cried in horrified tones, as if he'd not known what he was about before.

Araminta stepped into his embrace and rested her head against his chest as she looked up at him with an adoring smile.

"I've just agreed to be your wife, Mr. Woking. That's what just happened."

***

Snuggled together in the carriage, Ralph held Lissa's hand and, between kisses, explained that he was taking her to someone who "mattered" in government, someone he believed could help them.

"He was formerly attaché to Rear Admiral Lord Worthington, an MP who was involved in the initial case that never really got up against Sir Aubrey in which he was accused of Spencean sympathies," Ralph told her. "I've made extensive, *discreet* enquiries regarding the best person to deal with in this matter and was referred to Sir William Keane. He wants to learn everything he can about Lord Debenham, whom he suspects of being the real villain—not Sir Aubrey, as I think we both know—in the plot to assassinate Lord Castlereagh and bring down the government. So my dear, are you up to this?"

Lissa felt dazed, both with love for the darling, enterprising man beside her, and at the sudden turn of events. "I think that after climbing two stories down a rope in the middle of the night, I'm up for anything," she said, pretending mild indignation.

"That's my girl. Don't mind my question. Lip service, that's all it was." He grinned and gave her a playful dig in the ribs. "Of course I knew you were up to it. Now, aren't you going to tell me how clever I was to rescue you and to source someone who could help us?"

"Are you in danger, too, Ralph?" Lissa was suddenly worried. "Have *I* put you in danger?"

"I'm in danger every moment I work for that blackguard," Ralph responded pleasantly. He patted her hand and Lissa rested her head upon his shoulder and felt as if her heart really would burst for joy.

"If Debenham were committed for at least one of his misdemeanors—one that is technically against the law—I could seek another position without fearing retribution. But beggars can't be choosers, and I felt it safer to remain within the viper's nest rather than risk the viper's bite by going elsewhere."

"Yes, I do see that. And to answer your other question, yes, I do think you were astonishingly clever in rescuing me, and, yes, I *am* dying to know how you knew I was in danger."

His expression grew serious. "I knew you could be in danger after Debenham stormed in, furious that a sketch had been done without his knowledge. I fobbed him off with a false name but I knew it wouldn't be long before he tracked down Master Cosmo." He squeezed Lissa's hand. "The problem was, I was in Little Nipping, and unable to get home for a full day. Debenham had come on horseback. In fact, he'd only just arrived at his estate before he thundered back to London."

"Oh, Ralph, how awful! And you really were worried for me?" Now that she was safe, she couldn't help but want him to enlarge upon what he'd put himself through on her account.

"With Debenham on the warpath and Cosmo acting proxy as your...*protector*?" He shook his head, not smiling. "Lud, but I had the devil of a time getting back to London, myself. Little Nipping is not exactly on the beaten track. First it took me hours to arrange transport. And then all that was available was an ancient chaise which only got half way before an axle broke. It was dark when I arrived."

"And you came straight to the Lamonts'?"

"I did. That is, after having dispatched a missive to the gentleman we are about to see and with whom I'd already made brief contact." He tapped her nose, gently, with a smile. "Now, to save repetition, my love, no more questions, for all is about to be revealed."

Lissa lifted her hand to stroke Ralph's cheek. "You know, I've never met such a brave and clever man. And Ralph, you know I would believe anything you said. I don't think you could tell me a lie, even to spare me."

"Certainly not! He put his arms about her and hugged her close. "I think too highly of your intelligence to try and fob you off with sweeteners." He sighed, capturing her hand and gazing with intense earnestness into her eyes. "One day I will be in a position to support a wife, my darling girl. You really are quite astonishing, and despite all the honorable things I said about leaving you free to accept a well-appointed suitor, I do hope you'll be patient because I believe I shall be rising in the world soon. I have a feeling here." He tapped his breast. "That's another reason I had to kidnap you. Over my turtle soup the other night, I realized that I can be rather persuasive, despite my modest nature, and that you really might take me at my word and cast your net elsewhere."

Lissa twined her arms about his neck and kissed his cheek, her heart overflowing with affection. "After I met you, Ralph, I never for a moment entertained any ideas of finding anyone else."

With a heartrendingly grateful smile, Ralph kissed her back, and then the carriage jolted to a halt and Ralph jumped out first before helping her to the pavement. "We're here, dearest. Nothing to worry about, and yes, I'm sorry for the state of your dress, which I shall explain to Sir William, but as soon as I'm able I'll buy you a new one, and Mrs. Nipkins can fashion you up something in the meantime. Now, prepare to meet His Excellency Sir William Keane, British envoy to Constantinople, now briefly back on English soil. I believe he could just be the answer to everything."

Lissa wanted to ask how a diplomatist to a foreign court could be their answer to *anything* but then her thoughts became occupied by the damage to her gown as they mounted the stairs. When she caught sight of her face in the reflection of a large silver epergne on a low table by the entrance to the withdrawing room in which they were told to wait, she turned to Ralph in panic.

"I look like a costermonger," she whispered. "My hair is all over the place. What can I say that will be of any interest to a man like Sir William?"

It soon transpired that Sir William was indeed very keen to engage Lissa in what she knew of certain matters, but for a moment, all Lissa could do was stare and veritably tremble with shock at her meeting with this tall, handsome, broad-shouldered gentleman with the firm jaw and piercing blue eyes.

She had to blink three times in order to dispel the image of him sporting very few clothes and a pair of very well-formed thighs, writhing on a red-upholstered banquette in the supper house at Vauxhall Gardens with Mrs. Crossing.

She was aware of Ralph gently squeezing her arm while he repeated what had obviously been Sir William's question to her.

Lissa jerked into awareness to hear her beloved add, "Poor Miss Hazlett is still dazed. Until a short while ago, she was being held against her will by the man who claims to be the sketcher of the remarkable likenesses that have so interested the ton. The sad state of her dress is on account of a rather hasty exit from her attic prison. We came straight here, as you requested."

Sir William, who Lissa judged to be in his mid thirties, nodded. Despite his aura of authority there was a kindness about him. A kindness lacking in Mr. Crossing, that was certain. He moved the Argand lamp closer so that the light shone on Lissa's face. "Will you tell me who asked you to render these likenesses?"

Lissa licked dry lips. Would he deal so kindly with her if he knew she had sketched him with Mrs. Crossing? She tried to put out of her mind the image of the pair that kept intruding. She'd never seen anything like it. But now he was smiling kindly at her, soliciting information in the quest for justice. She had to concentrate on the facts that were relevant.

Taking a deep breath, she said, "Some weeks ago my employer's son asked me to sketch a young lady, as his efforts had failed to capture her likeness. I did so, and then gave him the drawing to present to her so he could claim credit and win her regard. After that there were a number of commissions, which I sketched on his behalf, for which he claimed credit."

"A number? Who else commissioned a sketch, Miss Hazlett?"

"Lady Smythe commissioned a sketch of her husband."

He drew a notebook towards him and began to take notes.

"Any other commissions?"

Lissa dropped her eyes then sent a panicked look at Ralph. But then, Ralph had no idea this was the man she'd sketched in company with Mrs. Crossing.

"Please, don't feel overawed by the situation, Miss Hazlett. You are not on trial here but it is my hope that your evidence will help put a dangerous gentleman in the dock. He is guilty of a litany of crimes and I hope that proof of his hitherto denied association with two dangerous radicals will help achieve the government's aim to ultimately keep our country safer than it might otherwise be."

"So you want me to tell you about my sketch of Lord Debenham? Of how it came to pass that I sketched him with Lord Smythe and another man I'd never seen before, though I remember one of them referred to him as Buzby."

"Excellent, excellent, Miss Hazlett. Your recollection is quite on the mark. Buzby is indeed the man you have sketched together with Lords Debenham and Smythe. Can you tell me the date, time and circumstances of this sketch?"

So Lissa told Sir William about the night at Vauxhall, of the conversations she'd overheard and of the accident that led to her sketching the three men, when it was only Lord Smythe whose sketch she'd thought was of any interest.

"And indeed all might have ended there had it not been for a colleague of mine, Sir Archibald Ledger, who knows of our suspicions and who happened upon your sketch when he picked it up after you'd dropped it in a passage. Immediately he was cognizant of the potential value of this sketch. Might I commend you on the astonishing detail and accuracy of your rendition?" Sir William paused to take a pinch of snuff, before asking her a number of other questions regarding the layout of the room and what she might have overheard.

Finally he leaned back in his chair, shaking his head. "My dear Miss Hazlett, you have been of inestimable value and I have kept you long enough. But before I let you leave, I suppose I should ask if there were any other sketches done, either that night, prior or subsequently?"

Lissa nodded earnestly as she leant forward. "Indeed, I *was* going to tell you this. You see, Your Excellency, a few hours ago, Mr. Lamont visited me in the room in which he was keeping me prisoner. He found my sketchbook, containing one of two gentlemen I'd done some weeks ago. I'd never intended that it be made public as I was practicing caricatures. But Mr. Lamont took it, saying it would prove a closer association between two men are under scrutiny for a close relationship they deny."

Sir William raised one eyebrow. "Mr. Lamont is a devious fellow."

"I know it," Lissa remarked as Ralph reached across to put his hand on her shoulder, muttering, "And you'll have to step over my dead body to return to that household, Miss Hazlett. Trust me, I will make arrangements for your safety."

Lissa looked at him gratefully, turning as Sir William asked, "And who were the two men in the sketch taken by Mr. Lamont?"

"Lord Smythe, Your Excellency, and…Sir Aubrey."

"My, my, how fortuitous for Mr. Lamont and the man he is working for to discover such a picture. Would you say it was a good likeness?"

"My future wife's ability to create a likeness with a few rapid strokes of the pencil is remarkable," Ralph interjected proudly.

"Oh Ralph!" Lissa cried, overjoyed at his reference to her altered status and her talent. They turned when Sir William cleared his throat.

"I'm honored to be a witness to what I gather is a rather oblique marriage proposal, but before you leave I have one final question for you, Miss Hazlett?"

Lissa steeled herself.

"Was Mr. Lamont requested to sketch any other personage? At the moment we are only interested in Lords Debenham and Smythe and Sir Aubrey."

Lissa was saved from answering when Ralph leaned forward to rest both hands on the table. "Forgive the interruption, Your Excellency, but I have not known, before, what to do with information I have that I believe is critical to the case regarding Sir Aubrey and Lord Debenham's involvement in the Castlereagh business."

"You have!" Lissa and Sir William spoke at the same time, and Ralph sent an apologetic look in Lissa's direction. "I didn't want to tell you, Miss Hazlett, as I feared such knowledge might endanger you. It's only been a very short while since I gained possession of it and I wanted to be sure I handed it to the right person. I now know Sir William is the man to entrust with something so important and sensitive."

"Well, what is this evidence?" Sir William sounded a trifle impatient and Ralph nodded, as if he understood the need to get to the point.

"A letter written by Sir Aubrey's late wife lays out the whole affair. It exonerates Sir Aubrey and incriminates Lord Debenham."

"But Miss Partington burned the letter!" Lissa cried.

Ralph turned from Sir William's shocked expression to Lissa's outrage, with a smile. "She burned what she *believed* was the letter. I had a copy made and paid the sum required to gain possession of the *real* letter. It's under my mattress."

"Good Lord! Well, this does alter matters. Pray, enlarge upon the contents of this letter."

After Ralph had given a concise summary of the whole affair, which did not implicate either Jem or Araminta, Sir William leaned back, laced his hands across his lean torso, and slowly shook his head. "My word, but this has been a profitable meeting. I shall be leaving the country soon but before that I will be meeting with some colleagues of mine to discuss the matter. Though I am now based in Constantinople, I will still be involved in ongoing developments with this case due to a...surprising connection." He shifted in his chair and looked intently at Lissa. "Do you have anything further to add, Miss Hazlett? I take it you have informed me of all the sketches you were required to do? Mr. Lamont is a devious miscreant. We need to understand the full extent of his activities in case he's involved in greater criminal activity. If he has been recruited as a spy, we need to know the names of everyone he might have spied upon."

He sent Lissa a questioning look at her quick intake of breath and she dropped her eyes.

"Your Excellency, I should have mentioned it, earlier, but I was too..." She shook her head, unable to finish until, at Sir William's prompting, she gathered her courage and said in a rush, "Mr. Lamont was asked by a certain Mr. Crossing to follow his wife. It was the same night I sketched Lords Smythe and Debenham. At Vauxhall Gardens. He requested that she be sketched with whomever we found her."

Predictably, there was silence at this pronouncement. Carefully, Lissa raised her eyes to find Sir William staring at her with an expression difficult to fathom.

He turned to Ralph. "If you will excuse us for a few moments, Mr. Tunley, I would like to speak to Miss Hazlett in private." Calmly, he led the way to the door, saying conversationally, "This is more serious than I thought. In the interests of national security, I cannot have her evidence given in the presence of a third person."

After Ralph had bowed himself out of the room, Sir William slowly returned to his seat, steepled his fingers and sent Lissa a long, considering look. "I take it you did not sketch Mrs. Crossing after all, else her husband would have made it a matter to bring before the divorce courts."

Lissa looked down at the great tear to her drab print skirts. Such a pity, for it was one of her most serviceable gowns.

Well, there was nothing for it. She'd have to be frank.

"I did, in fact, Your Excellency. I sketched her as I saw her. Mr. Lamont made me follow him to a supper box and she was there. With a man, Sir William, as you well know. As Mr. Lamont was looking over my shoulder, I had no choice but to sketch what I saw."

Sir William raised one eyebrow, but beyond that gave no further indication that he understood she recognized him as that man. "Then the sketch was not given to Mr. Crossing?"

Lissa shook her head. "Mr. Lamont anticipated a great deal of money for such sensational evidence. It's true that I sketched Mrs. Crossing with...the man she was with, however I had taken a great dislike to Mr. Crossing. He gave the appearance of being a cruel, vengeful husband. And when I saw how sweet and...vulnerable...Mrs. Crossing seemed, I was afraid he would hurt her."

"You are perfectly correct on all counts, Miss Hazlett." A nervous tic worked at the corner of Sir William's mouth. He dropped his voice and his look gentled. "Go on. I presume you found a means of denying Mr. Lamont what he wanted."

"Mr. Lamont wanted me to give the drawing to Mr. Crossing immediately but I made an excuse to keep it until two nights later, when I was fortunate enough to encounter Mrs. Crossing and warn her. I asked her if she had perchance a brother who could be substituted for her lo—"

Lissa blushed at nearly saying the word lover.

"I understand what you're saying. I also understand that a

fiery redheaded brother, if such coloring could be indicated, might have greatly aided her cause."

"That was indeed the case. I believe Mr. and Mrs. Crossing have been observed in great felicitation since."

Only the faintest flicker of an eyebrow indicated that this meant anything to Sir William. He rose with a bow, indicating their interview was at an end. "You have been of great assistance, Miss Hazlett. More than I can truly say." The tenseness behind his eyes relaxed and he smiled. "You are free to leave but I would request that you do not quit London for at least another three days—until I have been in touch with further questions." He hesitated. "I gather you will not be returning to the Lamonts, in view of recent events."

Lissa shook her head. "My belongings are still there but I would be afraid to go back."

"I would suggest it would be most unwise." He cocked his head. "Mr. Tunley appears to have taken on the matter of ensuring your safety. These are grave matters beyond your ken, Miss Hazlett, so this relieves my concern. I know Mr. Tunley is in Lord Debenham's employ but your young man is an excellent fellow. You'd be wise to follow his counsel."

Lissa smiled her gratitude as she prepared to issue out of the door and into the corridor. "I would trust Mr. Tunley with my life, Your Excellency."

"I do not think he would let you down, Miss Hazlett." Sir William nodded, then closed the door after her and Lissa felt the jolt of excitement to see Ralph coming towards her, appearing from the gloom like the good-natured savior he was.

"Right, my girl, I think we've had enough excitement for one day. Off to Mrs. Nipkins for a good night's sleep, eh? I shall arrange lodgings for myself next door. How are you feeling?"

Lissa exhaled on a huge breath that made her shoulders slump yet she felt strangely exhilarated. "It *has* been a big day, I will admit it, Ralph, but it's been exciting too. So much more exciting than being just an everyday sort of governess. Her smile broadened. "I'm so glad you're here."

"Wouldn't have missed it for the world." He threw his arms about her shoulders and pulled her into an impulsive hug before letting her go. "Now, off for some well-earned rest. The villains aren't vanquished but together we've almost saved the day. Aren't we a great team, Miss Hazlett?"

Chapter Twenty

Araminta awoke in a cold sweat. Was it only last night she'd felt so joyous with her dreams about to come true? Was it only last night that she'd received a marriage offer that would make her the wife of charming, rich and titled Lord Ludbridge?

Yet how had it all ended? With her agreeing to marry Mr. Woking. In fact, precipitating Mr. Woking's marriage proposal, which was only to add insult to injury. And, now, here in the dismal precincts of her garment-strewn room, which Jane had not even tidied properly, was an enormous bouquet of red roses with a card Jane was settling down to read.

Araminta pulled the covers up to her chin and muttered, "I don't want to hear it," but it appeared Jane did not hear her.

" '*To the incomparable Miss Partington, who has made me the happiest man alive by agreeing to become my wife. Ever your slave, Lord Ludbridge…*' That is rather romantic," Jane observed with a sniff, placing the roses across the seat of a small bentwood chair by the dressing table. "What a pity you couldn't have married him, after all. And, oh, my goodness, here's another one."

Araminta rolled her eyes at Jane's sarcasm and tried to block her ears as her maid read the card attached to a second enormous bouquet, this time of yellow roses. " '*Everlasting love to the sweet and ravishing Miss Araminta Partington who has conferred upon me the greatest of gifts: her undying loyalty. From her devoted husband-to-be, Mr. Roderick Woking.*' " Jane tossed the second bouquet rather unceremoniously across the first and sent a contemplative look in Araminta's direction. "You deserve congratulations, Miss Araminta, for you do know how to get yourself out of a situation." She bent to pick up a rumpled stocking. "That is, once you've already got yourself *into* a situation."

Araminta narrowed her eyes then pulled the covers over her

head. As soon as she was married, she'd get rid of Jane and her impertinence.

Married. She shuddered and stuffed her hand in her mouth to stop herself from crying.

"Oh, and in other good news," she heard Jane's muffled voice through the covers, "Miss Hetty writes that she is having the most wonderful wedding tour and that, happily, she is already with child."

"Argghhh!" Araminta cried from her stuffy nest. "Get out, Jane!" But when she heard Jane taking her at her bidding, she threw back the covers and called her back.

"Fetch me more water. I need to scrub myself." She shuddered at the memory of Mr. Woking's dirty paws and everything else contaminating her pristine—well, almost pristine—being. "Then you can lay out my jonquil pelisse and sprigged muslin. Mr. Woking will no doubt be on his way to make arrangements and to ask Cousin Stephen, who can act as proxy for Papa. Oh dear Lord, I can't believe I'm going to marry Mr. Woking! If only there were another way, but if there is I can't see it." She gave a little sob as she put her feet to the ground. "Mr. Woking wishes our marriage to take place imminently, as do I."

"You mean in view of what you did to him last night, miss?"

"How dare you speak like that, Jane?" Araminta stood up and whipped the dripping flannel from her maid's grasp. "Do not ever make reference to this again."

Jane ignored her as she sat to smooth out Araminta's other stocking. "Have you thought how you're going to explain matters to Lord Ludbridge, who is no doubt also happily making arrangements for your wedding in the belief you'll be his bride on his return? What might he say when he learns you've married Mr. Woking?"

Araminta tossed aside the stocking she'd been in the process of slipping onto her foot and threw herself onto her back on the bed to stare at the ceiling. "Why do you plague me with all these questions? I'll think of something in good time. I'll say…I'll say Mr. Woking attacked me, and to preserve honor, I believed the only decent thing was to marry him, since Lord Ludbridge insisted on leaving me just when I needed him. He'll never forgive himself, and nor should he!"

"Oh, you'd accuse Mr. Woking, would you, when I reckon the shoe was on the other foot? I can't say I like Mr. Woking overly but you can't blame a feller for som'at like what you gone and done."

"When did you start telling me what I can and can't do, Jane?" Araminta snapped, sitting up suddenly. She gasped as a wave of nausea engulfed her, opening her eyes to find Jane had already positioned the chamber pot under her nose. As it hadn't been emptied, she gagged more than usual.

Collapsing once more onto her back, she threw out her arms and wailed. If she'd had the courage, she'd have gone to visit one of those filthy creatures who got rid of mistakes like the one she'd made, but she'd been so terrified by the tales of almost certain death, which Jane had gleefully passed on to her, that three times she'd lost her nerve and Jane had said only last night it was too late.

Soon Araminta was dressed in her pretty afternoon gown, ready for the inevitable visit that she both welcomed and dreaded, since all her hopes hinged on this one necessary, dreadful union with a man she despised. She didn't want to think of the one she could have had. No, she'd have to spend some time in the country to save the pain of being confronted with what she'd lost through simple misfortune.

"No girl is as unlucky as I am," she muttered as Jane did up her buttons and a knock on the door proclaimed a visitor.

"Surprise!" called her mother, sailing into the room with a radiant smile and bearing a bundle of swaddling, which of course turned out to be the sister whose name Araminta couldn't immediately remember.

In Lady Partington's wake came Cousin Stephen, who was smiling more broadly than usual, for Araminta had certainly thought him a grumpy old thing to have about the place the past few weeks.

He was cooing at the tiny, downy-haired beast whose fat pink face was wreathed with answering smiles as she grasped his finger.

"Watch out, Araminta, she's going to rival you as a beauty to be remarked upon," he teased. "Though of course, you'll be in your dotage with, quite possibly, grandchildren by the time little Celia has her come-out."

"Don't vex Araminta like that, Stephen, you know she has no sense of humor when it comes to such matters," her mother chided him gently.

"Goodness, I have a sense of humor far more in evidence than grumpy old Cousin Stephen's," Araminta muttered. "I don't think I've heard him say one nice thing to me this whole season."

To Araminta's horrified disgust, her mother leveled a look of mock disapproval upon the young man. "Poor Araminta, she seems quite out of sorts yet she's looking as pretty as a picture. Indeed you look blooming, Araminta, and that's the truth."

Stephen became serious. "I've been conscious of the need to ensure we have no further scandals attached to the family's good name. Hetty's behavior was scandalous enough, and now I hear whispers circulating about you, Araminta, that trouble me, and I'm sorry for bringing it up now."

"Whispers?" Araminta sat down quickly on the edge of her bed and fanned herself, offering a bland smile at her mother and Cousin Stephen, who were now *both* looking quite censorious. "Goodness, what can you mean?"

"You were seen alone with Lord Ludbridge last night, dearest," her mother said. "I heard it from the dowager Dalrymple, who was most stern at the fact you'd slipped away from Mrs. Monks." Her mother took a seat beside her and stroked her hand. "You know how careful you must be of your reputation, and that the slightest bad behavior will bring the gossips around your ears. Do be careful, darling."

"Well, as a matter of fact, I'm marrying Mr. Woking, and if that's the door knocker I can hear it's probably him now to ask permission."

She could have heard a pin drop. Mutinously, she raised her face. "Well, aren't you going to congratulate me?"

Cousin Stephen didn't seem to know what to say. Her mother just looked confused. "Mr. Woking. I've heard nothing of this gentleman. Well, nothing...complimentary. Why, I thought you favored—"

"Well, it doesn't matter who I favored, I'm marrying Mr. Woking, who has been in love with me for two seasons and whom I finally have favored with my acceptance."

Stephen turned to her mother as he reached for the baby. "Mr. Woking is the nephew of Lord Debenham."

"Goodness...*dangerous* Lord Debenham?" her mother asked, uncertainly.

"The nephew is a different kettle of fish." Cousin Stephen began to rock the child, who was starting to grizzle. "Nothing dangerous about him at all," he added, though not in a tone that suggested this was a good thing. He looked suspiciously at Araminta. "Why are you marrying him?"

Araminta took a walk to the window. "Because it's nearly the end of my second season and I have to marry *someone*," she said breezily. "He's in line to inherit extensive landholdings, he's pleasant enough, and he'll be a good husband."

"You mean easy to manage," Cousin Stephen said.

Araminta bristled at his tone as she turned. "I have quite lost my heart to the gentleman," she said as a dreadful pang regarding lost Lord Ludbridge threatened to undo her. "I am going to marry him, and now you're going to come downstairs and give Mr. Woking your blessing."

"Don't you speak to your cousin like that," her mother admonished her. "I own I am just as astonished to hear this announcement. It's not like you to settle for…well, second best."

"Second best?" Araminta took a few angry steps into the center of the room and raised her chin. "I will *never* settle for second best and I will never *be* second best. This suits me in every way, and I will not hear another word to dissuade me."

She turned back toward the stairs and put her hand to her belly. Were those flutterings of fear or something else? No, Jane had said it took at least four months before any movement could be felt and she was only a little over one.

In the nick of time, she'd managed to find a father for her baby, even if she would forever pine for the one who'd got away.

And she wasn't referring to Sir Aubrey.

***

The entire bon ton, it appeared, had turned up to celebrate the impending nuptials of Miss Susana Hoskings and Mr. Edmund Dunstable at the lavishly decorated home of the bride-to-be. Swathes of red and gold silk adorned the lintels, enormous vases of luxurious blooms perfumed the air and the jewels of the richly-garbed crowd sparkled beneath the chandeliers.

Yet the uninvited might have been excused for thinking it a celebration in honor of Miss Araminta Partington and Mr. Roderick Woking.

"Congratulations, Miss Partington! Congratulations, Mr. Woking!"

The good cheer was abundant this evening as Araminta stood a few yards from the front door beside her new affianced, who was beaming like the cat who'd got the cream. Araminta looked at him askance and was about to remark upon the crumb clinging to his lip when she realized it was a pimple.

Yes, she was marrying a pimply boy. Her heart shriveled a little more at the thought.

"Everyone seems so pleased for us, I feel a trifle guilty." Mr. Woking—Roderick—picked up her hand and kissed it as another gathering of guests was announced. "Why, thank you, Mr. Crossing, Mrs. Crossing. So kind, and yes, I am the luckiest of bride grooms."

Araminta managed a weak smile as she responded to the latest well wishes. "Yes, such a lovely evening," she agreed before murmuring to Roderick, "Don't feel guilty. We've managed to steal the attention from Miss Hoskings' lackluster match. Look at the dreary girl, standing on the other side of the doorway. Doesn't she know she cannot wear that shade of puce with a complexion like hers? Yet she's made a decent match, can you believe it? Five thousand a year, though I can't imagine he'll want to spend much time away from his club. Nevertheless, she looks like she'd put up with anything. I'm sure tonight is the most exciting she's ever likely to have. She's lucky she received an offer at all, with such a hatchet-face, poor dear."

"The girl is nice enough." Roderick lowered his head and his eyes glittered. "Her aunt was ruined by my uncle, don't you know?" He gave a slow nod of his head, as if proud of the fact. "My uncle, Lord Debenham, has quite a reputation with the ladies. Don't think your family is the only one to be mired in scandal, though of course it's not the gentlemen who need to worry about reputations and that sort of thing. Your sister should have been more mindful of the consequences her actions had on you, Araminta, my love. Have no fear, however, that I hold her—or you—in contempt."

"I don't," Araminta responded acidly. "But can you really believe that a roly-poly like Miss Hoskings had an aunt who caught the attention of Lord Debenham?" The mention of the gentleman with whom she'd nearly courted disaster made her shiver.

"Appearances are deceptive, aren't they, my dear-heart?" He sent her a sly look, which made Araminta think she was going to be sick again.

When she did not respond, he went on, a trifle too eagerly for the fact they were in public—or anywhere, for that matter. "The manner in which you pretended to hold me in such disdain when in fact you were mad for me has made me all the wilder for *you*."

He'd dropped his voice to a rushed whisper and his normally pasty face, now shiny red in the glow of the candles, reminded her of an overripe tomato as he slanted an impassioned gaze across at her. "My goodness, but last night was magnificent, and I am so glad you see the merit in a hasty wedding, though of course we need not observe the abstinence that would ordinarily be necessary, given what has already occurred." He chuckled as he clearly dwelt on their grubby, thirty-second encounter on a banquette in his drawing room the previous night.

"Please excuse me, I'm suddenly not feeling quite the thing," Araminta whispered hurriedly over her shoulder as she left his side and dashed into the corridor in search of a chamber pot. This time she really *was* going to be sick.

She was not familiar with the house, and the labyrinth of passages presented more of a challenge than she'd expected. Finally she found what she was looking for and, whipping aside the curtain, gasped her stomach's contents into the gaping hole.

It took her a few minutes to gather herself. She walked shakily back into the dark corridor and leaned against the wall with her eyes closed, her head tilted upward.

What nightmare was this? Was she really going to marry Mr. Woking in three weeks? Right now it was almost as if God were punishing her. But why, when it was Hetty who had behaved so wretchedly—meaning Araminta had had to work so hard to save the family's wealth and reputation from ruin?

"Lost your way, Miss Partington?"

The voice struck real fear into her and she gasped, snapping to attention and opening her eyes to see Lord Debenham looming.

"I'm not feeling too well," she responded weakly.

"Too weak to return to the ball? Why, that's not like you. Perhaps you should come along with me. You definitely look like you need to rest. I've never seen you look so wan, when you're such a vibrant beauty on any other day."

Araminta put her hand against the wall to steady herself. "I really should go back. Roderick will be wondering what's happened to me."

Lord Debenham continued to stand before her in a disconcerting, slightly menacing way. She wasn't quite sure how to respond.

"Roderick. Yes." He drew the words out consideringly. "That *was* a surprise."

Araminta shrugged. "I don't know why. You were the one to cite his many qualities, I seem to remember."

"When I was rejecting your overtures, Miss Partington." He sighed. "My, how I've lived to rue the day."

She blinked her eyes wide in surprise. "You made your lack of interest quite plain, sir. And now Roderick is to be my husband, and you and I shall be cousins in marriage." She smiled, feeling more confident now she could speak like that.

"But what if that isn't enough for me?" He put out his hand and touched her cheek.

Araminta flinched, though a frisson of excitement made the contact far more exhilarating than when Roderick had pawed her.

"I don't understand you, My Lord," she whispered, repulsed yet irresistibly drawn to the danger he exuded. "I am about to be married."

"Don't play the innocent with me. You know exactly what I mean." He'd drawn closer now. He was playing with her, stroking her cheek, her neck, her décolletage with the tips of his fingers, his voice a soothing murmur as he led her along the passage. "If you are so weary, I can take you to a room where you'll be comfortable. I'm a regular guest of this house, in fact. Hoskings and I have enjoyed many a cribbage evening together and I'm not always in a position to return to my own bed. Let me take you somewhere you can lie down."

Despite every instinct screaming caution, Araminta's breasts tingled and she felt again that increasingly familiar throbbing desire between her legs. She'd thought she'd never feel it again except in Teddy's presence, but he'd left her, meaning pimply, groping Roderick was her only means of salvation.

"Here we are, my dear."

Self-preservation kicked in when he pushed open the door to one of the many guest chambers along the passage. She stopped, turning back toward the ballroom. "I must return to Roderick," she said, drawing on every reserve she had to make it sound as if that was what she truly wished.

Lord Debenham stood very close to her in the doorway. "Do you desire my nephew, Miss Partington...like you desire me?"

The suggestiveness in his tone was more thrilling than

terrifying. In the light of the candle resting in a sconce just above them, his eyes glittered like a satyr's.

"And like I desire *you*?" He grasped her hand and placed it on the front of his bulging black pantaloons.

Araminta swallowed, her body in a state of the wildest excitement. But she did not take her hand away. She closed her eyes and shuddered slightly. "My Lord, I am saving myself for Roderick," she whispered.

"That little sapskull? Why, you're too ripe and ready for half, aren't you, my tempting armful, but I don't think my nephew's the answer."

Araminta swayed as she felt his arms go about her. Giddy with desire, she was, this time, determined to cling to the safest course. That is, until he slipped his hand into her bodice, beneath her stays and chemise, and gently pinched her nipple.

This man was terrifying, but surely one taste of him would make no difference after what she'd already done? No, she'd not marry him if he were the last man on earth. He was far too dangerous to have as a husband—foolish, naïve girl that she'd once been to believe she'd have the necessary control over him that she required.

Heat engulfed her, her skin prickled and her breath came in short, desperate bursts.

One wild, wanton, wicked taste of this sinfully villainous blackguard while her pimply, boring, ghastly husband-to-be waited in the ballroom would be utterly and deliciously thrilling.

"You do flatter yourself, Lord Debenham," she whispered, as she pressed closer against him, angling her body to ease the way for his exploring hands. "Why would I give my virtue to you when I owe everything to Roderick for making me such a gallant and enticing offer before the end of the season?"

"An offer of marriage, maybe, but my offer is much more exciting, don't you think?"

His touch seared her skin as he kneaded her right nipple. Suddenly he pulled her against him and thrust his tongue into her mouth. She moaned, sagging against him, squeaking with delighted surprise when his hand went up her skirts and he cupped her heated mound.

"My, you *are* wet," he growled. "Wet and willing." Lightly at first, then with a little more pressure, he began to massage the swollen nub between her legs.

Araminta thought she would die from pleasure. "So this is what it feels like?" she gasped, shifting slightly to give him greater access. Seducing Sir Aubrey had been nothing like this. Though she'd been damp with desire, she'd merely plunged onto him and he, thinking she was...someone else—she shuddered as she reflected that that someone was her sister, though Hetty was welcome to Sir Aubrey—had then furiously berated her.

What a terrible man Sir Aubrey was to have led her on to believe he wished to marry her and now—she gave a little sob—she had no choice but to marry Mr. Woking. At least, though, Mr. Woking would be infinitely more pliable than this dangerous devil whose ministrations were nearly driving her insane.

She liked his roughness, and moaned again as he dipped a finger inside her before resuming his pleasuring, returning pressure to the outer lips of her secret, sensitive parts.

"Oh my, you are on fire," he muttered as he swept her into his arms and carried her into the bedchamber, where a single candle guttered on a chest of drawers by the large mahogany tester bed.

Without ceremony, he tossed her onto the crimson counterpane. Quickly, he unbuttoned the flap of his breeches, which he then kicked off, together with his shoes. Shrugging out of his tailcoat and waistcoat, he then threw himself—naked but for his shirt—on top of her.

Araminta managed to wriggle out from under him, gasping, "Not so fast, Lord Debenham. If I am going to gift you what by rights I should be gifting Roderick, I want more of what you were doing before."

Oh, she wasn't stupid. She knew how to get what she wanted at the same time as reassuring him that she was unspoiled. This was going to be even more important in a few months' time when the baby came a little earlier than it ought.

"More of this?" His satyr-like eyes bored into hers, only an inch away, but obligingly he supported himself on one elbow, his lean, hairy flanks fascinating her before she gasped in delight as once more he slipped a finger inside her entrance, then out, slowly massaging the ever-swelling nub of her desire.

"Mmm, more of that." She relaxed into the soft mattress and exhaled on a deep, satisfied moan at the exquisite sensations. So this is what she'd been missing out on? Closing her eyes, she was sinking into even more pleasurable euphoria when to her annoyance he stopped abruptly, rolled her over, and began to undo her buttons so that he could pull first her dress, then her petticoats, and finally her short stays and chemise over her head.

"My Lord!"

"Don't worry, I'll have you dressed in a trice when I'm done but *this* is how I want to see you."

She smiled coyly, enjoying her nakedness, or rather the raw appraisal in his eye as she flaunted herself without shame. "I suppose I'd better not spoil those if I'm going back to the ball," she conceded, glancing at the pile of her clothes as she drew the counterpane up to her chin.

"Now why do you suppose I went to the trouble of undressing you?" he asked, dragging it away again so he could look at her. He raised his eyebrows. "My, but you are rather a delectable little thing. Despite the fact you're insufferably haughty and immeasurably vain, you have the body of a racehorse. I shall enjoy getting used to this."

"Well, get used to it now, because this is the only time you will." She grinned up at him, feeling smug. Yes she had the measure of him. He was in thrall to her and she was—thank goodness—getting a little pleasure for once out of this sport.

"The only time? What makes you think that, Miss Partington?" He chuckled as he resumed stroking the swollen lips about her entrance, then bent to suckle her right nipple.

"I'm marrying Roderick in a little over a fortnight."

"Maybe I want to marry you myself."

"You're far too dangerous, My Lord, and besides, I've changed my mind about thinking that was a good idea. Oh! Ooooh!"

He'd caught her by surprise. Her body exploded with sensation and she bucked and jerked, but she was not ready to cast herself completely into the abyss of pleasure just yet. Lord Debenham had more work to do in order to make up for all the terrible things she'd been forced into, just to get respectably married.

She threw her head back and opened herself up even wider to him, making clear with her sighs exactly what pleased her. "Further up. That's right. Oh yes, just a little faster and a little harder. Yes, oh my goodness, oh my goodness!" Her climax was sudden and intense and the most thrilling sensation she'd ever experienced. Dear Lord, so this was why people got into trouble.

For a few minutes she lay there, gasping, then Lord Debenham took hold of a handful of her hair and drew her into a sitting position. She looked at him in surprise. He wasn't rough but it certainly wasn't a gentle act, either.

"My turn now," he said, thrusting apart his legs so his member sprang out before him.

She blinked as she was forced to wriggle onto her knees on the soft, though lumpy mattress. He was still gripping a hank of her hair. "What do you mean?"

"Take me in your mouth."

"What?"

"You heard me. Take me in your mouth. Like this," he said, pushing her head down so that his pulsing member nearly choked her. "And careful of your teeth. Yes, up and down, slowly, that's right."

She was horrified, but his pleasure was infectious, and soon she felt her own body swell again with desire.

The timing was perfect, for just as she felt her juices build up to nearly explosive quantities, His Lordship hoisted her up under her arms, pushed her onto her back and thrust himself unceremoniously inside her.

"God, this is magnificent!" he shouted joyously as he began to pump himself madly in and out.

The tension was mounting for Araminta, too. Every nerve ending was on fire as Lord Debenham continued his frenzied thrusting. She was vaguely conscious of the counterpane slipping to the floor, the protesting groans of the squeaking bed, the slapping noise of their thighs. She wrapped her legs about his waist and dug her fingers into his buttocks in her escalating frenzy as the tension tightened.

And tightened.

Then, with a gasp of utter rapture, she shattered once more as he exploded inside her.

The only sounds in the sudden silence were the chiming of a clock in the dim recesses of the house—and the protesting creak of the door as it was thrust open upon a horrified wail, a small shriek and a cry of anguished dismay.

Araminta wriggled up onto her elbows and peered over Lord

Debenham's shoulder.

She was met by the disbelieving look of her husband-to-be, the scandalized fury of her hostess, Miss Hoskings' mother, and the incredulous look of Cousin Stephen.

Dropping back onto the mattress—Lord Debenham hadn't moved, but still presented his bare buttocks to the assembled onlookers—her last sight was of the triumphant grin of her seducer.

Chapter Twenty-one

"*There's* a nice piece of court gossip." Ralph, standing at Lissa's shoulder at Mrs. Nipkins' round wooden dining table in the tiny parlor, reached across to point out a paragraph in *The Times* newspaper she was reading.

Lissa rested her head on his shoulder and nodded, more occupied with dreams of their happy, shared future, than gossip sheet news.

"What does it say, dear?" Mrs. Nipkins raised her head and smiled from where she was sewing the skirt of white sarsnet to the bodice of a beautiful ball gown. Her owlish eyes glittered with interest, but they were kind eyes and her interest was never inspired by prurient scandal.

Lissa enjoyed living with her. It was a small house but it pulsed with warmth and good humor. Since Lissa had arrived, Ralph had moved from the second bedroom to a tiny attic, while pretending he'd moved lodgings to next door. It broke Lissa's heart that she'd been the cause of his having to compromise his comfort, but he'd joked that Lissa's arrival was the instigator of him rising in the world. And from his attic room he could see the whole of London.

Lissa, caught up with affectionately tracing the veins on the back of Ralph's hand, let Ralph do the reading while she and her landlady listened.

"Miss Kitty La Bijou, who has taken London by storm with her sensational rendition of Juliet in Shakespeare's *Romeo and Juliet*, is rumored to have secured the forthcoming role of Desdemona—and the attentions of a certain Lord X."

He was about to continue reading when Mrs. Nipkins asked, "Ooh, yes, I have heard about Miss La Bijou. Very popular she is and quite the beauty. Have you see her? I know how much you like the theatre, Mr. Tunley."

"She was excellent when I saw her in *Romeo and Juliet*," Ralph conceded, "but she'd better not get mixed up with this Lord X. The gossip reporter is wasting his time being cryptic, for all the world knows he's referring to Silverton. And Lord Silverton is part of the fast set to which my not-so-very esteemed employer, Lord Debenham, belongs." He raised one eyebrow as he explained. "Debenham is fond of the gaming hells. So is Silverton."

Lissa couldn't meet Ralph's smile. Her mind was racing too fast.

Kitty La Bijou was the name her younger sister had always said she'd adopt if she ran away to London. A few weeks before, Lissa had received a letter from their mother admitting that Kitty had been gone for some weeks; that following another of their regular arguments, she'd stormed out of their cottage. Her mother said she'd been certain she'd return, however, Kitty had finally written to say she'd found work in London and wasn't coming back.

Kitty had never hidden the fact she loathed her life in the small village in which they'd been born. While Lissa and Ned had both kept a low profile and ignored the taunts from the village children regarding their shameful birthrights, Kitty had been more outspoken. Often, Kitty would return from having trespassed onto the grounds of The Grange, their father's estate, where she'd gone to spy on their half-sisters. Enviously, she would describe the lavish clothes and other luxuries their half-sisters took for granted.

Lissa let Ralph continue to read while her thoughts ran riot. *Kitty La Bijou.* It couldn't be *her* Kitty? Surely? Having her name associated with a man of dubious reputation, or any man at all, in a news sheet? No, it couldn't be.

Mrs. Nipkins bit off her cotton thread and put down her work. "Lord Debenham is your employer, Mr. Tunley. Regardless of what you feel, it's unwise to speak uncomplimentary of him."

"Even to the two ladies I trust most in the world?" He grinned. "Should I fear losing my job or worse because I confide intimacies to you?"

"Of course not, Mr. Tunley, but you never know who's listening or standing behind a door at this very moment."

A loud rap on the thin door to their cramped living quarters made them all jump. Now Lissa and Ralph did exchange fearful glances.

Just as Ralph reached the door to open it, the rapping

continued, and a lady's hurried, anxious voice intruded.

"Forgive me for arriving so late and with no warning."

Lissa watched with surprise as a slight young woman entered. With graceful hands their visitor pushed back the hood of her cloak, revealing, to Lissa's shock and incomprehension, the familiar face of Mrs. Crossing.

Astonished, she made the introductions and then Mrs. Nipkins rose to say goodnight, so that Mrs. Crossing could occupy her seat once it had been established that her visit was in strict confidence.

Immediately Mrs. Crossing folded her hands in her lap and leaned forward. "I am leaving tonight for France but I had to see you first." She looked at Lissa then nodded toward the window. "My carriage is waiting for me outside, and I shall be meeting Sir William in Calais in three days' time. He is returning to Constantinople and I shall accompany him."

Lissa wasn't sure how to respond. Perhaps asking the obvious question would help. "You are leaving your husband?"

"Sir William and I have planned this for some time. We were waiting for his position to be secured so that he would have a permanent residence where I could safely join him. Of course, our elopement is a closely guarded secret, and no one must know."

"Then, with respect, why tell us?" asked Ralph.

"Because Sir William desires your involvement, Mr. Tunley, in an important mission, which was the reason for his brief return to London."

Lissa jerked her head around to see Ralph's expression flicker between hope and concern. For her own part, she didn't know what to think.

"We know something of the matter about which you speak, but why is Sir William not asking me, himself?"

Mrs. Crossing handed him a sealed missive. "He entrusted this to me to deliver to you before I left London."

"Rather cloak and dagger." Ralph laughed uncertainly.

"It is," Mrs. Crossing agreed. "A new world to me, also, but I am slowly learning. Mr. Tunley, I understand you are still officially in the employ of Lord Debenham, who will be back from his wedding tour in a month?"

The scandal involving the elopement of Miss Araminta Partington with dangerous Lord Debenham had had London town agog and Miss Partington's name considerably sullied. Word was that the daring debutante had accepted a marriage offer from Lord Debenham's nephew, Mr. Woking, the night prior to her elopement with her betrothed's uncle.

"I am," agreed Ralph.

"It is Sir William's desire that you will accept his offer of a position as his attaché, as you will read in his missive. I shall be living in Sir William's household as his widowed cousin, and his hostess. There are other matters for which he has enlisted my help, and this is one."

Pain slashed through Lissa like a sword. This was the kind of work Ralph had always dreamed of. But there was no place in such a new life for her. An attaché was constantly roaming the world.

Ralph cleared his throat. "I would be honored, however, Miss Hazlett and I are affianced. I could not abandon her to live abroad."

Lissa gasped. He was refusing an opportunity that promised him so much? This was the most concrete affirmation of his loyalty and intention to keep her safely by his side that she'd received, though she had no doubt of his affection.

Mrs. Crossing cocked her head. "When are you to be married?"

Ralph shifted uncomfortably. "No date is set for, alas, I have not the means to support a wife, but as soon as that situation changes, yes, Miss Hazlett and I will be married."

A warm glow suffused Lissa, even as she knew she couldn't be the means of standing between Ralph and his rising in the world. She gripped his hand. "You must accept, Ralph. Our time will come."

The light in Mrs. Crossing's eye brightened as she leaned farther forward in the cramped parlor. "I believe it is greatly to everyone's benefit that the two of you have such an understanding." She smiled her sweet smile at both of them. "Miss Hazlett, your astonishing skill at rendering a likeness with a few rapid strokes of a pencil will be of enormous benefit in the work Sir William is doing. I had not realized there was such a definite understanding between you but this is wonderful." She hesitated as doubt clouded her brow. "That is, if you are amenable to the proposition I'm about to put to you, speaking as Sir William's, proxy. Although it is not something he has not yet endorsed I am confident of persuading him of the merits."

Lissa could feel Ralph's interest sharpen while her own heart beat harder.

"What proposition?" Ralph's voice sounded dry and tense.

"As you are well aware, there are a number of dangerous gentlemen—indeed, several who are peers of the realm—who are under suspicion for past misdeeds, including the attempted assassination of Lord Castlereagh. It is thought these same men are involved in a more heinous plot that threatens our country's sovereignty."

Lissa felt her hands go clammy.

"Lord Debenham is their principal person of interest, together with a small group of close associates whom the government believes to be involved in a conspiracy with several foreign operatives." She took a breath and looked at Lissa. "It was your drawing of Lord Debenham in company with Lord Smythe and Mr. Buzby—men who have hitherto denied any close association—that reignited a suspicion long held by Sir William. I do understand you already know this. However, his investigations have, to date, revealed nothing that would result in a conviction. Nevertheless, he is anxious that these men, and several others with whom they associate, be watched closely."

Lissa must have revealed her confusion for Mrs. Crossing gave an apologetic laugh. "Sir William would have explained this a great deal better than I am doing, which is why he is the diplomatist."

Lissa and Ralph waited for her to elucidate.

"As you already know, Sir William wants Lord Debenham watched. Debenham claims Mr. Lamont falsified the sketch in which he was seen in close consultation with Lord Smythe and Mr. Buzby."

"A good thing Mr. Lamont's duplicity has finally been revealed," remarked Lissa before being struck dumb by Mrs. Crossing's next words.

"Surprisingly, it would appear that Mr. Lamont is now in Lord Debenham's employ. Furthermore, Lord Debenham had Miss Partington testify that she spent the entire evening with him in his supper room at Vauxhall that evening."

"Good Lord!" Lissa and Ralph spoke at once, and Lissa went on in shocked tones, "So, he gave her no choice but to elope with him? I gather she'd set her sights on…" She blushed as she turned to Ralph, adding, "Lord Ludbridge who is Mr. Tunley's eldest brother."

"Teddy made a lucky escape," Ralph muttered, rolling his eyes before appealing once more to Mrs. Crossing for more information. "Where am I to be based, if I accept Sir William's extraordinary offer?"

"Initially you are to remain in Lord Debenham's employ." At Ralph's crestfallen look she added hurriedly, "However, you'd be well remunerated for doing so as you would, in effect, be working for both Debenham and Sir William."

"A double agent?"

"Oh Ralph, but spying is such an ungentlemanly pursuit," cried Lissa.

Mrs. Crossing raised one pale, finely arched eyebrow. "Even if it is to safeguard the British people?"

Lissa conceded her point, reluctantly. She felt both nervous and excited for Ralph, yet disappointed, too. Ralph would be sent to the Continent to work for Sir William at some stage and what would become of her?

"Miss Hazlett, you are no longer employed in the Lamont household, I gather. I am fearful of putting this proposition to you, for there *could* be dangers associated, however, you have already proved yourself both daring and loyal, as well as gifted. Is it possible you could entertain the idea of being installed as governess in the household of a man whom Sir William believes is heavily involved in dealings with Lord Debenham? Dealings that threaten the safety of this country."

Lissa pressed her lips together in surprise.

Then, at her suddenly interested look, Mrs. Crossing went on, "Lord Beecham has a ward—a young lady who will have her come-out next year. In the interim he is, I understand, looking for a governess to instill in this young lady the…er…graces which her previous half a dozen governesses have failed to do. It is perhaps a position that will not be of long tenure, given Miss Martindale's hoydenish reputation, but even a few weeks ensconced in his household would give you the opportunity to sketch his associates. The position does not come without danger but it would be well remunerated."

Lissa turned shining eyes to Ralph and found his were dark

with concern.

"If it's dangerous, I could not possibly consent."

"How dare you tell me what I can and cannot do when I am not yet your wife!" Lissa cried indignantly, turning back to Mrs. Crossing to say with great determination, "I would be delighted to accept. If Mr. Tunley is to be in any danger in this operation, the least I can do is to show him my support."

"What, by agreeing to put *yourself* in danger?"

Ralph shook his head but Lissa leaned over and gripped his wrist. "Please be glad for me, Ralph. If you're going to be involved in all manner of dangerous havey-cavey affairs, I need to know I'm doing my part. And how could being governess to a little hoyden be more dangerous than being a governess in the Lamont household?"

"Lord, Lissa, but why am I not surprised?" Ralph stared at her, admiringly. "When I dragged you from that carriage accident I thought you a dashing, daring debutante."

"Only to discover me a lowly governess." Lissa smiled as Ralph gripped her hand.

"And, when I rescued you through the window, I discovered you to be a very *daring* governess."

"But still a lowly governess."

"Well, perhaps," Ralph conceded. "Now, though, you'll only be *pretending* to be a lowly governess, living a life cloaked in danger and mystery and intrigue. And that, I think, is far more to your taste." His tone was jocular before he revealed his concern once more. "Are you sure you're up to this, Larissa? I could not forgive myself if harm came to you."

"Working for my country to keep *you* safe, Ralph, is the best alternative to not having you with me." Lissa sent him an arch look and Ralph in turn grinned a quick apology at Mrs. Crossing as he took his beloved in a quick hug.

"Ah, my mysterious governess, you will never stop surprising me."

Lissa sighed happily. "And when we have worked together to fulfill our joint mission on behalf of the government and have brought these dangerous men to justice, I hope I won't stop surprising you."

She pushed herself out of her chair and fully into Ralph's arms as he rose, too. Over his shoulder she caught a glimpse of Mrs. Crossing's expression. There was understanding and compassion there as their visitor stood up and covered her hair once again with the hood of her cloak.

"Thank you for your visit, Mrs. Crossing." Ralph broke away to bow to her in farewell and to raise the candle to light the way as he opened the door for her. "I am very happy to accept Sir William's proposal and to serve the kingdom to the best of my ability."

Lissa nodded. "And I, too, will do whatever I am asked to keep this country safe." She smiled and reached for Ralph's hand. "Even if it's to become a spy, which it seems is what I must be in order to assist my dearest Ralph."

As the door closed softly behind Mrs. Crossing, Ralph wrapped his arms around Lissa and kissed her deeply.

Suddenly the tiny, cramped quarters, which was all they could afford, seemed like the first step in a whole new world opening up before them. The moment they stepped over its scuffed threshold and into the cobbled alleyway, they'd be embarking on the adventure of their lives. Lissa couldn't wait to taste what the real world was like, knowing her brave, darling Ralph was her greatest ally. Even when they could not be together.

"I cannot tell you how thrilling it is to learn of the depths to which you're prepared to sink for me, my most beloved," he murmured against her lips.

"You say that in jest, Ralph darling, but who knows what challenges this new adventure will throw at both of us. *Then* you'll realise how much I'm willing to sacrifice for you, and the true depth of my love," she whispered, before deepening the kiss.

THE END

Note about the Series

Her Gilded Prison is the first in my five-book *Daughters of Sin* series which follows the intertwining lives and sibling rivalry of Lord Partington's two nobly born - and two illegitimate - daughters as they compete for love during several London Seasons.

With Hetty and Araminta both falling for men on opposing sides of a dastardly plot that is being investigated by Stephen Cranbourne, now a secret agent in the Foreign Office, you can expect lashings of skullduggery and intrigue bound up in the central romance.

What Readers are Saying About the Series:

"The reader will find themselves thrown into a world of lies, misdeeds, treachery, and romance. What an impressive story! Ms. Oakley has a unique way of telling her stories, bringing unknown heroes/heroines into the spotlight, as they navigate a world of espionage, and intrigue, all while trying to survive and find their HEA. Magnificent and mesmerizing!" ~ **Amazon customer, April Renn**

"Full of secrets, murders, intrigues and you feel you know the characters and want to strangle some of them, especially Araminta!!! I have since read all the series and can't wait for Book 5... This is a series I will read again and again." ~ **Amazon Customer**

Below is the order of the books:

Book 1: Her Gilded Prison
Book 2: Dangerous Gentlemen
Book 3: The Mysterious Governess
Book 4: Beyond Rubies
Book 5: Lady Unveiled: The Cuckold Conspiracy

Dangerous Gentlemen

Find out what happens next to vain and beautiful Araminta and plain, shy Hetty as they embark upon a London season full of intrigue and scandal in Book 2 in the *Daughters of Sin* series.

Shy, plain Hetty was the wallflower beneath his notice...until a terrible mistake has one dangerous, delicious rake believing she's the "fair Cyprian" ordered for his pleasure.

***

Shy, self-effacing Henrietta knows her place—in her dazzling older sister's shadow. She's a little brown peahen to Araminta's bird of paradise. But when Hetty mistakenly becomes embroiled in the Regency underworld, the innocent debutante finds herself shockingly compromised by the dashing, dangerous Sir Aubrey, the very gentleman her heart desires. And the man Araminta has in her cold, calculating sights. Branded an enemy of the Crown, bitter over the loss of his wife, Sir Aubrey wants only to lose himself in the warm, willing body of the young "prostitute" Hetty. As he tutors her in the art of lovemaking, Aubrey is pleased to find Hetty not only an ardent student, but a bright, witty and charming companion. Despite a spoiled Araminta plotting for a marriage offer and a powerful political enemy damaging his reputation, Aubrey may suffer the greatest betrayal at the hands of the little "concubine" who's managed to breach the stony exterior of his heart.

"Dangerous Gentlemen takes you on a seductive ride while still staying true to the character of London society." —*Romantic Historical Reviews*

"The excitement and danger leading up to the climax will have readers turning pages long into the night. "—*Night Owl Reviews*

Save when you buy the boxed set of Books 2 & 3

The Mysterious Governess
Book 3 in the *Daughters of Sin* Series

Two beautiful sisters – one illegitimate, the other nobly born – compete for love amidst the scandal and intrigue of a Regency London Season.

***

Lissa Hazlett lives life in the shadows. The beautiful, illegitimate daughter of Viscount Partington earns her living as an overworked governess while her vain and spoiled half sister, Araminta, enjoys London's social whirl as its most feted debutante.

When Lissa's rare talent as a portraitist brings her unexpectedly into the bosom of society – and into the midst of a scandal involving Araminta and suspected English traitor Lord Debenham – she finds an unlikely ally: charming and besotted Ralph Tunley, Lord Debenham's underpaid, enterprising secretary. Ralph can't afford to leave the employ of the villainous viscount much less keep a wife but he can help Lissa cleverly navigate a perilous web of lies that will ensure everyone gets what they deserve.

"Uniquely designed, and cleverly executed. Spies, traitors, deception, betrayal, mystery, suspense and romance, bring together a intriguing Regency Romance, with many twists and turns, and an abundance of adventure." ~ **Amazon Reviewer**

ABOUT THE AUTHOR

Beverley Oakley was seventeen when she bundled up her first 500+ page romance and sent it to a publisher. Rejection followed swiftly. Drowning one's heroine on the last page, she was informed, was not in line with the expectations of romance readers.

So Beverley became a journalist.

After a whirlwind romance with a handsome Norwegian bush pilot she met in Botswana, Beverley discovered her "Happy Ever After", and her first romance was published in 2009.

Since then, she's written more than fifteen sizzling historical romances laced with mystery and intrigue under the name Beverley Oakley.

She also writes psychological historicals, and Colonial-Africa-set romantic suspense, as Beverley Eikli.

With an inspiring view of a Gothic nineteenth-century insane asylum across the road, Beverley lives north of Melbourne with her gorgeous husband, two lovely daughters and rambunctious Rhodesian Ridgeback, Mombo, named after the Okavango Delta safari lodge where she and her husband met.

You can find out more at www.beverleyoakley.com or follow her on Facebook at https://www.facebook.com/AuthorBeverleyOakley/

Printed in Great Britain
by Amazon